A Fawcett Crest Book

R538

JON GREEDHAM

SORRY, I DIDN'T MEAN TO KILL YOU

S&W SPFLD,MA
U.S.A.

"The kind of book you read slowly because you don't want it to end ... Jon Greedham takes ⟨⟨⟩ of this literary category just as forcefu⟨⟩ castaway thrillers with 'Look Alive Eh'..."

—**Entertainment Weekly**

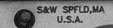

THOUGHT YOU WERE DEAD

Also by Terry Griggs

Quickening (Porcupine's Quill, 1990; Biblioasis, 2009)

The Lusty Man (Porcupine's Quill, 1995)

Cat's Eye Corner (Raincoast, 2000)

Rogue's Wedding (Random House Canada, 2002)

The Silver Door (Raincoast, 2004)

Invisible Ink (Raincoast, 2006)

THOUGHT YOU WERE DEAD

Thought You Were Dead

A NOVEL

Terry Griggs

Illustrations by
Nick Craine

BIBLIOASIS

FIRST EDITION

Library and Archives Canada Cataloguing in Publication

Griggs, Terry
    Thought you were dead : a novel / Terry Griggs.

ISBN 10: 1-897231-53-9
ISBN 13: 978-1-897231-53-1

    I. Title.

PS8563.R5365 T48 2009   C813'.54   C2009-900927-7

Cover design and illustrations by Nick Craine.

Canada Council   Conseil des Arts
for the Arts   du Canada

Canadian   Patrimoine
Heritage   canadien

ONTARIO ARTS COUNCIL
CONSEIL DES ARTS DE L'ONTARIO

We gratefully acknowledge the support of the Canada Council for
the Arts, Canadian Heritage, and the Ontario Arts Council for our
publishing program.

For me

1

FAQs

THE DOGHOUSE that Chellis currently found himself in was meant for a much smaller doggie, a bad pup the size of Bunion or Hormone. Two miscreants if ever there were. Rats with ruffs and canine pretensions. *Their* messes on the floor were substantial, considering, and not metaphorical in the least. Why was censure made of such inflexible material? The doghouse was clamped on his back, and he could feel it chaffing and wobbling as he edged snailwise toward the ringing phone. (Rotary – none of this trilling and burbling for Chellis.) And guilt? It was the toxic pressure-treated wood of the psychological lumberyard. *Hello?*

Elaine, *finally*. It had been weeks.

"Laney." Hey, hey. Forgiven.

"Chel. What are you doing?"

"Eating my crusts."

"Good boy."

End of conversation. But still. The molecular structure of the doghouse shifted. It was not exactly spandex yet, nor a swish little retirement home for his misdeeds, but matters were clearly improving. Weren't they?

Mrs. Havlock called next. What a sociable afternoon.

"Are you free, Chellis dear?" A summons disguised as a question.

Would he like to eat something other than humble pie? And crusts? "As a bird."

"A body is involved." She pronounced this *bawdee*, incarnating it in his ear, making it all vowelly and fat.

"*Another* one?"

"Don't be cheeky. I'm not quite sure what to do with this one."

"I'm sure you'll think of something brilliant."

11

"*Exactement*. Six for drinkies?"

"Six it is, Lady MacBee." That woman had *so* much blood on her hands.

Midday and Chellis was still in his jammies. Now that there was some cause to, he sloughed those off, and stepped into his Jolly Roger boxers, jeans, and pulled on a no-logo T. As Mrs. Havlock required maturity in the footwear that crossed her threshold, he slipped on his vintage Beatle boots over a pair of cotton Happyfoots. Black jacket, can't go wrong with that, especially one with potato chips in the pocket. He performed a quick *vanitas* scan in the bathroom mirror. Ears, eyes, lips, teeth – nothing missing or untoward. *Hunkus bolus*. Not Dead Yet anyway, which was the family motto . . . of the extant members that is, of which he happened to be the only one. Orphaned by the whole irresponsible lot of them. Forget the Sunday roast, crokinole and Trivial Pursuit at Christmas, hand-me-down, crumb-ridden toasters and all of the other dubious fringe benefits of family life, he was a free radical circulating in the social blood stream.

Chellis tipped his head back for a nose hair check, and stared admiringly up nasal canals so clear he could see all the way to Mars. Wait, that was his brain, a marvel in itself, red hot and whirring away, formulating question after profound question. Why, why, why? So many synapses were firing that his head sounded like a bug zapper. Here was a puzzler: how *could* she love someone with beige hair? That's what he couldn't quite grasp. The stuff was scarily synthetic. It looked as if it belonged in the bathroom, a hair doily for the one-ply, or something you might use to exfoliate your chest with. He traced the shore of his own darkish (more or less) hairline (okay, less), but respectfully, so as not to give it migratory ideas. His friend Hunt's forehead was now so vast, you had to walk clear round the back of him to confirm its conclusion. When had that happened? He'd have to call Hunt and enquire. But later.

There were no epiphanic moments to be had driving through town, although Chellis kept his sensitivities on high alert. What would an epiphanic hour be like, he wondered? Or a whole day? Blow your brains out. He addressed a query to the Almighty Celebrity above, nothing too taxing, just making conversation, "*Mein Gott*, isn't this a sleepy town?" In an effort to redeem a life sample, he scrutinized painfully tidy houses with buff siding and seamless eaves troughs, lawns Killexed into astroturf, sidewalks blindingly white, cracks cleaned with a Q-tip. Where *was* everyone? Playing hockey? He flicked the dreamcatcher that was dangling from the rearview mirror (former owner) to keep it from getting clogged and sticky from the town's subpar dreaming. Ah, but heading his way? Approaching his silver, second-hand, generic auto was another silver car, newer but exactly the same model, with a dreamcatcher dangling from *its* rearview mirror. Chellis gave the driver a comradely two-finger salute. His *doppelgänger* glared, attempted recognition, failed, drove on.

"You shit," he said mildly. "Carbon monoxide breath. Dangling participle." As that was all the road rage he could muster, he motored on, satisfied.

Was he too early? Mrs. Havlock didn't appreciate early. Or late. He consulted his Vulgari, as Elaine called his ten dollar mall watch. At least it covered the vile and seemingly permanent rash he'd gotten from her Anti-Insomnia Bracelet. He should know better by now, but had unwisely agreed to test it out for her. With the cursed thing clamped on his wrist like a manacle, he *had* fallen asleep, but then woke up ten minutes later, screaming. After which he'd spent the rest of the night marinating in a vinaigrette of worry about unlikely occurrences involving asteroids, mice, and a severed head on a cake plate. It was only fourish, way too. Chellis didn't want to end up in Mrs. H's bad books, of which she had a few, although through no fault of his own. He does his bit. Clearly there was time for a detour, possibly down Elaine's street, an accidental drive-by. No stopping? Not even if she happens to be standing in the middle of the road and flags him down? Not on your life. He sighed . . . *my* life.

He hit the gas and came up behind a hybrid car with a *Save the Adverb* bumper sticker. Green sentiment, sense of humour, worthy cause, potential pantheist behind the wheel, bisexual haircut, colour that didn't match the upholstery, *man*, Chellis approved of the whole package. His spirits lifted. He honked the horn as he peeled past, rolled down the window, and shouted, "Ya done good!"

He pulled into Pnin's Variety for a package of breath mints in preparation for a possible communicative incident. It wasn't out of the question, conversation could ensue. Hypothetically. Elaine had been known to stand stock-still in her driveway for minutes on end, clutching a bag of groceries, thinking. He'd arrive on the scene and awaken her from her reverie with his minty sweet breath – Zephyrus on wheels. Her bag of groceries would hit the blacktop, causing the eggs to tremble perilously in their carton and damaging Vaughan's zucchini, or his bananas, whatever. They would engage in intercourse. Swift and hard, for she would promptly tell him to *fuck off and die*. Turns out smarty Elaine will have been working on the final, crucial details for her Axiomatic (a labour-saving device for the Lizzie Borden's of the world), or some such invention, and he will have interrupted her yet again, sending her Go Train of thought zipping out of the station. Again? Yes, *again*, and would he *please just go away*.

At least she said please. Hypothetically. And that was nice.

Mrs. Pnin was behind the counter, looking grim. He had to wonder if the little Pninheads had pninworms again. Chellis chuckled, and she offered a tight smile back.

"Murder, Chellis." She held up a *Star* and pointed to the front page colour photo of two policemen and a suit crouched over a blanket-swathed lump on the ground with its feet sticking out. Unshod and bluish, none too fresh.

"*Tsk*, terrible. Well, that's Toronto for you."

"No, no, it happened in Claymore."

"Claymore? Good heavens!"

"Practically next door."

"What does it say? Some family dispute? You know what they're like over that way. Domestic deviants all, even the toddlers." So *that's* where everyone was, rubbernecking at the scene of the crime.

"A man, unidentified. Not a local. A knife." She stabbed a finger into the middle of her forehead. "Got that from Richard, you know Richard Major? He's over by the low acid orange juice."

"Um." Chellis almost broke his neck snapping it to look the other way, toward the door, thinking *run away, run away*. But he'd already been spotted and tagged. The guy was headed down the aisle toward him moving with a slick strut, as if his ankles were oiled.

Richard Major, aka Dick Major, aka Major Dick, set a slim, shapely bottle on the counter – some ginseng-ginko-green tea-EDTA concoction with writhing serpents on the label – and gave Chellis a brisk clap on the shoulder. "Chilly Willy, man, is that really *you*?"

"Hey, Dicker." High-school acquaintance, say no more. He'd check for a bruise later.

"Man, this I cannot believe. Someone told me you were . . . uh, gone."

"Been keeping a low profile Dick, but not that low."

"Ha, so you back for a visit, or what? Can't believe we all used to *live* in this hick town, eh?"

"Yeah, ha. Yourself?"

"The Big Smoke. Reputation management. Love it." Dick gave the pocket of his slinky, pricey suit a promiscuous pat, slid his hand in, and pulled out a platinum card. This he presented to Mrs. Pnin, who was furiously scratching her head. "You?"

"Me? Consulting." Chellis delivered this not-entirely fabulist piece of information in a brusque, manly tone, as if blocking a punch. "That Lexus out front yours, Dick?" The one he'd dinged ever so slightly on the passenger side while wrenching open his own cheap, piece-of-crap car door?

"Yep," Dick smiled.

"Nice." Chellis smiled back.

While waiting for Dick to sign for the drink, Mrs. Pnin was now absentmindedly scratching her plump white arm with his card, scooping her DNA onto it like dip on a cracker. This reminded Chellis of that cadaverous appetizer Elaine made last year for Halloween, goblin green it was and served in a cunning pottery skull. Exhumus she called it. It was quite a hit.

"Say, what about this murder business?" Chellis asked. "I hear you've got the inside story, Dick?" And didn't he always?

"Nah, not me. Know some of the cops involved, but they don't give much away." He turned to sign the receipt and retrieve his card. His signature amounted to nothing more than a tail with a tiny head, a perky sperm. "Thanks, Mrs. Pnin. Gotta go. Good seein' you again, Chilly. Wait'll I tell Di, man, she always thought you were hilarious. Ever in the city, eh, look us up."

"Sure thing." How about that, old Dicker had gotten hitched to Diane Ryder. One of the glyceride twins, Di and Mona, very bad for your health. And now it was Dick and Di? There was a moralistic little slogan for you. "Drive carefully," was his chirpy addendum. It was the most bruising thing he could think to say, but apropos, considering that Richard Major had killed Elaine's best friend.

Chellis perused the breath mints, moodily. "So, Mrs. Pnin, how are the kids these days? They enjoying school?"

Mrs. Pnin resumed her grim expression. "Lice," she said.

*

Chellis entered the Twilight Zone, the nob-hilly part of town where the Big Bad Wolf didn't even bother to stray, for the houses were all made of brick and solidly mortared with privilege. Here serenity lay so thick it had a nap you could rub between your fingers. The windows were bowed, the gardens lush, the maples towered – although not for long, seeing as the trees were being quietly undermined by the Asian longhorned beetle – the meek busily inheriting the earth. Elaine resided in this luxe neighbourhood thanks in part to her Comedo Vac, SuckZitUp, one of her more lucrative inventions, but mostly because of the Perfect Man's pedigree and inheritance. He *did* also have a joblet. What was it, again? Oh yes, lawyer. Patents mainly. The Perfect Man's perfect part-time play profession. Otherwise he picked pecks of pickled peppers. And being 100% ideal, he uncomplainingly performed other menial chores, and to prove it there he was in the driveway of 13 Hitchcock Crescent washing his Jag.

Having forgotten his shades at home in the pocket of Uncle Bob – his leather jacket and only relative – Chellis was attempting to peer out of the corners of his eyes without turning his head. He didn't want to get caught gawping. Viewing dear Vaughan was like observing luck incarnate. So much good fortune had been invested in the man that it was hard to see how he contained it all. No wonder his muscles bulged. Chellis did feel that muscles in general, and the Perfect Man's in particular, were highly overrated. There was something alarmingly geographic about them. High maintenance, too. If Chellis wanted a six-pack he'd head for the beer store, as would any intelligent individual. Vaughan had on a Stanley Kowalski undershirt (as

16

played by Marlon), a pair of Khaki shorts straight out of some Asian sweatshop (go beetles go!), and appeared to be wearing a shammy cloth for a hat. No, wait, that was his *hair*. Perfect. He could polish the car with his head. Might as well use it for something.

No sign of Elaine. She'd be hard at work, ferreted away somewhere deep in the house, hand sunk up to her elbow in a bucket of wingnuts. Chellis considered stopping on some fictional pretext. He could ask to use the phone – there was that urgent matter to discuss with Hunt – or the bathroom, speaking of urgencies: *veni, vidi, wee wee.* Although it was usually a bad idea to venture into Elaine's bathroom, locus of many trial-inventions. One's most valued extremities were always in danger there. Stepping on a weigh scale could be like stepping on a land mine. The last time he'd visited, he stuck his finger in what he took to be a sample of Vaughan's hair product – a clear gel substance prematurely ejaculated from its fancy tube onto the counter – and had ended up dancing around the room in excruciating pain as his finger sizzled and burned. Nah, no stopping. He was already in *her* bad books, and only today apparently had begun to worm his way out. No point in blowing it. He *had* been unjustly accused, mind. How was he supposed to know? And . . . what was *that*?

Having finally divested his gaze from the spectacle of the labouring husband, Chellis noticed a peculiar conical-shaped, tent-like structure on the front lawn. It appeared to be made of straw (Big Bad Wolf take note). What, the Champions had company? From the South Seas? Mysteries were compounding as the day progressed. The thing shuddered slightly as he drifted past.

Time to kill, he drove up and down the streets of the well-heeled on the lookout for an Open House. Finding a Hunt Realty sign stuck on one of these prim lawns would be sweet, for that would amount to a Wide Open House and possibly some liquid refreshment. No dice. There wasn't a single faux-Georgian or pseudo-Tudor on the market. Everyone happy happy happy. Not an itchy foot in the whole place. Unless the residents had already fled to their play houses in Tuscany, where they could live more intensely and experience anecdotally rich crises with the plumbing, their lean cheeks plumped out with *fatta in casa con il rosmarino e la salvia*. Seems Chellis remembered a time when KKK stood for something else other than the price tag of a house.

Hunt wouldn't mind getting his hands on one of these babies, but usually got stuck with the handyman specials over in their part of town. Funny, you didn't really need to travel halfway around the world for cheap wine, colourful peasantry, and no-show contractors. The other side of the tracks would suffice.

He dawdled along, taking in the scenery, and spotted two Beware of Dog signs, and one Beware of Human. Beware of Wag, more like, although some jokes did constitute useful advice. How *did* someone end up with a knife slotted in his head like one of those wooden kitchen blocks? Too busy watching his back? *Montenegro*, he thought. Good film, although the only part he could recall was the guy wandering around with a knife stuck in his forehead, a genuine sinus buster. He decided that it was a shade corny this murder, as far as genre goes. A cozy – if not for the victim.

Tempus fugit and so did Chellis. Somehow he'd messed around too long and was late. He sped out of town toward Mrs. Havlock's country place. The town sign pleaded ingratiatingly in a tourist script, begging for a return visit: *PLEASE COME AGAIN, WE'D LOVE TO SEE YOU!!!* The flip side was even worse:

WELCOME TO FARCLAS!
CANADA'S PRETTIEST TOWN
HOME OF THE CHAMPION POWER TOOL
BIRTHPLACE OF DELORES 'SHAKE IT' DELANGE
FRIENDLY, SAFE, FUN!!
A GREAT PLACE TO GROW YOUR HAIR!!!

Oh yeah?

2

Chez Anonymous

THE GATEKEEPERS of Havlock House were snarling and yipping behind the dungeonesque front door, hitting the high notes like tiny aggrieved castratos. Although only Bunion qualified for that role, seeing as Hormone was a *grrrrl*. Chellis could hear her nails clicking on the foyer's parquet floor as she danced and yapped, her nails painted some trendy canine colour, like Bitch Black.

"Potato I have," he called out. If they were so smart they'd catch the reference. Bunion even resembled a Joyce scholar he knew. Knew of, that is.

The doggies instantly shut up. Either Mrs. Havlock was striding down the hall like Darth Vadar, silencing all before her, or they had stopped to reflect and scratch their little heads.

Chellis tried the handle, which turned easily enough. He was expected after all, and this *was* officially rural Ontario where doors were not locked, or locked only by those reckless enough to have read *In Cold Blood*. Who would dare waltz into Mrs. Havlock's house uninvited anyway? He opened the door a crack and peeked in. Two short, trembling, keen-eyed individuals with spindly legs and insufficient fur stared up at him. Moistly – eyes lubricated with interest. They resembled a pair of eccentrically designed and animate end tables. Assured that they would not chew off his ankles, he slipped in. They watched him carefully. One false move and there would be an ear-cracking volley of complaint. He retrieved two still-intact potato chips from his jacket pocket, one of which was shaped remarkably like Kissinger's very own potato head and would have brought a small fortune on eBay, but there was no reneging now. With a priestly flourish he offered each doggie one of these misshapen hosts, comprised of grease, salt, and genetically modified unknowns, which caused him to

ponder who and what else the Body and Blood Himself had to jostle along with nowadays. How much of St. Monsanto, that other miracle worker, gopher genes and whatnot, did the faithful have to swallow in their transubstantiated wheat wafers? The pooches accepted their treats with delicacy and good manners, then skittered off in opposite directions to devour them in privacy. At which point Chellis was greeted by the lady of the house, appropriately titled, as theirs was a feudal relationship.

"*There* you are, Chellis."

"Sorry, Mrs. H. I'm a nanosecond late."

"Don't apologize."

"Okay. Sorry."

"Never apologize."

"Right." *Sorry.*

"Unless you kill someone by mistake."

"Got it."

"I wasn't serious."

"Of *course* not . . . sorry."

"You don't look sorry."

"What can I say?" *Whaaa. Jesus!*

"Come along then. The stopper's already off the bottle."

Mrs. Havlock led the way to her den (lions and tigers and bears) which gave Chellis the opportunity to observe her better half (oh my). She was tall, aristocratically slim and trim, with great legs for a geezer babe. Her white hair was shorter than usual, the cut post-punkish, expensively so. Ominously, she had on her dress with the twitchy white figures on a black, silky background. The classic, but plain little black dress, anonymous as night and as common, was insufficient for someone as distinctive as Mrs. Havlock. This particular dress, with its pre-linguistic design, signified gestation on her part and imminent labour on his. In this endeavour they were a couple with an almost embarrassing number of progeny. A disturbing metaphor, but there had been private occasions when Mrs. H had stood a chubby manuscript on its feet, bounced it up and down, tidied and patted it, and then smiled at him with enormous maternal pride.

"A body," she said, once he was uncomfortably settled in the minion's armchair. This was the chintz chair with short legs and the strategically-placed spring poking up in the seat. If this spring ever sproinged, ripping through the fabric, it was guaranteed to ream the chair's occupant, giving new meaning to the word colonize.

She poured him two slim fingers of Lagavulin, and for herself two heftier ones, then seated herself in her burgundy leather arm chair, and proceeded to loom.

"I thought you'd go in for something different this time," he said.

"Yes, as did I. But I keep seeing this body. It simply won't go away. It's under a Flowering Judas bush."

"Could be mulch."

This earned him a stern, school-mistressy glare. Followed by a sigh. "A *body*. Male. Who is it?"

Chellis sipped his drink, watching her the way the doggies had watched him. *Please* no anthropological forensics, he silently begged, his yearning for a tidy corpse set on internal whine. Let's keep the maggots out of the poor bastard's nose, the slugs out of his mossy, scooped-out eye sockets.

"So," he said.

"So," she said. "Forensics are popular right now. That would be new territory for me."

"Overdone. Interest is going to bottom out soon." If he didn't bottom out first.

"In gore? With a scientific twist? I doubt it, dear, but you might be right. I'd much rather lead than follow a trend. Why are you squirming like that?"

"I'm excited."

"Oh, goody."

"Does this body happen to have a knife slotted in its forehead?"

Eye-rolling this time. Athena Havlock might be waging a fair battle against cliché in her prose, but her facial expressions could use some revision and updating. "This is *not* a comedy, Chellis. I can't see his face, he's lying on his side, turned away from me."

"Not a very co-operative dead man."

"They rarely are."

"A job for Lazar, then?"

"Yes, I believe so."

Okay, now he got it: she wanted to play with *him* again. Marcel

22

Lazar was Mrs. Havlock's Perfect Man, but at least he had the decency to be fictional. Lazar had a full head of firmly-rooted black hair, a curling strand of which generally tumbled sexily onto his forehead (forelock foreplay) à la Ted Hughes – a forehead so smoothly granitic that a knife blade would snap like plastic if some witless criminal tried to sheath it there. Lazar was built like the poet, too (in his vital, earthside days), although unlike another famous colleague in the mystery genre, he himself did not indulge in any lyrical sidelines. Mrs. H had cordoned that area off, announcing brusquely that, "Writers should not write about writers and writing." Chellis could see how this might lead to some linguistic redundancy, but her complaint had more to do with her belief that such a subject was self-indulgent and imaginatively lax. The latter was not a failing of hers, so she was tough on it as a deficiency in others. Besides, she occasionally broke her own rule by using the odd short-lived, ink-slinging character, primarily it seemed for the pleasure of wiping out the competition.

In any event, Lazar was not her only playmate. While Chellis had only leathery Uncle Bob to embrace him in his lonely moments, Mrs. Havlock was surrounded by an extensive family – all invented, but what could be better? One whole wall of books in her den was a shrine devoted to them. Gazing up at it now, he spotted veterinarian and amateur detective Lenny Scott's series: *Dead Fly*, *Monkey Business*, *Fish Bait*, and his favourite, *Pig Latin*, in which Lenny meets that studly cop and they have *antasticfay exsay* on the operating table directly after she neuters his whisky-drinking police dog, Rebus.

Very few people knew that Mrs. Havlock, writing as Betty Mac-Beth, was Lenny's mother, or that she had also pseudonymously given birth to corporate crime buster Sitwell Z. Barker, star investigator of misdeeds in the beauty industry, *In Your Face*; real-estate development, *Rubble Without a Cause*; the world of theatre, *Am Ham*; waste management, *A Brown Study*; the fast food business, *In Bad Taste*; and religious cult leaders, *Holy Shits*. Mrs. Hav laboured efficiently and tirelessly in the cultural service industry, supplying enough material to satisfy vast vermi-composters full of bookworms. She wrote literary thrillers, literary mysteries, literary mainstream, and occasionally even something literary, for which she allowed interviews and picked up awards. The latter category she produced under her own name, but the rest was strictly under the table. Not that she regarded the populist novels as slumming; she simply enjoyed the secrecy and free-dom involved – and the cash. Publicly, she was known for her philo-sophical and linguistically challenging works, and consequently was not in much demand. Just the way she liked it.

Besides, being prolific was highly suspect.

In a sense, Athena Havlock's real name – if it *was* her real name – was her pseudonym, the nominal shield that protected her various other identities and allowed her to infiltrate the shelves of bookstores like an occupying force, if undercover. For this, she usually chose pen names that positioned her books cheek-by-jowl with the bestsellers. Mrs. Havlock was Stephanie Kinglet, Dan Beige, and Jon Greedham – she was everyone's evil twin. Whether she did this out of business acumen or mischief, Chellis could never quite tell.

"Wakey, wakey, dear."

"Unh. More please." He held out his glass, doing his best Oliver Twist imitation, and she indulged him with a smile and generous tip-ple. He preferred Laphroaig, which naturally she knew, but he was prepared to suffer the classier scotch.

"Thinking?"

"Non-stop."

"Good boy."

Hadn't he been praised thus once already today? But then, he was her good boy, her Jack Horner who sat so quietly in his corner pulling out plum after plum for her. Such as . . . the behavioural effects of frontal lobe damage (inappropriate euphoria, vulgarity, rudeness), the substance used by Victorian women to restore colour to silk (hartshorn), the number of bones in the face (fourteen), the name of Sir Isaac Newton's dog (Diamond), the parts of the claw hammer (cheek, eye, face, claw, handle), the antidote to Brown Recluse spider bites (ice), the slang term for wattles, human (neck drapery). Or he might be required to plumb the many and more extensive subjects that added ballast and authenticity to her work: the invisible stitching involved in corporate malfeasance, the skinny on high-end fashion models, the formal constituents of an operetta, the how-to of condominium construction, the cutthroat politics of just about anything that involved more than one person. Whatever it was she wanted, he'd find it, for he was her little researcher on the side, the secret agent she sent out into the wide informational world of detail and particularity. Lazar was basically a dumb-fuck, an empty head that Chellis had to fill like a candy jar book after book. That old writing adage, write about what you know? Well, Athena wrote about what he, Chellis knew. An exaggeration, of course. She was a sharpie, no doubt about it. Nor was he unhappy in his work, for it was the one job in the whole of his misdirected and pointless life that fit him to a T. A dream job and he hadn't even done anything to deserve it. Mrs. Havlock had picked him up in the local ValuMart one day along with the gherkins and Melba toast. She bagged him and carted him home.

He had been working at ValuMart stocking shelves for about a year, the lost-in-the-ozone year that followed Rennie's death. Rennie was his faux-mum (her term), and she'd bought it while clowning around on a back road bicycle tour. Her bike was clipped and sent spiralling into the netherworld by an SUV driven by an SOB, some country-dwelling executive too busy yakking on his cell and picking his nose to notice 23 cyclists travelling in a tight, roadside-hugging pack ahead. Even for those still in shock, the wake had been a blast – the Stones, Muddy Waters, Van the Man – but the aftermath was all downhill. For Chellis, mindless employment had been just the thing. After work every day he helped himself to one of the trashy novels in the rack beside the freezer that held the microwavable dinners. He'd grab one of those, too, and that would provide his two squares: a tasteless Turkey à la King to go with the other King (admittedly the better fare). He'd return the book the next morning, then later choose another, one of which happened to be a fattie by Sitwell Z. Barker, involving skullduggery in the confectionary business. *Blood Sugar* it was called, and it wasn't half-bad, a cut above its kind. This put him in the uncommon position of being qualified to recommend the book to its author the following day, while wrestling a monstrous package of Cushy Tushy toilet paper out of its carton.

He'd been observing her, a classy-looking older woman, who was assessing the book rack with a keener level of interest than it warranted. Most shoppers, if they stopped at all, did a quick scan for their author-brand, then tossed it in the cart along with the back bacon and the cheese doodles.

"That one's worth a look," he offered. She was running her fingers over the raised lettering on the cover of *Blood Sugar*.

She turned to him, evidently pleased. "You've read it?"

"Yep." Stockboy eloquence.

"What did you like about it?"

"Unhh, the complexity of the narration, the shifting points of view, the strong character development, the intricate plotting."

Raised eyebrows. "Was there anything you *didn't* like?"

"Sure. Lots."

Eyes narrowed. "Such as?"

"Well, it's not *Madame Bovary*, is it?"

"No, it isn't."

"Not even *Flaubert's Parrot*."

"Not meant to be, I expect."

Chellis then listed the book's many factual slip-ups and inaccuracies. "It's pretty sloppy in that respect. Cheap copy-editing. Still worth a read, though."

"How do you know all this?"

"Dunno. I like looking things up."

"*Do* you? What on earth are you doing here?"

Ho hum. Spanish Inquisition. "Working."

"You're wasting your life."

"That's the idea."

"Come with me," she ordered.

He followed her obediently to the checkout counter and that was that. Mrs. Havlock informed the manager that Chellis had a new position. "Concierge" was how she described it. Let someone else unpack the arse-friendly, but environmentally toxic Cushy Tushy. He had graduated to a whole new level of stockboydom.

"You have a list for me then, Mrs. H?"

"Indeed, I do."

She handed Chellis a sealed envelope. Within would be the seeds for the newest tome, seven or eight words scrawled in vernal green ink that he was to nurse and nurture until they were plump with potential. It didn't always make sense to him, what she wanted, until he read the final product and saw how cleverly she served up the raw materials of his sleuthing efforts.

"One other thing," she said.

"Oh?"

"What do you make of this?" She swivelled her chair toward a rolltop desk, seized a folder that was sitting on top of a pile of proofs, and flipped it open. From it she retrieved a five by eight photograph which, swivelling back to face him, she held out, her expression unreadable.

He took the photograph and studied it closely. Further inspirational material, he assumed, although this was a new tack for her. The photo, black and white, was that of a graveyard, old style, with mossy, picturesque markers and stones. Lichen by the bushel. Cherubs, clasped hands, and roses were a dominant decorative feature, unlike the guitars and transport trucks one sometimes encountered etched on polished black granite while strolling through the more modern cemetery to visit one's eternally amused mum. *Died Laughing*. If his own wit hadn't been petrified at the time, he would have had that inscribed on her headstone. The script on these venerable ones, where visible, was an elegant italic or a chunky Roman. Verses abounded, heaven was repeatedly invoked, and entire families were gathered in the earth below, not infrequently sharing luckless and proximate death dates. Families of mounds, and too bad for you if you had in life despised your whole clan. This party was forever.

"What's wrong with this picture, you're asking?"

"Precisely."

"The gravestone off to the left."

"Yes?"

"Family name, 'Strange'. Cool name, but that's not it."

"No."

"Alistair Strange, husband, 1851–1899. The children, Elizabeth, Alwyn, Duncan, and Nora. The wife, Bethea Strange 1865 – . No death date. I wonder why?"

"So do I, dear."

"Where did you get this?"

"That's what's so interesting. Someone left it in my mailbox, but

27

in a blank envelope. No return address and no further information of any kind in it. Only the picture."

"Some wacko fan."

"This residence is known to so few, as you're well aware. Not even to my publishers. Business mail goes to my Toronto address. Locally, I'm known simply as that wealthy old bag from the city. And you wouldn't blab."

"My wallet's lips are open, but mine are sealed."

"Good. Speaking of secrets spilled, how is your inventor friend?"

Chellis winced. "She called."

"Entirely understandable, her pique. Secrets do have to be kept. I wouldn't be very happy, either, if someone were to divulge mine. Don't know *what* I'd do."

"Mine are so secret, *I* don't even know what they are."

She sipped her whisky, and gazed at him over the rim of the glass. "I'm intrigued."

"Thanks."

"Not by you, dear. You're an open book. The photo, find out about it will you?"

"What do you want to know?"

"Who sent it, and why? Where *is* this boneyard? Who were these 'Strange' people? That sort of thing."

Wonderful. "I'm not a private investigator."

"Read up then. That's your job, is it not? Get one of those *Dummies'* books on the subject." She gave him one of her commanding, imperial looks. "And before you go . . . do you have any more of those potato chips?"

3

Crime and Punishment

"SO WHAT DO YOU THINK?"

Careful, careful. "It's . . . ridiculous."

"*No* it isn't. What do you mean *ridiculous*?"

"A full-body sun hat?" Chellis tried to keep a straight face. "You think someone is actually going to *buy* something like that?"

"One size fits all."

"Even a very *big* someone? A giantess?"

"One size fits *two*. It's romantic. *And* healthy, full protection from UV."

Elaine wasn't listening to his ultra-sensible advice, as per, and this after having asked for it, also as per. She had already moved onto the marketing angle.

"Maybe you can sell it to CSIS."

"I wasn't spying on *you*, darling. I wasn't the one cruising by at 0.1 klicks while ogling Vaughn's physique."

"Ah, Von Yawn."

"Drop dead, Chelly."

"I just might." Chellis tried to snag a piece of cheese from the circulating Roomba, but the blasted thing shot to the other side of the room and got stuck under the couch. It began to whir pathetically and grind its little robotic brain. Elaine jumped up and walked over to free it. She repositioned the plate of cheese and crackers in the centre of the vacuum's metallic flat top. The Roomba responded with a beep of gratitude and careered away to snorfle up a strategically positioned pile of Pinky fluff. It began to circle around and around, zeroing in on its prey. At least the Roomba was getting something to eat. Chellis had been invited to lunch with the Alpha couple, but had been finding the appetizers somewhat elusive.

"Where is the famous physique anyway?"

"Making lunch."

"Perfect."

On cue, as if drawn by the magnetic force of his personal adjective, Vaughn himself appeared. Chellis noted once again that Elaine's mate gave much support to Eric Von Danekin's theories about aliens kick-starting the evolutionary process.

"You're looking very clean today Vaughn," he offered by way of a pleasantry. "Bright and shiny."

Elaine groaned, but Vaughn, ever the gentleman, responded with a wholly non-ironic smile. "Why, thank you Chellis. Care for a drink?"

"Iwouldthanks." Chellis's response followed so hard upon the question that it sounded for a moment as if Vaughn had answered it himself. The ultimate in courtesy.

"It's only 11:30," said Elaine. "A.M."

"Who are you, the Liquor Control Board?"

"Ha, ha." This was Vaughn. "You two." Pause. "Mixed drink, Chellis? Imported beer? Wine? I have a lovely Châteauneuf-du-Pape decanted."

"Surprise me, Vaughan."

Vaughan did. "Oh look!" he said, after reaching down to flick a mote of imaginary dust off the arm of the chair in which Chellis was seated. An irregularity in the world's order had caught his eye. "You seem to have something . . . " his observation lumbered out, bottom-heavy with concern, "er . . . on your . . . footwear, Chellis. I believe it's . . . it's . . . oatmeal."

All attention was then rivetted on the pointy toecap of Chellis's Beatle boot.

"You didn't tell me you'd *eaten* today," Elaine accused.

"Breakfast, Laney. An old custom observed by the fortunate of the human race. Happened hours ago." Actually, the porridge had been dinner the night before. What was good enough for Goldilocks was good enough for him.

"Days ago by the looks of that glob."

"It's not a *glob*. Globs have girth." He tried getting rid of the offensive, slob-confirming evidence by rubbing the boot against the back of his pant leg, but the hardy Scottish comestible stuck fast, like cement.

Vaughan, satisfied, announced, "Do excuse me for a sec, I best check on that ragout." Before sweeping out of the room with a manly and purposeful stride, he added, "Isn't Elaine's newest invention, the full-body sun hat, simply brilliant?"

They observed a moment of silence.

"Nice guy," Chellis finally said.

"Yes, he is." Elaine was taking this straight-up, no ice.

"Very supportive." Like a jockstrap.

"Always."

"Is he, you know, interesting at all?"

"*Yes*. Extremely."

"Doesn't leave pubic hair embedded in the soap, I suppose?"

"Never."

"I'll be checking later, you realize."

"You'll be sorry if you go snooping in the medicine cabinet."

"Packed with marbles again?"

"Not telling."

"Your robot is leaving crop circles in the broadloom, by the way."

The Roomba, fixated on the now fluffless spot, was circling and circling like someone with an unresolved neurosis.

"I wish it *were* mine. I'd work out the bugs, add a few more features, it'd be terrific. Vacuum, circulating hostess . . . ."

"The floor's the limit."

"Exactly."

Elaine walked over to the Roomba again and gave the machine a nudge with her shoe. It hurtled off and began to bounce erratically along the baseboard. The plate of cheese and crackers slid off the top and it was on them in a flash, sucking up every last crumb. Next it tried to inhale the plate. It began grinding away at this task, shortly made a distressed choking noise, beeped once, and shut itself off.

"Greedy thing," said Chellis. "That cheese must've gummed up the works."

"It's sweet. It's in love with Pinky. Follows her around everywhere."

"Where is the old fluffball, anyway?"

This query occasioned another pause, a thoughtful one. "I don't know, now that you mention it. Haven't seen her all day."

They both gave the Roomba an appraising look.

"You think?" asked Chellis.

"Surely not." Elaine continued to study the machine. "It's not a bad idea, really."

"What? Having Pinky for lunch?" Chellis might dislike and resent Vaughan, and wish to send him back to his ancestral home in outer space, but he was exceedingly glad that reliable old V was the one in charge of the ragout. An invitation to dine with Chef Elaine was usually a traumatizing lab rat experience. How could he forget the bologna fried on her curling iron, the 'tie' food made of edible (not quite) string, the casserole composed of post-consumer, cheese-like, simulated-protein product? The *grass*?

"That soap idea. Soap that ejects pubes. Icky, shed bits won't stick to it."

"Don't use oatmeal in it then."

Elaine was gone. She'd vanished into that mysterious, but bountifully equipped laboratory in her head. This shouldn't take too long, he reasoned, soap not being of a high imaginative order. He sat back, drummed his fingers on the arm of the chair. Vaughan materialized like a genie by his side, slid a glass of red wine into his hand, then tiptoed out of the room. Chellis gratefully guzzled half the glass – swell stuff – and looked around. A conventional hoity-toity living room rendered quirky with invention. It was more like Pee Wee's playhouse. If, by way of his own experiment, he were to pour the rest of his wine onto the carpet, Ruggy would doubtless deal with it. Elaine had been working on an advanced Scotchguarding process not too long ago – now that *was* brilliant. It froze the spill on the spot and you then swept it up and tossed it away. Not that he would ever dream of tossing out frozen Châteauneuf-du-Pape spillage; he'd scoop it up and lick it like a flat pane of puddle ice. Slowly he tipped his glass and a fair measure of wine, more than he intended, splattered onto the rug with a crime-scene finesse. It soaked in. The rug was white. Emphasis on was.

"*Chellis*," snarled Elaine. "For Christ's sake, no wonder you never get invited anywhere."

"I do too."

"What, you don't approve of the vino? Not your usual proletarian plonk? I can find you a Margaret Knight and a bottle of Baby Duck if that would help."

Margaret Knight was the inventor of the square-bottomed paper bag. Elaine gave credit where credit was due – unlike Chellis.

"Science, Laney. Experiment, right? Your sort of thing. I thought you'd treated the carpet with your . . . what did you call that gunk?"

"You mean the 'gunk' I stopped working on because of someone's big mouth?"

"I didn't *know*, c'mon be fair."

"Blab, blab, blab. It's hard to get a patent if everyone already knows about the invention, isn't it? Even supposedly secret details of the formula, which I'm amazed you even remembered. Dickhead."

"I was proud of you, that's all."

"Keep it to yourself."

"Okay, okay. I said I was sorry, didn't I? I bought you flowers."

"Mums. From ValuMart. On special. There was a big orange sticker on the plastic pot."

"Yeah, so?"

No comment.

"I'm glad you liked them."

Still no comment.

"All is forgiven, then, eh?"

"Not quite."

Shit. "No?"

Elaine smiled, but it was not a smile to gladden Chellis's heart.

Shit. Not *that*.

She raised the lid of the licorice red hassock in front of her, a Pandora's Box decor feature, and pulled out a clipboard. This she waggled invitingly, if somewhat menacingly, at Chellis.

No, no, no. "*Not* the Mall?"

She nodded slowly, still smiling.

Shit.

4

Mommie Dearest

"SO, HUNT. YOUR HAIR?"

"Got me, Chel. It was there twenty years ago. You're the detective, you tell me." Hunt raised his voice. "Eight feet, by ten, by eight."

Chellis dutifully wrote down the figures in Hunt's spiral notebook, but awkwardly on account of the bandage. "No I'm not."

Hunt pressed the release on the tape measure and both men watched with delight as the tape zimmed back to home base, concluding with a decisive *snap*.

"Your hand, what happened?"

"Bathroom."

"What, your dong's so weighty you pulled a muscle?"

"Laney's bathroom."

"Say no more."

"I don't intend to." Chellis walked over to the closet and peeked inside. It was empty except for a single dress hanging on a rusted wire hanger. The dress was a faded grey and brown polyester, pilled from wear, light as moulted snake skin. It exuded a stale, powdery, *je ne sais quoi* odour. "Ew."

"Yup, place smells. Let's do the master bedroom."

"Small master."

"It's a doll's house."

"Timeless in design."

"Enduring in value."

"Charm to spare."

"Loads of character."

"*Very* unique!"

"Fabulous opportunity!"

"Hardwood floors!"

"Genuine antique fixtures!"

"Teeth in drawer!"

"Yeah? The old lady's dentures?" Hunt walked over to have a look.

"Too tiny." Chellis had opened the top drawer of the vanity. That and a three-quarter bed, stripped of covers, except for a cheap, yellowed mattress pad, were the only pieces of furniture remaining in the room. "Rat's teeth."

"Baby teeth," Hunt concluded. "But you're not far wrong if they belong to Sonny Jim downstairs, swinging his biz deals even as we speak. Not too choked up. When was the last time he visited his poor old Ma? Eight, nine years ago, why, he can't quite recall."

"He told you that?"

"No shame." They stared at the teeth scattered in the drawer, a baker's dozen of misshapen, discoloured canines and incisors, the molars resembling dried corn kernels. "Neighbours finally twigged to the fact that her cat was hanging around for days outside, shredding the screen door and getting no joy."

Chellis reached out his bandaged hand, fingers protruding like roots sprouted from a potato. He was drawn to move the teeth around, stir them into a different configuration, interfere with their disorder. They wanted touching.

"Don't," warned Hunt. "They might bite."

"Maybe she was an old meanie. Beat the kid stupid."

"Hope so."

"He'll ask an arm and a leg for this dump, eh?"

"Natch. He's the type. Then gripe when it doesn't sell. Switch agents, drop the price, same old, same old."

Arm and a leg, Chellis continued to riff on that. Such was the visceral price one had to pay to shelter the remaining bits of oneself after a realty siege. He wondered how much the filial ingrate downstairs got for his teeth way back when. Had he enriched himself even then, or did he carry a lifelong grudge for having sold himself so cheaply? Each miserable little artifact will have been attached to some memory for his mother: the string on the doorknob, the misfired Junior League hardball in the kisser, the dentition-defying rump roast. Her son's gap-toothed, con artist smile. For her, these teeth may have still been rooted deeply in the past and alive – all, finally, that she had of him. Did unsentimental Rennie have a stash of suchlike relics? Vestiges of his younger self could be chattering away in some distant drawer of the archeological midden he called home. If he went on a dig, what would he find? As a boy, he had been aware, if dimly, that she had ever been on the lookout for his real mama, who she feared might one day appear at the door. This fabled woman, as unreal to him as the tooth fairy, come to snatch the warm, bloodied tooth from beneath his pillow and grab him as well. His worth? What would she leave Rennie as payment? A thin dime. As it turned out, the parental abduction arrived in a form that neither he nor Rennie had been expecting.

"What happened to the cat?" he asked.

"Mr. Nice Guy shipped it off to the pound." Hunt quickly scanned the room, took in the urine-coloured water stains on the ancient wallpaper, the wow in the hardwood, the dearth of electrical outlets. Unmentionables that either made the potential buyer's heart beat faster, your can-do fixer-upper personality, or induced a particular quality of silence in which one could almost hear the customers' hearts quailing. He expected a surfeit of the latter. Viewings with an asphyxiating burden of dead air. "C'mon Chel, let's get this done and get out of here. Treat you to lunch."

"My turn with the tape measure."

*

"*Sláinte*," Hunt raised his pint of Guinness.

Chellis did likewise. "May the sauce be with you." Being a cultural bastard, despite what his name might suggest, he couldn't bring himself to appropriate the Celtic salutation. He'd feel like a dork. Hunt, bless him, had a dork immunity.

"Looks good." Hunt had flipped open the menu. "I like their motto – 'Never trust anyone under thirty.'"

They had decided to try out a new restaurant downtown called The Age Spot. It was run by a couple of greying and brindled Boomers, had a bracingly cranky ambience, and retro fare. The menu was heavy on the fried, the trans, the bleached, and the non-to-inorganic. There didn't appear to be a speck of bran or a flaxseed in the whole place, and the offerings were rife with anti-antioxidants. The choice of drinks were highly sugared, caffeinated, or alcoholic. If you wanted bottled water they'd stomp off and fill up a brown stubby from the tap. True, smoking was not allowed, but there were ashtrays on all the tables filled with complementary candy cigs and it was not forbidden to reminisce fondly and with an unrequited ache about the nasty practice.

An elderly waitress, definitely *not* a server, headed their way at a brisk clip. She had high, stiff orange hair, a squint that belied an advanced case of macular degeneration, and a name badge pinned to her pink smock that read 'Bev.' She slowed down when she bumped into their table, this causing the clerical collars of foam on their drinks to slosh over the glass rims and pool on the flecked arborite.

"Youse ready?" she growled.

"Aaah . . . Bev . . . Beverly, is it? " Chellis stalled, cracking open the menu and performing a hasty scan.

"Got that wrong."

"Oh?"

"Name's short for Beverage. Sister's name is Brandy. Parents were drinkers."

"Really?"

"Of *course* it's Beverly, you tithead. Now whaddya want? Make it snappy."

"I'll have the Heart Attack Special," said Hunt.

"Got it. You?" She stared hard at Chellis's head, but misfired, puncturing a hole in his aura. He could feel it sagging onto his shoulders like a burst balloon.

"Okay, okay . . . I'll try The Big C, no, wait . . . what's this one? The DOA?"

"Fried spam, instant mashed potatoes, boiled veg, side salad with brown iceburg lettuce, a dried carrot curl, and a dead tomato slice. Plus a pickle left over from the last guy's lunch."

"Wow, Rennie's own cuisine. That's for me."

Bev gave a sharp nod and hurtled off, smacking tables and chairs that were in her way. Human pinball.

"The tough love school of waitressing," Hunt said.

"Yeah, frightening. Bet she'll make us sit here until we finish everything on our plates."

"Not a problem, Moe's gotten over her homemaker phase. No more mac and cheese or marshmallow salad the way Mum used to make. You've heard of the Slow Food Movement? She's into it. I can hear the stuff idling in the cupboard, lazing around, but it never seems to make it to the table."

Maureen was Hunt's ex-wife and girlfriend, in that order. The divorce had been her idea, and the staying together afterward in post-matrimonial bliss had also been hers. She was the ideas person in their coupling and Hunt usually went along with the latest, as he regarded her notions, however crackpot or pointless, as the creative byproduct of a stable union. Besides, she shouldered an inordinate amount of the world's happiness, and small though this was, it was yet a burden. He surely didn't want her to unpack it. What preceded the divorce was her "affair" affair – her extramarital project. She had decided that their marriage, for the sake of its health and vibrancy, required some free range coition and had selflessly volunteered to do the dirty work. She planned the strategy and manoeuvres for this bit of hanky-panky, all the ins and outs, as it were, and then discussed them earnestly with the cuckold-to-be. Hunt wasn't overly concerned because he knew that she would drive any auditioning adulterer and homebreaker nuts. The real problem was that no one would venture anywhere near her. Moe didn't lack in looks, pulchritude, or social graces, but she gave off the wrong kind of pheromones – virtuous and clean as soap – and her zeal had a clinical, thrill-dispelling effect. The nuanced and grotty joys on offer in a truly sordid arrangement she simply did not get, nor would get. In a last ditch effort, Hunt had privately solicited the help of his pal, who, though protesting loyalty, was perhaps more ready to weigh in than he should have been.

She turned him down. Thus:

"Aw, gee, Chel. I can't, not with *you*. Sorry."

"No, eh? Hmph. That's okay, Moe . . . it's just . . . why, though? Because of Hunt?"

"No, that's not it."

"So, what is it? The fangs, the goiter, the killer BO? I had to stop using that deodorant Elaine concocted. It scorched all the hair in my armpits."

"See, *see*, that's it! You're funny."

"Funny?"

"Yes, ha ha funny, you know that. Don't take this the wrong way, but . . . I've always kind of thought of you as Daffy Duck."

Nods. "I'm honoured."

Moe beamed at him, her excess of well-being plumping her cheeks and making them glow in an adorable, neotenic way.

"And who'd want to fuck a duck, right?"

Chellis had consoled himself with the insight that she would have turned down any nookie-suitor no matter how impressive the performance CV. She had only wanted *to be asked* and he, Lothario of the spoken word, had satisfied her. Moe and Hunt's amicable divorce had followed hard on. *As it were.*

"How are your folks?" Chellis asked.

"Both cackling away, making money hand over fist."

"No kidding?" He had to smile at the thought of Hunt's parents. Had to. Now *they* were funny, if unintentionally. Hilariously, they *both* bore an uncanny resemblance to Mother Teresa; they were like a matching pair of salt and pepper shakers, complete with holes in their heads. They had provided so much comic relief over the years that Chellis could only be grateful to them. Less so Hunt, who had frequently envied aloud his friend's orphan status, averring that *families are not vehicles built for pleasure, Chel. You ride in them as far as you need to go and then you bail out.* Recently, his folks had sold their house in town, placing it on the market with another realtor, so as not to show favouritism, and moved north to cottage country, where they bought a defunct slaughterhouse that they turned into a B&B.

"People actually stay there?"

"Apparently. Big demand."

Chellis shuddered. Animal terror, rivers of blood. Surely the ghostly, skin-em-alive, head-lopping, and trotter-severing ambience would not be particularly restful for even the most hard-hearted tourist.

"Like that Lizzie Borden B&B in the States," Hunt said. "Very popular."

Forty whacks.

Chellis jumped. Bev had suddenly appeared with phantom stealth and slammed two plates of food on the table. They were not, mercifully, commanded to Enjoy!, although she did order Chellis to sit up straight – "You'll get round shoulders!" – and then she turned on Hunt.

"How *many* times have I told you not to lean back in your chair like that?"

"Once?"

"And wipe that smile off your face."

"Mad Cow," whispered Chellis, giving his plate the once over after she'd rocketed away. The side order of coleslaw was hemorrhaging mayo.

"For sure. She'll slap you up the side of the head if you give her any lip. Love that Velveeta hair colour, though."

"I mean that's what this dish was called, wasn't it? The one pound burger, fries with gravy, onion rings. The Mad Cow."

"Hey, you're right. Bev's short-term memory must be shot."

Chellis glanced around. "Everyone here has exactly the same order."

"So *that's* what they mean by 'No Catering.' Eat what you're served and shut your trap. Very Fifties."

They dug in up to their elbows. It was fantastic.

*

"Bad boy, you're gonna catch it."

Hunt was leaning back in his chair and casting a sly look in Bev's direction, but she was busy chewing out some other customer. He rubbed his belly and belched. "Man, I've go so much meat in here I feel like I'm carrying a kid." The buttons were straining on his shirt, revealing eyelets of skin tufted with black curlicues of hair.

"That was definitely the mother of all burgers." Chellis studied his friend. "I believe I've solved the mystery of your missing locks."

"Christ, yeah. Stuff grows everywhere, except on the old noodle." Hunt sat forward and grabbed a pack of candy Camels from the ashtray. "Speaking of old noodles, how's Madame Twatski?"

"Now, don't be rude." It was not exactly true that Chellis had kept completely mum about the true nature of his employment, or of his employer, insofar as he could divine the latter. Hunt and Elaine

41

had both been apprised of his secret service and both marvelled at his luck. A qualified marvelling, however. On this his friends agreed: how very like Chellis it was, with his half-degree in Eng Lit and his half-assed ambitions, to have landed such remunerative and effortless work. In Hunt's view, anyone who knew that the Web existed, especially a clever old spiderwoman like Athena Havlock, did not require a personal researcher. He was convinced that Chellis was nothing more to her than an informational boy toy (and he dearly hoped that info was as far as it went). As for Elaine, she felt that there was something fishy about the arrangement. The job was too easy, too unstructured, too undermining of a character already prone with sloth. Rennie had been a piss-poor mother, all that palsy-walsy stuff, all those gifts and toys in lieu of discipline. Trust Chellis to somehow find an equally indulgent replacement.

Back off Protestants! He *did* work, night and day. His approach was simply more meditative and circuitous than it was for most wage slaves. He was a hunter and gatherer, a sifter and sorter, a delver and deliverer of the goods. And the goods were often a genuine pain in the rear to find. There was an intuitive knack to this business that Chellis was pleasantly surprised to find himself in possession of. A highly sensitive Nosey Parker, he was receptive to that which others – a realtor or an inventor *for example* – might shrug off as insignificant and not worthy of sniffing out. God *is* in the details, Chellis knew, because he had often seen His Big Old Fuzzy Face staring back at him, tipping him the wink, from the deep core of matters minute and particular.

Certainly there was more to conquering Mrs. H's requests than the occasional browser search or trip to the library. He had come to know what she liked, what provoked her interest and fired her mind. Much of his work was customized to her imaginative style, and was even on occasion anticipatory and preemptive, like the time he spent a whole day researching the devious wonders of identity theft and credit card scams and had the information on hand the very moment she asked for it. That the apparent simplicity of his assignments did not reveal the labour involved was evident when he offered up one of her request lists to his friends' amused inspection. Elaine: *I suppose you have to eat these instructions after reading them?* Yuk, yuk. Or Hunt, dismissively: *Should take ten, twenty minutes tops.* Then, handing the list back, *And since you're not doing anything, I've got this open house over on . . . .*

"Brand new assignment." Chellis patted his shirt pocket where the current list reposed, the sheet folded into a tidy quartered document. With its loose collection of words, he almost expected the paper to rattle like a packet of magic beans. But then he recalled the photo and his irritating secondary quest, which was currently sitting on the top of his fridge under a pile of Canadian Tire money (5 cents, 10 cents, it adds up) and a weeping can of no longer frozen orange juice. "Say, Hunt, wasn't Moe tramping around in graveyards a while back looking for some forebears of hers?"

"Cripes, the genealogy phase. Glad that one's over. Two years work, buckets of cash down the toilet, and all she managed to dig up was a farmer from some bog hole in Ireland. Made her happy, though. Why?"

"Need to find something for Mrs. H. A gravestone inscription she wants checked out."

"Pray she doesn't get bitten by the ancestor-hunting bug, or you'll spend your days in some dank library vault scrolling through miles of microfiche. Talk to Moe. Believe me, she's an expert on the dead and buried. Speaking of which, you think your boss knew that guy they found over in Claymore?"

"Should she?"

Hunt shrugged. "Heard he was some sort of literary type."

"A literary type in Claymore? That's asking for trouble."

"Obviously." Hunt took a pseudo-drag on his chocolate ciggie and blew out an imaginary cloud of carcinogens. "Uh-oh, here comes Bev with the bill. How little d'you think we can tip her?"

"How much allowance did you get as a kid?"

"Not a friggin' cent."

"That sounds about right."

5

Mallaise

CHELLIS SHOT UP from the bench and stood at attention. Despite the soporific, soul-sucking atmosphere, he'd been having a decent enough time watching pallid, blank-faced teen girls dressed in their baby clothes drifting past in packs, yards of midriff exposed, rolls of fat wobbling on the waistbands of low-slung jeans. Breasts were everywhere, aggressively prominent in tiny T's. It was a cannibal's marketplace. No, it was the mall, and Elaine should know better than to exile him here with nothing but a clipboard for self-defence.

But *what ho!* the inventor herself was steaming toward him with a headlong velocity that was all too familiar. He decided not to bother with the jocular greeting.

"Aha! You're checking up on me. You don't trust me."

"Damn straight."

"That hurts, Laney. I honestly don't think you know how sensitive I am."

"Dry up, Chel. You're *selectively* sensitive. When it suits. What do you have for me so far?"

"Hmm, well, let's see." He consulted the clipboard. "Ten people told me to fuck off."

"What country are we in, Chel?"

"Okay, yeah, they said *please* fuck off."

"The usual, what else?"

"One woman laughed so hard she had to rush to the bathroom."

"Turn off the charm, will you. The questionnaire is very straightforward. Let me see."

Elaine snatched the clipboard out of his hands, and read aloud, "Totally stupid . . . Heavens, I'd never buy one of those . . . Are you serious, man? . . . Sounds, like, ya know, too flimsy, too, like, weird . . . Sorry, not interested . . . You one of them religious nuts, one of them Morons?" She tapped the board, driving invisible drill bits into it with her forefinger. "You filled these in yourself, didn't you?"

Chellis affected his best expression of incredulity, placing his innocent and formerly injured hand flat on his chest. "You bet."

"You're hopeless."

"I prefer to think of myself as 'a challenge.'"

"I thought you wanted to earn your way back into my good graces. I also thought your hand was, how did you put it, dangling off your wrist by a mere sinew?"

"I heal quickly, one of my many talents. It's the venue, Laney, you expect to get a decent survey here? Malls are awash in spiritual chloroform. Get a load of that couple over there. Both string-theory physicists before they stepped in here and now look at them – totally strung out. They could be extras from *Dawn of the Dead*."

Elaine studied the couple as they wandered past, a middle-aged, conventionally attired ma and pa with identical fixed expressions, botoxed tip to stern by the material glut on display.

"Why, I wonder?"

"Why do malls invariably stupefy people like too much TV and what can you invent to cure it?"

"Yeah," she smiled.

Oh man, this just about finished him off, this rare, fleeting, and utterly beautiful phenomenon.

"Do that again," he pleaded.

"Do what?"

"That thing with your mouth. You know, you stretch your lips a bit, and then curl them up at the ends."

"Piss off."

"Okay, where to?"

"Who cares." Elaine glanced around, eyes widening slightly at the commercial come-on. "Since I'm here I might as well do some shopping."

"Great, I love shopping."

"Excuse me, but you hate shopping, Chelly. Shopping with you is like having a bag of wet sand tied to my ankle."

"Mind if I write that down?"

"Yes I do. Hands off. Why is it that when I read your employer's books I run across sentences, even whole paragraphs, that sound incredibly familiar?"

"You read her books? *You*, Brainy Elaine?"

"Beach read."

"Is *that* what you were doing in your humongous sun hat? Reading trash? Hey, you're blushing."

Elaine made a *mnph!* sound of compacted exasperation, internal gears being stripped, and stalked off. Chellis followed at a discreet distance, ducking behind slow-mo mall-crawlers, practising his gumshoe trailing technique. She strode purposefully into a lingerie shop, which he knew was a bluff. Elaine never shopped for sexy underwear, being a devotee of no-nonsense, 100% cotton granny pants. If Vaughan was getting to pull lacey thong undies off Elaine's lovely rear with his perfect teeth, Chellis was prepared to shoot himself. But he didn't think so. Peering through the store window and observing her as she flipped through racks of scanty, silky merchandise, he could tell that her thoughts were running more on practical, inventive lines than on erotic ones. He *knew* her. She was the girl-next-door. Literally at one time, when they had all been growing up together, she and he and Hunt. In those days, the door of her house had been painted an eyeball-peeling red, whereas now, on uppity Hitchcock Crescent it was an elegant, mist-grey – creating an illusion of easy entry – and heavily, brassily beknockered. (As was the woman who swished past him into the store. Two highly convincing power points! She gave him a sidelong, knowing look.) Elaine may have exchanged one door for another, and one raucous, brawling working-class family for a small, smug, nouveau rich set, but she herself had not changed . . . much.

Her head swivelled sideways like an owl sensing a minute, but telling, disturbance in its personal space. Chellis ducked down and ooched along until he was beyond the store window and its pornish, *get-with-it-prudes* display. He found himself facing the open entrance of the next shop, which happened to be a bookstore, which also happened to be what he needed. Heck with Elaine. She'd come looking for him anyway, annoyed that he wasn't still shadowing her. Crouched, he was well-positioned to perform a zippy Russian Cossack dance – a suitable bit of ethnic, mall entertainment – but instead, knees creaking, he rose and stretched. He could stretch willfully all day and not achieve a truly towering height, but contented that he'd been restored to his full, dignified self, he entered this commercial establishment where the clerks might not have gained any intimacy with the wares on display, but at least rarely asked if they could *help you*. Not bloody likely, was the only true answer to that.

What a relief, this linguistic oasis, even if it was a chain and pervaded by a mallesque unreality. Here be books. Here be books to slake and concentrate and revive the wandering and dehydrated mind. Here be books *on sale*. Last season's must-haves heaped on front tables and reduced to the price of bum wad. Buy a stack and stock your privy; be blessed with piles of a more edifying nature. Chellis was not immune to the lure of a good bargain when it presented itself, but he found the remainder table depressing and indecent. Words *are* cheap. He hustled past, eyes averted in case he got snagged by a title he'd meant to read when it was all the rage. He wandered more slowly through the fiction section, Mrs. Havlock's contributions winking slyly at him as he passed by. As previously instructed by the author, he stopped to place a few volumes face out, dimming the lights of the competition by either smothering their books with hers, or misfiling them. He occasionally did this for lesser-knowns as well, obscure writers he happened to like. Chellis, the Robin Hood of literary distribution – or the Puck.

In the genre section her volumes were all spine, but these did not require his gallantry. Her darlings here had grown legs, as they say in the lit biz. Legs! They were veritable centipedes that scrambled off the shelves and into customers' hands, where they dug in their little heels and clung fast. These books could not be put down, as they also say.

Chellis skimmed past the kids' section, letting himself be tangentially seduced by covers burgeoning with magicians, pirates, bears in pants, and a worm sporting a Tyrolean hat. He was seriously tempted to sit down on the juvenile chair provided and have a long, lingering read of *Goodnight Moon*. That bunny, now *there* was character development. And mystery. And a bowl full of mush. Chellis knew that his inner child would be thrilled and his outer one becalmed, but he did not pause. The How-To books were beckoning.

But, *goodnight brain*, the *Dummies* and their ilk had apparently conquered and wiped out the humble, no-nonsense indigenous species. How did this work? You tell people that they're stupid and inept and they can't get enough of it and make you a millionaire? Right, so, Chellis perused the wares on offer: *The Cro-Magnon Guide to Accounting*; *The Bonehead's Book of Autopsies*; *Meatloaf Instruction for Meatheads*; *Modern History in Monosyllables*; *Checkers for the Cranially Challenged*; *The Little Book of Aphorisms for Little Minds*; *Lafs for Losers*; *The No-Brainer Guide to Advanced Calculus and Gardening*; *The Sun Also Rises, eh? Astronomy for Assheads*; *You Wittle Wascal: Tantric Sex for Fuddists*; *Clueless: The Dolt's Manual of Detection* . . . wait, Chellis paused over this last one, then reached up to pull it off the shelf.

"Thought I'd find you in here. What are you looking for?"

He instantly retracted his hand as if he'd singed his fingers.

"Hand still sore, is it?" Elaine glanced at the titles and didn't even try to repress her smirk. "Having some trouble with your self-esteem, Chel?"

"Research." He attempted a neutral tone with a spritz of hauteur.

"Everything's research."

"My philosophy exactly."

"With you, I mean. It's your excuse for not doing anything else. Your bolthole."

"Pardon me, Mrs. Champion, but perhaps you'd like to add to this shelf: *Laney's Tiny Tome of Lite Psychology*. I'm here because I'm working. What are *you* doing here, besides harassing the customers?"

"I need a book of baby names."

"*What?*" He was aghast. Not *that*, surely not. Naturally the virile Vaughan would be a walking talking sperm bank, up to his eyebrows in reproductive equity, family jewels clanking wealthily every time he moved his perfect thighs.

"Calm down Chel, it's for the cat."

"Ah."

"Which I didn't want, by the way. I have a cat, Pinky, remember."

"The Roomba's lady love. I thought she was a goner."

"But the cat came back, yes, and now her nose is really out of joint."

"She'll get over it. He'll be her partner in crime, her best boy.

Soon she'll be washing his pretty face for him and wondering where he was all her life."

"Since you like him so much, and since you were the one who rescued him from the pound, why don't you keep him?"

"I already have pets."

"Chel, flies aren't pets."

"I know that, sheesh. They're food."

"Oh, God."

"For my spiders, those friendly arachnids on the porch. They bring me my slippers every evening when I come home from work."

"Work, ha! And spiders aren't pets, either. Likewise mice, cockroaches, and whatever other abhorrent creatures-in-residence you're subsidising at Vermin U."

Chellis smiled, glimmering beneath that carapace of crabbiness was a half-decent sense of humour. "Marry me. I'll save you from your snotty existence."

"Sorry, I'm taken. Funny you didn't pop the question when you could have."

"My popper wasn't working at the time. Besides . . . I was busy."

"I know. Research."

"You would have turned me down."

"You're right about that."

"Can I help you?"

This query, directed pointedly at Chellis, issued from a pimply youth who'd slithered up beside them, drawn by the glow of invective. Or possibly he sensed a plug in the flow of book product out of the store caused by these conversing customers.

"I wish," muttered Elaine, moving off.

"Why, yes you *may*, if you think you *can*." Chellis offered the clerk this gentle grammatical corrective without apparent effect. "I'm looking for, gee, I've forgotten the title, but I think the author's name is Tolstoy. Yes, I'm pretty sure that's right."

"Canadian?"

"I believe so." In his heart of hearts, all that bygone socialism.

"I'll check the computer."

"Thanks."

"No problem."

Chellis sighed. He could either grab the kid by the throat and squeeze a good old-fashioned *you're welcome* out of him, an expressive spurt as antique as Hopalong Cassidy Toothpaste, or he could go and bug Elaine some more. He opted for the latter and found her in the mystery section.

"Call him Noir."

"Who?"

"Your new black cat."

"You can't name him, he's not yours."

"Okay, okay, I'll take him."

"Can't, you had your chance. Besides, Vaughan likes him."

"Vaughan likes him?"

"Do I hear an echo? As a matter of fact, Vaughan adores him."

"Vaughan adores him? I did something nice for Vaughan?"

"'Fraid so." Elaine was flipping through one of Mrs. Havlock's paperbacks from the Marcel Lazar series. "This is you, you know."

"Who, Lazar? Don't be ridiculous, he's a drunk."

"Uh-huh."

"Get lost, Laney. A couple of drinks a day."

"Before breakfast?"

"Whenever, don't be picky, it's good for my health. I don't look anything like the way Mrs. H describes Lazar."

"True, she *has* made him a lot more handsome than you. Taller, smarter, way sexier. Why is your bottom lip trembling like that?"

"Keats was five foot two, Pope was *four foot six*."

"The Pope?"

"I'm a veritable giant among men, with a giant's male accoutrements. But look, even you must know that these detective types are pure formula. Male *and* female fantasies. Lone wolves, shit-kickers, slightly disreputable truth-seekers, tall, dark and available. They're never married, are they?"

"You're not."

"That's beside the point."

"She's using you."

"Yup, it's called being an employee, which you don't happen to know much about. She's allowed to because she pays me. Very well I might add."

50

"Don't get all huffy, only wanted to warn you."

"And *you* don't of course? Use your old pal, that is."

"Wouldn't dream of it, although . . . I do have a favour to ask, almost forgot." Elaine slotted the book back with its brethren on the shelf, and began to dig in her massive handbag, home of wrenches, springs, hockey tape, unidentifiable whatsits, and several semi-invented gizmos. "Here," she pulled out a plain white bar of soap and handed it to Chellis. "Be a sweetheart and test this for me, will you?"

Chellis weighed the bar in his hand. It was suspiciously light. He sniffed it. "Smells like that cereal you concocted once. Otiose, stick to your ribs, and that was no lie. Any side effects?"

"Such as?"

"Skin hanging off in strips. Death."

"Chel, it's only soap."

"Ours is a risk-averse culture."

"Well, take a chance, live a little . . . wash your hands, have a shower." A tiny alarm sounded from within the depths of her handbag. "Oops, gotta go. Meeting Vaughan for coffee."

"Swell, you talked me into it, I'm busy, but I can spare an hour or two – "

Elaine was gone, the *fata morgana* of the mall.

"Hey, sorry." It was the spotty clerk. "Our copy sold out when the author's book was on Oprah. I could try to reorder it."

"That's all right. Too expensive anyway."

"Yah, really."

"Say, would you like to try this?" Chellis offered him the bar of soap, passing it on with relief to the next sucker in this experimental relay. "I understand it's excellent for certain, er, skin conditions."

"Sure, hey why not. Thanks, eh."

"No problem."

6

RIP

EYES CLOSED, but not in slumber, Chellis was perusing a brief, back page newspaper article recently composed and published (about a second ago) in his very own head: *While attending a slow-food luncheon at the home of Ms. Maureen Hunt, a Mr. Chellis Beith of Burke Street, Farclas, was unexpectedly eaten by an orc. At the time of the occurrence the victim was said to be feeling no pain. The orc, dressed in the latest couture corpse-wear, including a designer Ulcers-R-Us T-shirt, requested a Rolaid from the hostess before beating a hasty retreat. "Poor Chellis," a shocked Ms. Hunt sympathized. "He didn't get a chance to try my homemade pita made from wheat grown in my own backyard and ground by my very own unhurried hands." A brisk service will be held for Mr. Beith downtown at The Age Spot. Donations to the Bev Retirement Fund gratefully received, although not by her.*

No wonder Hunt was putting on pounds these days. He never ate at home, and Chellis had discovered why. His first mistake had been accepting Moe's invitation to lunch, instead of inviting her out to eat. She could have picked censoriously at her fast food while he picked her brain, and the drinks bill wouldn't have mounted stupendously if he were paying. At her place, during the pre-luncheon period, which was comparable in length to the Precambrian, Chellis had slowly, *slowwwly* but surely gotten plastered. Not only had he dislocated his head (lost it!) knocking back tumblers of grappa, but he had the queasy impression that somewhere along the line, assured of the health benefits of the Mediterranean diet, he'd knocked back a bottle of extra virgin olive oil as well. Lunch, when it had finally arrived, resembled molten Shrek on a plate. Offering it a pension seemed more appropriate than saying grace. At least the meal had been colour-coordinated with Moe's necrological chatter. He'd had no idea that she was such a ghoul. This cold, bubbly internal spring of hers might even be the secret source of her terminal good cheer. Mrs. Havlock was a bit this way, too, for there was nothing like the subject of death to bring colour to her cheek and a sparkle to her eye.

Presently he was a captive of his front porch easy chair and as motionless as an expelled orc pellet, hair of the dog resting loyally on the floor beside him. This geriatric piece of furniture was bulky with cellulite and had Jiffy Peanut Butter lids for feet, but ever-welcoming arms. As long as he could remember it had functioned as the household grandma surrogate, a place for either he or Rennie to retreat to for consolation, bottle in hand, as often as the punishing vicissitudes of life demanded. To be nine years old, home sick from school (exams and overdue assignments, very sick-making), and sucking back a Carling's Black Label on the front porch, had been a great consolation indeed. Chellis got achey-hearted recalling it, his youthful, boozy Black Label days enthroned in this seat of anti-authority. He'd spent many contented, wastrel hours here simply watching the foremothers of his current arachnid clan – the original slow-foodies – as they fastidiously assembled fly wraps. The only multi-tasking he did involved harkening to Elaine's rowdy relations next door as they pounded on walls, slammed doors, threw sharp objects at one another and bellowed abuse. How he missed them, the Borrings, a family name that occasioned one too many jests for their liking. They had certainly never lived up – or down – to it. His lively ex-neighbours had been an extended family of sorts (they threw sharp objects and bellowed at him too), extended a safe enough distance anyway. At the first opportunity and never mind her feminist sentiments, Elaine had handily dropped her surname into a white trash receptacle. If Vaughan were a real gentleman, he would have exchanged names along with the marital vows. Elaine Champion. Vaughan Borring. Too right.

After the kids next door had flown from the nest – and outside of Elaine, their flight paths took them directly to employment/incarceration in a) Wal-Mart b) a Ford Automotive Plant and c) the Kingston Pen – the parents had sold up, bought an RV with the funds, and rattled off to live in some outlaw, drifter colony in Nevada called Slab City. The house sale had been accomplished with the assistance of Hunt Realty, a perfidy compounded when the very same and only realtor in the company lured a couple of over-achievers into the neighbourhood, a nice-nice young couple who worked all day and renovated most of the night. Any ruckus Chellis now heard from that direction was utterly drained of passion and drama. Painting their perfectly fine red front door a cowardly neutral colour (Clotted Cream? Xenophobic White?) and then hanging a flowery twig wreath on it, was about as violent as things got. The cops no longer came screeching up to that door, although by rights they should, for to be hammering nails into a wall with the objective of displaying a Thomas Kinkaid painting was a much greater offence than knocking a few heads into it. Chellis realized that trouble lay ahead the day he spotted the couple in their driveway, measuring it with a ruler and staring worriedly at the encroaching crabgrass. His crabgrass. Soon enough they'd be rapping his knuckles with that ruler and hauling him to court for attempting to make a land grab.

He did truly miss the Borrings, Frank and Mary and brood, and he especially missed the slightly tubby and bespectacled and determined child they had somehow conceived. (Exceedingly attractive came later, and how had she managed that? Sheer willpower.) Elaine had been so different from the rest of them – reserved, studious, proper – that the usual corny family jokes circulated: the mix-up at the hospital, the cuckoo in the nest, the postman/milkman service with a smile. Although Chellis did sometimes more seriously speculate about her origins. It wouldn't have surprised him in the least to discover that she too was a foundling, a lost sister perhaps that fate, with Dickensian plot-engineering, had landed in the house beside his. (O Fate! Listen up, and land her there again! Rout the gentrifying invaders! Be tasteful though, eh.)

Chellis fondly recollected the countless summer afternoons that he and Elaine had sat together companionably on this porch, he reading *Mad* magazine, or Archie comics, or P. G. Wodehouse, and she reading *Popular Mechanics*, Richie Rich comics, or Virginia Woolf. A room of one's own? She'd occupied one from birth, if only in her head. Rennie had been amused by Elaine, calling her Little Miss Einstein and Professor Borring. Elaine, for her part, had never been much amused in return. Not because of the teasing, which she was inured to, but because Rennie's temperament irritated her. She had enough to contend with in her own boisterous and lax household without having to humour a mother who steadily slipped through her definition of what a mother should be like a ghost walking through walls.

Rennie, slight of frame, fine-featured, pale complexion, hair dyed black, fingernails painted a glossy white (*perlaceous!*), leaning against the porch railing, smoke in hand, staring out far beyond the crab-grass, tardier then in its world takeover. A birthday party raging inside, Chellis's tenth maybe, kids roaring through the house, jumping on the couch, the beds, and Elaine in the bathroom fixing the toilet that had been running non-stop for days. Or hunkered down in a corner building a Frank Gehry gas station with the Meccano set she'd given him, or playing pin the tail on the donkey all by herself, and not even cheating, and still winning. Or in the kitchen washing a week's worth of dishes so they would have something to put the cake and ice cream on other than their grubby hands and laps. Elaine scrubbing and scrubbing, a self-appointed Cinderella, and Rennie smiling faintly, mysteriously, vanishes.

If, say, Vaughan also vanished – *poof!* – and Chellis made a face at the neighbours and frightened them away – *boo!* – and Laney moved back next door – *yes!* – then their houses could get married. Not in the Montague and Capulet sense, but a union more architectural in design. This would leave the individuals within the wedded structures at liberty to stretch themselves existentially. They would not have to be fused like Siamese twins by the royal and marital pronoun – we did this, we did that, we went shopping, we bought a bra, we went *we we we* all the way home. How did Philip Larkin, that cheeriest of Twentieth Century poets, put it? "He married a woman to stop her getting away/ Now she's there all day." Dead on, Phil.

Well, a plague on the house next door, Chellis thought, athough *please* not on his. His had enough problems. In fact his house already resembled a plague site. If he were capable of movement, he might even do a little housework as certainly he had been meaning to do for about a year now. Housework itself was made for procrastinators, a deluxe, four star excuse-hotel that he rarely checked into. Was it even possible to feel like a non-virtuous and guilty slacker whilst down on one's knees plucking specks of grit off the heated slate tiles with a pair of tweezers? Not that he had tiles of any description. He'd have to go next door for that, tweezers generously extended.

Gingerly, he inclined his head to take in his immediate surroundings. He spotted an unfamiliar leaf collection in the corner and grime thick as ultrasuede on the floor. He noticed that an enterprising squirrel had stuffed a slit in the cushion of the other chair, a lame and faded wicker rocker, full of pine cones. (*Brilliant*, thinks squirrel. *No one's ever gonna find this.*) The loafer's classic empties and pop cans, several toppled over, were much on display, as well as a plant pot studded with cigarette butts. The neglected resident of the pot was so desiccated that it was unrecognizable as a former respirating and chlorophyll-producing member of the upper world.

Chellis spied (with his little eye) a shoal of unread newspapers beside his empty recycling box (not entirely empty, as something furred and foul was growing on its blue bottom). *Do* people actually clean their porches, he rebelliously began to wonder. Wasn't that Mother Nature's job? Surely he hadn't been abandoned by her, too? He scooped up one of the newspapers, intending to toss it in the Blue Box, when a two-paragraph article on an extreme corner of the front page caught his eye. Big enough news still for the front page, but shrinking quickly and about to sink out of view in the obscure depths of the paper, therein destined to stand briefly in the shadow of Goliath car, computer, and cell phone ads before being wiped out completely.

"Huh," he said, feeling no compunction to say anything more intelligent, seeing as he was expressing mild surprise only to himself. Having plunged on past the headline, *Slain Man Identified*, he was informed that the body discovered in Claymore had been that of one Jude Thomas. *Hey Jude!* The name didn't ring a bell even though the piece described the victim as a freelance reviewer, copy-editor, and most recently, part-time production assistant at the prestigious Culloden Press in Toronto, one of Mrs. Havlock's publishers. In other words, the poor bugger had been a literary limpet clinging tenaciously to the skirts of the publishing world, and it *was* mostly skirts. *Who* would want to kill a lowly book reviewer? Only about a thousand people Chellis could think of offhand. The police were in for some excruciating interviews. Cop: "I understand, sir, that you're a writer."

Suspect: "Indeed, I am, and my talent was evident from my earliest years. . . ." Or a copy-editor? Obviously it had been some escalating dispute over commas, or the vicious culmination in an argument involving the use of the word "career" instead of "careen." Or a production assistant? Book not ready for the author's much-anticipated launch? Case closed and sealed tight as an uncut folio.

Lord, Chellis sighed, what a world, and how difficult it was to remain in it, even for the meek and mild. Especially for the meek and mild. He was practically crowbait himself, having barely survived Moe's lunch and the suffocating amount of information on matters posthumous that she had heaped on him. Morbidology, she could open her own university department. Death Studies. No doubt such already existed, considering the number of journals, indexes, newsletters, books, and periodicals that were devoted entirely to the learned exhumation of the permanently inert. Even for the necrologically curious hobbyist extensive resources were available, whatever lugubrious subject might tickle one's fancy: funerary art, memorial photography, body snatching, cemetery tourism, burial customs, postmortem misadventures of the famous (Laurence Sterne, Gram Parsons, Alistair Cooke). The U.S. even boasted a National Museum of Funeral History. Rest in Peace? Fat chance.

"What fascinates me," Moe had said, sipping her post-prandial bark tea (her tree), and studying Mrs. Havlock's graveyard snap, "is this fuzzy halo thingy on the left-hand side. You might have some supernatural activity here."

Sweet Moe. No wonder Elaine called her the airhead of the house. Women could be exceedingly and sneakily mean to one another. Men were much more direct. And death was occasionally the result.

"About the circumference of a can of orange juice?" he'd said, chirpily.

"*Yeah*, it is."

"It's pollution, Moe, your super-unnatural activity. Very scary it is, too. So any ideas?"

Forget the ditsy reputation, Moe had come up with ideas by the score. If only he could retrieve some of them from the sodden files in his recently flooded memory bank. Elaine claimed that alcohol turned your brain into lace, but that opinion came from her prissy side, not her scientific one. (Which was only two sides to a woman who was tetrahedral in complexity. In portraiture, only a Picasso would be able do her justice. Thus reflected her spaniel.) If his cogitations *were* like tatting, then there'd be plenty of vents for the irrelevant to drain away. Of what Moe told him, he did recall the bit about how the location of a cemetery could be pinpointed, or at least narrowed down to a particular country or county or settlement, if the tombstone offered enough idiosyncratic clues. This involved sussing out the kind of material used for the stone, the type of script and contents of the text, the decorative embellishments, the flora that grew around it and on it, the physical context in which it was set. Local stone carvers may have worked in an identifiable style. Bless her, she had made his quest seem somewhat less impossible.

Moe had tapped the photo with a bread stick that looked suspiciously store-bought. "If this gravestone had a winged death head carved on it, or a crescent, which would indicate heraldry, then it's Old Country, a dead giveaway."

"So to speak."

"Exactly."

"Bob's your uncle."

"I thought Bob was *your* uncle. Where is he, anyway?"

"Home. Hangin' loose. Hasn't come out of the closet yet this year."

"Right, okay, you're lucky the script on this marker is Roman. Italic doesn't weather very well. It wears away, which can be totally frustrating. This stone has to be granite, though. See all the lichen, it loves to grow on granite, moss too. If you magnify it, you might be able to identify the species, which could be a help."

"Moe, are you showing off?"

"A weeny bit. Hunt isn't interested in any of this and it's so much fun."

"Careful, I'll tell Hunt you called him a weenie."

"Chel, I think you've had too much to drink."

"No!"

"Seriously, the best place to start is where you would have started anyway without my help, right? There's tons of death stuff on the web, lots of cemetery sites, it's fantastic. This could be way easier than you think. A quick search might lead you right to the spot, and to this person you're hunting for, this woman."

"She flew the coop."

"They do sometimes." Moe patted his hand and then slid a piece of paper between his fingers. "Ready for dessert?"

"Is it green?"

*

He delved into his shirt pocket, where the paper she had given him was resting flush against Mrs. Havlock's list. He didn't want the two lists to get overly intimate, thereby producing even more work for him to do. Retrieving Moe's, he read over the urls she'd made note of (Url, now there was an orc moniker if ever he heard one). What undreamed-of riches the cyber-world had to offer if one had the patience of a prospector. Moe had listed a site called, eerily, City of the Silent and another, the more upbeat Funeral Central and, most promising, Find a Grave. One site dealt only with haunted grave-yards, another archived tombstone photos, and one even allowed you to leave messages for loved ones (or the not so loved) that would be delivered to them after your funeral. Imagine the surprise – *I'm baaaack!* – and the potential for recrimination. The thought of leaving a gag message at this site for Elaine was so stimulating that Chellis stretched, yawned, and considered going inside to boot up.

He took a deep breath, life beginning to reassert itself in his person. *It's a beautiful day in the neighbourhood*, he hummed. And unusually quiet. He could practically hear Joe "Roach" Caruso's weed growing in his backyard, embraced by a sisterly stand of gently rus-tling sweet corn. A faint alien sound did however begin to register. A distant truck, Chellis decided, attending closely. The sound grew louder as the truck turned off MacAbre Street, and then much lou-der as it headed down Burke. *By gar*, it was a FedUPS truck, a rare enough sight in this part of town . . . and what do you know, it squealed to a stop in front of his place. *Not* next door, where the lit-tle achievers reigned and a courier might be expected to show up with biz homework or bags of cash. Chellis was thrilled. What could it possibly be?

59

The guy took his time, dicking around in the truck with his clipboard, but finally stepped out and headed toward the porch. He moved cautiously, glancing warily aside, keeping an eye out for any local gangs that might spring suddenly out of the unmown crabgrass. The delivery was small and squarish, an engagement ring perhaps from an secret admirer? But no, as the courier got closer Chellis saw that it wasn't a small intriguing box, or anything that a normal human being who had been minding his own business on his own front porch might expect to receive. A normal human being would not have Elaine for a friend. The delivery was a bar of soap with a Post-It note attached. After the guy had handed it over – eyebrows arched as he regarded Chellis signing for it, an unexpected feat of literacy for a local resident – he hustled back to the truck and peeled away, taking no further time to sightsee in the vicinity.

The Post-It note read: *Wrong soap. Use this one instead. E.*

Chellis had been thinking about calling Elaine, as he'd forgotten to tell her about his encounter in Pnin's Variety with Dick Major. She despised the dude, and the mere mention of his name was enough to make her blow a fuse. But now he had a better idea, and getting up stiffly out of his chair, he lurched inside the house like a revivified Lazarus to execute it.

7

Decomposed

CHELLIS WAS UNACCOUNTABLY HAPPY. Was, that is, until the silver Lexus slid soundlessly past his own silver vehicle. *Hi Ho Silver*. His was more the colour of tin, whereas Dick Major's glowed like cool cash. Like Ralph Lauren's numinous locks. Like no vehicle that would ever augment Chellis's own lowly status unless he stole it. Not that his car was completely worthless, considering that a loonie he'd placed on the dash a while back had slipped into the air vent and reliably clattered there, the lonely coinage in his squealing piggy bank on wheels.

It might not have been the Dicker who passed him. It was almost impossible to scope the driver, the smoky-windowed Lexus worn by its occupant like a full-metal burka. On the other hand, Chellis was as fully visible behind the wheel of his car as an Amsterdam hooker in a storefront display. He felt his good mood execute an abrupt U-turn and head back to the unknown source from whence it had come. This joy-dispelling, ships-passing-in-the-night event occurred at high noon on Mrs. Havlock's driveway. Mrs. Hav and Major Dick? A mini-tightening in his solar plexal region told him that these two separate spheres of his life should not be intersecting. A gurgling plaint from that same intestinal site also told him that it was high time for lunch. Sadly, there was no reason to think that any would be on offer chez Athena's, as it had never happened before. As far as he knew, she was a confirmed grazer and more likely to hit him up for a snack, even hazarding whatever well-aged, lint-enrobed, grocery store sample he might produce from his pocket.

As Chellis stood at the front door, envelope in hand and waiting for admittance, he noted that all was silent within Havlock House. There was nary a *yap* nor a *yip* to be heard. Bunion and Hormone

61

must have succumbed to the sulphuric fumes emitted by the previous guest. He tried the handle . . . locked. He knocked again and the cold metal of the door knocker slipped a chill into his palm. It was one of those knockers shaped like a hand, a severed hand holding a ball the size of a plum. He imagined the hand casually tossing the ball away and then snatching at his own hand, refusing to relinquish it, sticking to it as frozen metal does to damp flesh. He liked this creepy bit of fancy, but had the feeling he'd poached it from some higher literary source. That was the problem with being educated, even semieducated, one's originality was compromised.

Without the prelude of approaching steps from within, the door opened abruptly. Mrs. Havlock had been standing there the whole time.

"You're early." The greeting was not overly welcoming.

"You said noon."

"I said one."

"Must have misheard, Mrs. H." He had not. His hearing was as sharp as Spock's ears. "I'll come back in an hour, then."

"No, no, come in."

"Where are the furry greeters?"

"The vet's. Tummy upsets. Poor babies got into something."

"Not serious, I hope."

"They have delicate constitutions, but I'm optimistic they'll pull through."

Delicate? Those two tiny toughs? They were in the Keith Richards/cockroaches category of the indestructible.

"How do you know Dick Major?" He followed her, not to her den this time, but to her front sitting room. The style here was Early Ice Age: impersonal, formal, uncomfortable, unthawed. Chellis sank onto the settee that his boss indicated. It was made of some kind of stiff, red-veined material, tight as a new facelift. He swept his hand over it. If he were a lycanthrope (or a masturbator, heaven forbid) this stuff would shear his hairy palms clean.

"Never heard of him." She settled opposite him on an equally forbidding French Provincial chair, misanthropic in its demeanor.

"Richard Major?"

"No again, why do you ask?"

Was she being cagey? He couldn't tell. "The Lexus I passed on the way in. Thought it was his."

"Unfortunately cars do turn around in my driveway once they realize that there are only miles and more miles of cornfields to be had out this way. I've been meaning to install a gate, and will do."

They stared at one another, but not so long that it amounted to a contest.

"I must say, Chellis, that you're looking awfully hale . . . considering."

"Considering?" *Damn*, she'd seen it.

"In the *Penny Pincher*. The obit?"

"Oh *that*."

"Not the usual venue for such a grave announcement."

"What were you doing reading the *Penny Pincher*?"

"I like a bargain as well as anyone, my dear, but don't change the subject. That was quite a work of fiction."

"All true." The obituary he'd composed while in the grip of unprecedented inspiration was a work of gritty realism. He hadn't mentioned orcs once, he'd stuck to the facts, albeit facts dressed up in their Sunday best for the occasion.

"Except for the small matter of your death."

"Just a prank." A *dumb* prank, even he had to admit.

"I do hope you realize that your peculiar sense of humour is going to get you into trouble one of these days."

"Yes, ma'am."

"Don't be smart. I have to admit I did find it funny. Especially that bit about the soap. A skin-dissolving compound, was it? Not so much Dial as *Dial M for Murder*. Oddly enough, your prank wasn't far off-base with that detail. I read in the local paper only this morning about this poor young fellow, a bookstore clerk I believe, who'd been admitted to emergency with a bar of soap stuck fast to his cheek. They had to operate to remove it and do a skin graft. He said that some psycho-customer had given it to him."

"No guff, eh." *Jesus*. "What a weird coincidence."

"Isn't it?" Mrs. Havlock entrusted him with one of her inscrutable smiles. "So, what do you have for me? Given your recent demise, I imagine you're now an expert on morbidity."

"Pretty much." Chellis handed the envelope to her, his home-work completed, and watched as she performed the reading glasses ritual: unsnapping the case, cleaning the lenses, slipping them over her long, elegant nose, index finger and thumb on the frame making the final comfort adjustment. She pulled out the sheaf of papers and began to read quickly through them, pausing here and there, nod-ding, the occasional twitch or pursing of the lips.

"Good," she said. "Very good."

It had been a grim list this time, but no less involving for that. The stages of decomposition, rates of decay, putrefaction. A guaran-teed lunch-spoiler. Not that any seemed immanent, as he had sur-mised.

"*Livor mortis?*" This pleased her.

"Blue death. A lyrical term for postmortem lividity." Actually he thought *livor mortis* sounded more like a menu selection from The Age Spot. "When the blood stops circulating, it pools in those parts of the body that are closest to the ground. It clots, turns blue, and leaves a pattern that becomes fixed after about four hours. The extent of it gives some idea of the time death occurred, but it also indicates whether or not the body has been moved. It's all there in the report, how it works, lots of grisly detail." Good thing Mrs. H didn't watch TV, or she'd be much less impressed with his fact-finding. This forensic stuff was everywhere, and what did that say about us as a cul-ture, he thought? Ghouls, ghouls, ghouls. Topless, headless . . . the burlesque of death.

"Wonderful. I see you've been thorough on insects as well."

Insects, the real strippers.

"I've got a soft spot for the under-appreciated. Particularly mag-gots, but then don't we all. There's a mathematical formula you can use to figure out time of death and all that. If you're going to get into this entomological thing." Blowflies, beetles, wasps, ants, mites arrive in waves and dig in like avid diners at a popular new restaurant. All the bug sprays and pesticides humans lavish on them and they still get the last licks. "Mere *minutes* after death, flies are on the case, the soul-case, that is. If it's exposed to the elements, like your guy. Did you know that a pregnant female fly can sense chemical changes in the environment a *mile* away, whereas a human can walk within thirty yards of a dead body and not even notice?" He did wonder if he was telling her anything she didn't already know.

"Nature is most efficient."

"We're nothing but recyclable material."

"Well, *you* are, dear."

"Uh, yeah?"

"Just kidding."

"Ohh-kay."

Mrs. Havlock skimmed through the last of the pages.

"How *is* your corpse doing?" he asked.

"Hasn't budged an inch."

"Your first case of writers' block?" He at least tried to make this sound like an innocent query.

"Now *you're* kidding, Chellis. Writers' block is for amateurs."

"Your man should be picked clean by now, his bones carried off by wild animals. Or stomped on by deer. They do that to get at the marrow. They're thugs, ask any gardener. First your deer antagonist wipes out the Flowering Judas, munch munch, then stomps the hell out of the guy underneath. Hey, maybe he died of lyme disease."

"Thank you for the plot accelerator, Chellis, but do stick to research, will you? My corpse is preserved at the moment in my superior imaginative formaldehyde."

"I'm crushed." He hugged himself in an attempt to generate some heat. "While we're on the topic of *rigor mortis* . . . ."

"Are you cold? I suppose it is a bit frosty in here."

"Like a morgue. But my desires were running more along the lines of having a stiff one. If I may be so bold."

"You may. Excellent idea." She rose from her chair – it emitted a crotchety groan – walked over to a mahogany cocktail cabinet, bent down to open its double doors, and reached in. The room seemed so much like a stage set that Chellis half-expected her to produce a cut glass decanter of port and matching crystal glasses . . . which in fact she did. Were there any other writers in the land who actually owned these heavy, post-suave, banker-style wares? She poured two hefty portions of port, an aged, clot red. He'd have much preferred a warming tumbler of whisky, but beggars can't be choosers. Unless they happen to be the hostess.

"What did you bring to eat?" She handed him a glass.

"I was supposed to pack a lunch?" He patted his pockets. "*Nada.* A few pre-chewed sunflower seeds."

"Never mind," she sighed. "I'll check the kitchen. There must be something."

Chellis watched her depart, trusting (for no reason he could think of) that this wasn't going to be the same "something" that the doggies had gotten into. He sipped his drink, *decent*, and mused about how broken-up Elaine was going to be when she read the obituary. He knew she would as she was a faithful reader of the *Penny Pincher*, a reliable source of cheap machinery, parts, tools, and other inventor materials. He supposed that's what had made him so fleetingly happy, his childish prank, his goofy hybrid of revenge, silliness, yearning, and . . . death wish?

The unexamined life may not be worth living, but he felt that if he examined his too closely, the revelations would not be delight-inducing, or even useful. Much better to examine something else. At the moment this only left him with the room in which he was slowly being freeze-dried. He took another, deeper drink, and smacked his lips with a lordly Churchillian gusto. He shifted in his seat, which was about as comfortable as sitting on a stale cracker. The fireplace was cold, the mantel bare, no personal trophies or mementoes on display. A glass case in the corner did contain three Royal Doulton figurines, but they were of no distinction (were they ever?) and not, he suspected, the sort of conventional gewgaw that meant anything to her. The wallpaper was off-white, the curtains those shroudy, balloon-types, the rest of the furniture straight off the high-end sales floor, including a pair of love seats in a matching, glossy pink fabric, skin tone. There wouldn't be any point in sliding a hand down behind the seat cushions in an exploratory gambit, for bottoms had never graced those virgin pieces of upholstery, those chaste love seats. The drinks were the only sincere props in the whole room.

What could one deduce about the owner of this minimally, or evasively, decorated cell?

Nothing. It offered a blank face, a concealment, a rebuke to the enquiring eye. Chellis *had* been in several such rooms before, tagging along behind Hunt in his capacity as a helper and snoop, but the decor in those rooms had been less deliberate. What you saw, was basically what you got – the couch constructed of the same obvious, aesthetically-challenged material as the accountant who reclined upon it. You are what you sit on. That old woman's house he'd helped Hunt with last week had been as barren as this room, but it was a barrenness that told a story. A sad story, too, yet a whole life had been there for the taking. *This* room wasn't telling.

"I enjoyed your description of that interior." Mrs. Havlock was flaunting her mind-reading abilities. She had re-entered the sitting room and was placing a tray on a coffee table unencumbered by magazines, books, fossilized pizza crusts, or beer-glass rings, unlike his old warhorse of a table at home. One of the other requests on his research list, less unsettling than post-mortem breakdown, had involved some house-hunting for her faceless, nameless corpse.

"I'm not certain if it's the right domestic locale for my victim," she said. "He would have to be blue-collar, a truck driver, a janitor."

"Socio-economic lividity." Chellis surveyed the offerings, which weren't four-star but not entirely inedible, either. A miscellany of the pickled, the salty, the spicy. He went for a banana pepper, hoping for some heat.

"Clever boy."

Wasn't he just, though. The trusting and unassuming residents of Farclas had no idea how often their homes had appeared in the various works of Athena Havlock. On his rounds with Hunt he had lifted settings intimate and safe and cozy, had described them faithfully in photographic detail, and shortly after they had appeared exactly so, only with gore splattered on the walls, or a body with a smashed head sprawled on the new Kilim carpet, or a smoking gun upended in Aunt Maddie's heirloom candy dish. When a Farclas citizen placed a Hunt Realty sign on his or her lawn, thinking perhaps of making a killing in the current market, they were selling much more than they realized. Yes, the dark underside of Monopoly.

Chellis choked, turned red, and felt much better.

"I was going to warn you about those."

"Thanks." Yeah, sure. "They'd make a good murder weapon. Is that a banana pepper in your pocket or are you just glad to . . . ."

"Tsk. Chellis grow up, will you."

"Why? There's nothing to recommend it, is there?"

"Not much. Where were we? Ah yes, the list."

"You have a new one for me?"

"Sealed and signed. But first tell me about the photograph, any luck with that?"

"Are those olives?"

"I believe so. They were when I bought them. A local product."

"Olives? Local? That explains the fur, I guess." He chose a Brazil nut instead. "The photo? It's in the bag."

"Truly? That was fast."

"Like that dead guy from TO. In the bag . . . body bag, that is. You must have known him?"

"Knew *of* him. He reviewed a book of mine once, one of my literary efforts."

"Positive?"

"Dismissive. He referred to me as one of the 'blue rinse crowd.' Like most of my readers."

"Ouch."

"Dear, I'm not thin-skinned. Indeed, my skin's so thick after all these years in the writing business, I don't even need leather pants. The man was simply another neo-misogynist. He won't be missed."

"Is that like being a Neoplatonist?"

"Did he hate women, too? Everyone does, you know."

"Come, come, Mrs. H, that's not true."

"Deep down everyone does, even other women. You do."

"What? That's crazy. I love women. Or would, if I could get my hands on one."

"Are you sure? Think about it, your mother abandons you as a baby, your adoptive mother dies, foolishly, unnecessarily, your girlfriend leaves you and marries someone else, but still uses you for test-marketing, and you are employed, dominated shall we say, by another female – me. Your experience of women has been nothing but abandonment and betrayal."

"Is this a roundabout way of saying you're firing me?"

"Wouldn't dream of it."

"Good. Let's change the subject. I found your grave on the internet. The one in the picture you gave me. I expect that's where your secret admirer found it, too. It's outside of a small town called Kinchie, about 120 kms from here."

"Splendid. When can you go?"

"Go?"

"Precisely. I want to find out more. I want the dirt on this family, this town. Who knows, maybe I'll write one of those generational sagas. It's the woman I'm particularly interested in, this Bethea who has no death date. What an old-fashioned name. She was part of your assignment, too, if you recall."

"Do I have a choice?"

"Only as regards the goodies on the tray. Eat up." Her eyes widened slightly. "My!"

"What is it?"

Chellis knew it was too much to hope that she'd suddenly recalled something else she wanted done, an urgent and much closer-to-home investigation. Or that having dislodged a crown in biting down on a petrified heel of hundred-year-old cheddar, she desperately needed him nearby for dental advice and consolation. He hated travelling. Driving out to Havlock House was his version of a world tour.

Her expression was beatific, self-delighted, a writerly look he recognized.

"I've thought up the title!" she said. "As you know, once I have that the rest follows as a matter of course."

"And, it is . . .?"

"*My Hands, Your Death*." She smiled. "Isn't that brilliant?"

Chellis nodded, considering it. "I dunno, I sort of favour *Redneck Pygmy* myself."

8

Terrae Filius

TRYING TO GET PAST VAUGHAN was like trying to sneak past Cerberus at the gates of the Underworld.

"Hi, Chellis. Hey, *wait*. Gosh, we thought you were . . . holy smokes. We saw the obituary."

We? Would he be referring to his multiple perfect heads, or to himself and the little woman? Hard to tell over the phone.

"Yeah, yeah, that's what I was calling about. Somebody's idea of a joke."

"Why, that's terrible. No joke at all . . . it's sick. Elaine thought it might be your idea."

"*My* idea?"

"I told her you'd never do anything *that* stupid and thoughtless."

"Thanks a mil, Vaughan. So, how did she take it? Was she terribly upset?"

"Not at all. You needn't worry about that."

"Well, great. Great. What did she say exactly?"

"Let me think. As I recall, she said . . . *good*. Yes, that was it."

"Good? She was glad to hear that I was done like a dinner?"

"I wouldn't say she was glad. Elaine doesn't always show her emotions."

"So I've noticed. Look, it's been swell talking to you Vaughan. Can you put her on?"

"Not at the moment, I'm afraid. I have strict orders not to disturb her. She's working on something. Sorry."

"Okay, fine. How's the cat?"

"Noir?"

"You called him Noir?"

"Elaine's idea. Purrrfect, isn't it?"

71

It was theft of intellectual property was what it was, but Chellis let it pass. As he also did Vaughan's hilarious wordplay. "Listen, I have to go away for a few days, will you let your lovely wife know?"

"Sure thing. Have a good trip."

"See you next fall."

"Next fall? I thought you said you were going for a few days?"

"I did, Vaughan, I did."

See! The guy's sense of humour wasn't even grade school level. How *could* Laney stand it? Chellis replaced the phone in its cradle. Did phones still have cradles? He doubted it. The baby, along with the baby's accessories had been tossed out with the bathwater. All that was left were rapidly shrinking cells, more forensic evidence of a culture in decline.

But . . . much to do. In preparation for his journey into the wasteland, Chellis locked his doors, front and back, sealed the windows with weather-stripping, made a bag lunch to take with him, ate the bag lunch at the kitchen counter, then flumped down on his saggy, pre-owned couch to watch a whole season of SpongeBob Square Pants that Elaine had taped for him. Aww, she wasn't so bad. He wondered if he should try calling again to let her know that she was an acceptable human being. Her guard dog would still be on duty, though. Didn't the guy ever *work*?

Once he was replete with entertainment (why *did* SpongeBob's friend Patrick remind him of Vaughan?), Chellis began to consider a renovation project. Leaning back on the couch, feet up on the coffee table, he surveyed his living room, an on-the-spot virtual tour, a little realty TV. He had time to knock out a few walls. Open concept, he was all for that, in philosophy *and* decor. Already he could sense the swirling eddies and crashing breakers of *feng shui* upon which his enlightened spirit would surf the room. He could see his hair fluttering silkily as he performed some interpretive dance or some action yoga in his revamped and energized personal space. Gone the pop crate end tables, the stolen Men At Work sign, the dust-encrusted lava lamp . . . .

On second thought, he wasn't too sure about the fluttering locks. In an ad for shampoo currently playing on the tube, a model was flinging her head around like a ball on a stick, long blonde tresses aswirl, turning her grey matter into paste. What if everyone did that, tossing their manes hither and yon as they went about their daily business – *whap, whap?* Consider the blizzards of dandruff. And if you queued up too close to a hair-flinger at the grocery store you'd get a mouthful of flaxen-waxen keratin. It'd be like living amongst a herd of horses. Horses! What if one stepped on him during his enforced rural sojourn? Worse things could happen, he supposed, convinced that they would.

The chances of dying on the road? About 99 out of 100. Nor was this an unreasonable estimate: transport truck, guy on uppers, driving for days on end, Shania's midriff stretched across his mind's eye like a sleep mask, flattens Chellis's car into a tin disk, Chellis's lonesome hurtin' heart squelches through his freaked-out pores like meat through a grinder. No matter, his destination is a graveyard anyway. Unless he could fictionalize his current mission with a little armchair research. Nah, his boss would catch him out – *she'd know*. It was too bad he'd made so many wise-guy cracks over the years about astral travel; his psyche wouldn't be capable of taking seriously his request for an out-of-body lift to Kinchie.

He clicked the remote to a news channel, checking for world-ending events occurring due north. Wars, HIV, mud slides, wildfires, Avian Flu, tornadoes, floods, enraged solitary men with guns . . . yes, yes, all that was occurring this very moment, but not anywhere near the calm, bucolic vicinity into which he was about to plunge. Potholes on the road would be his most grievous concern. Not that one should underestimate the power of potholes to suck the unwary into the bowels of the earth. Out there on some treacherous stretch of black-top lurked a pothole that went straight to hell. Roadwork of the devil.

Clicking the remote again, searching searching, he wished there was a Chellis Channel that he could tune in to find out what he should expect in the next 24/7, what forecasts and comic-tragic personal programming might be on the roster for him. He landed on a local cable channel, so starved for news, especially of the titillating variety, that it was covering the Claymore murder again, granting that poor sod small town fame, while the horrors happening in the rest of the world thundered on, crushing all in their path.

A baseball-capped, bat-eared, tuberous Claymore resident was being interviewed. Chellis turned up the sound to hear him imputing the crime to a) terrorists, b) street gangs from Farclas (*ha ha – at least we have streets*), c) the baby-killing, pro-choice contingent, and d) his mother-in-law. Using the discordant conjunctions of the sub-literate – like, ya know, get it? – the guy was gumming together these stray strands of conspiracy theory into a single nut cluster. Chellis was placing his bets on the mother-in-law. Witches *were* once very useful for this sort of thing, but they'd gone out of fashion. No one would suspect the publishing world, barricaded behind their mountainous slush piles, of bumping someone off, but for all anyone knew, their office life could be as vicious as that of academe. Besides, murder required some competence, didn't it? (Mrs. H frequently vented on the subject of publishing screw-ups.)

Chellis was enjoying the interview – can't beat local produce – until he spotted something irksome that was momentarily captured on the screen. A flash of silver and a Lexus slid slowly by behind the interviewee. *Him* again? Chellis leaned forward, squinting at the screen. Because of the car's smoky glass, the driver was obscured, as if wearing a hangman's hood, but did briefly turn his head to take in the interview set-up, which caused his face to be illuminated by the television lights. Him again. *Cripes*. Chellis hadn't seen Major Dick in years, and now he couldn't go to the variety store or to Mrs. Havlock's or repose in the privacy of his living (for lack of a better word) room without being subjected to Mr. Rep Management cruising along in his trusty egomobile. Was Toronto suddenly so crime free that Dick had to do his rubbernecking in the sticks? And bring his date along for the ride? The über-observant Chellis *had* noticed a female on the passenger side, slouched down, her head buried in shadow.

He flicked off the TV in disgust – a defiled medium, no longer cool – and peeled a book off the top of the pile that Moe had given him. Genealogy. His immediate opinion of the hobby was curmudgeonly. He decided that he and Nabokov were of like minds on this subject, even if VN's mind in its present form – an elegant cupful of dust, alas! – was yet vastly superior to his own. "A game for old people," the great man had pronounced, an exercise in vanity and nostalgia, whereby the "Christmas tree of one's childhood is replaced by the

Family Tree." What would VN have made of the burgeoning industry that genealogy had become? The thousands of books devoted to it, the tourism, the bulging archives, the heraldic crests and aristocratic connections gladly provided by genealogical entrepreneurs and hucksters. But then, everyone loves a mystery. Some people were simply so clan-besotted (family values! outsiders need not apply) that they wanted to embrace and honour the whole lot, especially the dead relations who, unlike the living ones, no longer raged or bored you stupid.

Chellis pictured armies of family historians swarming over the lands of the past digging for roots. The horticultural term made him grind his teeth, which was the only part of his anatomy – hair, nails, and other hardware aside – that could honestly lay claim to roots. He grimaced as he read the title of the book, *Rooting for Yourself*, which seemed to place it in a motivational-genealogical-self-pleasuring genre. The prospect of what lay within was almost as alarming as that of the tiny, whimsical volume he'd spotted in the New Age section of the bookstore: *Elf Love*. (Might have been a title typo, though, and *that* wouldn't have surprised him. Also might have been part of a series: *Elf Help*, *Elf Sacrifice*, etc.) The book in hand had been written by some pinhead who had appended B.A. to his name. *Oh well, in that case, an expert.* Better give it a read. It was bound to provide plenty of fodder for a bracing sneer session. Even in its tender, twiggier forms, sarcasm was a worthy and enlivening branch of wit, and one shouldn't pass up a chance to indulge. And since he was paralysed with procrastination, a few pages of this book might be all that was required to speedily propel him out the door. He cracked it open, prepared to receive the gentle gift of amusement, if not a more robust hit of hilarity. Surely no dangers lurked within for those whose shallow, hair-thin genealogical roots had been plucked out and sent whirling away down the root canal? Wrong.

First off, Chellis was informed that he was a private investigator (he was *not* – now even complete strangers with B.A.'s were insisting on this) and the subject of his investigation was his personal past, the deep past, the anonymous loam in which the bodies of his forebears were entombed. His was to be a thrilling, albeit challenging, quest involving the disinterment of his great great grand sires (*so* illustrious they lit up the ground) stretching all the way back to the first clever monkey who had the foresight to envision an atom-sized Chellis bopping around on the future's horizon.

Absorbing stuff for some perhaps, but leaves of the book fluttered by unread as Chellis, in his investigative role, searched out the more practical information. About mid-text he landed upon a required exercise which involved filling in an initial genealogy chart with the known family members. A blank insert was provided for this and he dutifully unfolded it and pencilled in his name – the fruit, the nut, the sole product of a generic family tree. He could practically hear the distant roar of his bloodline, the vast red sea that had pooled (puddled? dried up?) within him. Him alone. The end product of what exactly? He stared at his name, afloat on the page by itself, potential connecting extensions barbed as a burr but hooking onto nothing. Depressing or what. His spirits began to sink. A sudden spiritual incontinence took hold and he could feel them sluicing through his boxers. They slid down his leg, leaked through a hole in his sock, through a crack in the floor and into the basement where they formed into condensation on a metal pipe from which they slowly dripped into a faded-yellow margarine container, collecting there like mouse piss, a spa for spiders.

So okay, he thought, what we have here is an existential genealogy chart. And after all, he wasn't entirely alone in a world that for everyone else was webbed and fibrous with family connection. He wrote in Rennie's name and let it hover angelically above his own, and in a far corner, giving him a cold shoulder to cry on, he pencilled in Elaine.

He hastened on to the next exercise: "Write a short account of your own life."

Short? Short he could definitely do. He could sum up his bio in a condensed *Reader's Digest* version, as condensed as a spoonful of Moe's mushroom soup (which she had *claimed* was homemade, as if he didn't recognize the commercial staple of his childhood). He could express his whole life in a haiku, his family saga in a mini-miniseries. He'd been born as the sixties were swinging into the seventies, his mother a free spirit. She'd been as visible as a spirit at any rate and certainly free, for she had buggered off mere weeks after his birth, leaving him on the counter of Lloyd's Burger Stand encased like a pet hamster in a Sorrell boot box. She'd stuck a note to his foot with Elmer's Glue that read: *baby beith*. Lower case, which didn't conclusively point to e.e. cummings as a paternal suspect, although years back the poet had been guilty of spawning a considerable number of literary progeny. Rennie had been in the back of the stand, teetering by her slim waist on the edge of the deep freeze and hacking away at a lump of frozen weiners with an ice pick. She thought she heard a customer at the counter. She had. Him, requiring some maternal service and kicking the shit out of his cardboard bunting. (*That* box, which later did become a hamster home for Charles I and Charles II, the end of that particular royal line, went a long way in explaining his claustrophobic tendencies, he felt, although it did nothing to account for his several other unacknowledged phobias.) Rennie had instantly whipped off the lid and . . . he saw her for the first time. *New mummy!* She laughed with surprise, and he would have, too, but he hadn't learned how to do that yet. His lips had other requirements and were puckered in a *suck-suck*, come-hither fashion, a yearning, little blue-eyed foreigner. Using the tip of the ice pick, she'd delicately lifted the note up and read, *baby beith*. Was this his name or a Biblical-flavoured declaration of his existence? Or maybe, given the legibility of the script, the faint, maiden pink, lipsticked letters, it was 'keith,' not 'beith.'

"You don't look like a Keith," she'd then said. "But you look like mine."

Such was the astonishingly accurate memory of a newborn. Chellis wrote 'foundling,' and left it at that. He took some comfort in the word itself, which was suitably literary and had a long history, even if he did not. *Illegitimus*. He'd encountered that designation, too, in this book, a term one might expect to find in old parish registers and courthouse records. The term sounded more like something a hoary, warty midwife might hiss the moment a luckless bairn tumbled into the world without the safety net of wedlock to break his fall. *Bastard!* A curse to knock you on your arse and ensure that you never got up, while the legions of the legitimate stood deeply rooted staring down at you – scrawny weed!

But surely those days were long past. He'd been born at a time when attitudes were enlightening up. *Some* attitudes about *some* things in *some* quarters. Those quarters getting smaller and smaller of late, the small change of liberal sentiment, a much devalued currency. He flung *Rooting for Yourself* on the coffee table. The freaking thing had gifted him with nothing more than a tension headache. He wasn't supposed to be looking for himself and his wily, slacker ancestors anyway. Why would he bother? It was his impression that the general populace could care less about their forebears and would be only too happy to be shot of their present family. His birth mother hadn't wanted him? Fine by him. Rennie had wanted him, and gave him a good home, and a good lax upbringing: he still liked to jump on the bed. No, he didn't need to go on an ego dig. But he did need to chase down his employer's whim if he wanted to pay the bills and keep the home that Rennie had given him. Bethea Strange was his sole prey, another vanished woman. What was it with women anyway, couldn't the slippery creatures stay in place? Always running off, dying, getting snatched and hacked to pieces.

God, he felt as though someone had nailed a spike into his forehead.

His eye fell upon a small metal container that he'd tossed onto the table a couple of weeks ago and had forgotten about. Laney's newest invention, if you didn't count the soap, which he wasn't counting, seeing as the replacement tester bar had migrated to his neighbours' antique copper mailbox, and, if it was anything like the first one, had likely bonded permanently to the box's pricey interior. This new product Laney had christened *Calm Balm*, some guck you rubbed on your temples while listening to ambient music and snorting incense fumes, all in a quest for inner peace. Vaughan had already tested it and had deemed it *amazing*. Or so she claimed. She had crossed her heart and sworn to the truth of this on his *OED* and smiled in that way that unbalanced him and made him sway like a palm in a sultry breeze, ready to drop his coconuts. He picked up the balm and unscrewed the lid. A fragrance, no an *odour*, wafted out that made his nostrils twitch like a rodent's. The stuff smelled faintly, no *strongly*, of carbolic, brine, and peat, a smell he found thrilling for some reason. Its consistency resembled a cross between Vaseline and Turkish Delight. All right, nothing ventured, nothing gained . . . a prescriptive that had thus far never bagged him a single thing in his life. He braced himself, dipped his finger into the slimy stuff and rubbed it gingerly on his temples. It eased his tension headache immediately by transferring the pain to the sides of his head. A searing pain. When his temples began to smoke, he not only defeated his lethargic funk, but broke his record for the 10-yard bathroom-dash. *Fuckfuckfuck*, he snarled, dousing his head with water. *That's it, I'm done with her, finito, no more, she's lethal, she's a bloody crank.*

Got him moving anyway.

*

Ready to roll, he double and triple-checked to see that everything was in place. His copy of *On the Road* was grooving in the seat beside him, his leathery partner, Uncle Bob, was slumped in the back, first aid kit in the glove compartment, the latter in the event that he became the unwitting subject of another experiment or met with the inevitable car accident and had to reattach his arms with Band-Aids. He also brought along his *very* recently invented Home Psychiatry Kit: marbles, screwdriver, yogurt-dipped nut bar. Ha! Laney wasn't the only mad genius around. He planned on dropping this off at her place on the way out of town.

He snapped his seatbelt clasp into the buckle, started 'er up, and after backing out of his driveway idled for awhile gazing affectionately at the house. Affectionately and achingly because he had a uneasy feeling that he would never see it again. Good thing he hadn't bothered to mow the lawn. He *did* have roots dammit, and not just those of the ineradicable crabgrass system that held his front yard in place. His house, Rennie's house, it contained their whole lives. Home, he had one, why was he leaving it?

He couldn't stand it. Go, *go!*

He pressed down on the gas pedal, lightly, as though he were flattening a peeled banana . . . and drove around the block. There it was! His house! He loved it so much. Was that a rat squeezing out of the gap under the porch? Nae problem! He'd recite poetry to it, an old and surefire method of ridding the house of rats. A few lines of Robert Frost and they'd run screaming out the front door. He drove around the block a couple more times, delighted to be arriving home again and again . . . until he noticed that one of his next-door neighbours was watching him, the female half of the equation, adorned in a trim pinkish tweed suit and matching Italian winkle-pickers. She was standing beside her mailbox holding the bar of soap. Was that a *glare* she was aiming his way, was her precisely cut blonde hair actually bristling, or was that only the wind fooling around, making a nuisance of itself? Chellis didn't wait for an answer. He hit the gas once again and took off, tires squealing as the hitherto unsuspected ties to his home place, his twining clasping *roots*, unreeled, snapped, and trailed behind him, fluttering as gaily as tickertape.

9

Accessory

THE FIRST DISASTROUS THING that happened was *nothing*. Self-fulfilling prophesies were usually so reliable, but so far no delivery. No ten ton weights had fallen out of the sky and smucked his "swiftly" moving vehicle. His trusty car swept along, a largely imagined blur of silver, a Gerhard road Richter, but not yet an artful highway smear. Could it be that too much TV exposure had primed him for calamity? No, too much Elaine exposure had done that. He swore to himself that the farther away he got from her the better off he'd be, and to his dismay, he found that this was true. He was actually enjoying his outing, his newfound rustication.

The scenery was pleasant and unthreatening, especially if one didn't think about the countryside's pesticide-induced glow. The farms he drove by were well-tended and prosperous, the farmhouses modernized and huge, with triple garages and indoor pools. He was enormously grateful not to have to reside in one. He could see himself wandering from one cavernous room to another, lost in space. Or sitting in one of those up-to-the-minute farm kitchens and over slabs of homemade lemon pie and man-sized mugs of coffee engaging with the informed residents in brain-cracking conversation about the latest Noam Chomsky. (Right-wing, scarlet-necked, Christian Fundamentalists, minds narrowed to a sharp pleat? Mythical beings, surely?) Then he couldn't see himself . . . he was *gone*, which was a relief, since he hadn't quite gotten around to any Chomsky yet. Farmers had earned their renovations at least, the salt-of-the-earth in upscale shakers, and their digs weren't quite as disheartening as the vinyl-clad developer-barracks that loomed on the edge of Farclas, frightening enclosures with names like Sissinghurst Downs and Wankers Rise. And while he was ruminating about wankers, he reminded himself that the homicidal mover-and-shaker who'd bumped Rennie off and gotten away with it lived out this way in pretentious rural splendour – a monster in a monster home. Chellis sincerely wished the guy apoplexy while reading his energy bill, brain cancer from his cellphone. This accelerating session of ill will and revenge fantasy, about which he felt not the least speck of guilt, kept him amused for some kms.

The fields that stretched away from the road on either side were immense: deep squares of swishing yellow plant matter or chewed greenery, with fat cattle grazing here and there, as blissfully unaware of their final destination as Chellis was of his. Perchance he and these beasts would meet again at The Age Spot and become more intimately acquainted. *Lord*, his personal sky darkened. *I hate humans . . .* but it was a fleeting moment of misanthropy, possibly a mental transmission picked up from the one handsome Charolais who had raised her head (Noam on the range) and gazed thoughtfully at him as he cruised by.

In the spirit of public service, the slender aesthetic side of it, he stopped twice to dismantle two roadside memorials, one with a Raggedy Ann doll tied to a mouldering Styrofoam cross. He knew where grief belonged (second rib to the right, and straight on into the dark night of the soul), and he did not believe it should be installed on the side of the road where it could suck up car fumes, flicked butts, clouds of dust, and the appalled looks of strangers. On average there was more than enough grief to go around; no honestly, you didn't have to share yours with others. He tossed the works into his trunk and continued on. Rennie had not had a kitsch immunity herself, but she would not have wanted to be memorialized by some tacky readymade from death's arts and crafts bazaar. Quietly borne pain was sheer and dignified.

He then engaged in another selfless act by taking a side trip to Claymore to pick up a couple of bottles of plonk. Who knows, he might have to do some entertaining later. He was a firm believer in the twelve-step program, which is how he got his exercise, walking those twelve steps from the car to the door of the liquor store. Sometimes he ran, even better. Monday afternoon, and Claymore's confirmed drinkers had all come and gone, including the realtor Hunt had told him about, who drove out here every day for his forty-ouncer of vodka so that word wouldn't get around Farclas. Words do, though, they have a way.

In the nearly empty LCBO parking lot, he executed a smooth landing, sliding in beside a truck the size of a small house. It so happened that the owner of the truck chose this moment to emerge from the store carrying a case of 24. He gave Chellis a dirty look, which Chellis gave right back. The guy had a wispy grey ponytail, tightly cinched (rural facelift), a grog-blossom (red nose), and what is known in the Hick Lit genre as a slackened jaw – gravity exerting itself on the trans fat packed into his jowls. Surely it wasn't the burden of too many dental fillings that was making his mouth hang open to that extent? Not that Chellis had expected anything more debonair from a Claymore resident. The one thing he couldn't fault, however, was the agility with which the guy scaled the truck's cab and seated himself inside, all without getting a nosebleed. In recognition of this athletic feat, Chellis gave him a friendlier nod, and was himself rewarded with a one finger wave, nor was it the middle finger. If their relationship continued improving at this rate, they'd soon be tearing into that case of beer, but as it was, the guy pulled out of the parking lot and peeled off downtown to the law firm of Dyer Nutt Maroon LLP, where he was a senior partner specializing in litigation.

That's what the clerk in the store said anyway when asked, and Chellis laughed merrily, always appreciative of a good joke. He got along so well with the clerk, a young man named Suzie, according to his bronze name tag, that Chellis honoured the store with a grander level of his custom and bought two bottles from the vintages section. This being Claymore there *were* only two bottles in the vintages section, a Côtes du Rhône and a Barolo. (So *there* Vaughan!)

At the cash, Suzie expressed sympathy for Chellis's injuries, the ones on his temples that were now concealed beneath two round bandages the size of poker chips.

"Someone shoot ya in the head?"

"Not yet."

Suzie continued his scrutiny, so Chellis offered, "Shock therapy."

"Yeah? Awesome."

It only then occurred to Chellis that his anxieties had diminished considerably since applying the Calm Balm to his beleaguered noggin. He felt more centred, more focused. Downright genial. "You haven't noticed a silver Lexus in town lately, have you?"

"Sure. Bogus car. Guy stopped here yesterday, bought a bottle of Veuve."

"Alone?"

"Nah, had some old lady in the car. Know how fast those babies go?"

"Old ladies? Pretty fast. Especially if you're chasing one with a golf club."

"Yeah, eh."

"What did she look like, this old lady?"

"The usual. White hair, I dunno, old. You shoulda seen the hubcaps on her."

"Whoa, sorry I missed those." Cars were individuals, whereas women over a certain age were a genre. "Lots of excitement in town lately?"

"I'll say." Suzie finally rang up the sale and bagged the wine. "Bin like a movie."

Such was modern life. "Who did it, do you think?"

"You did."

"*Me?*" Calm blue oceans, calm blue oceans.

"Joke."

Compound joking and from a genuine Claymoronian. "Whew, you had me worried there. Where *was* I the night of . . .?"

"Like, I know you're a detective, eh. Can't fool me. You wanta know what I think?"

"Tell me, Suzie."

"Suzie?"

"In my professional capacity, I noticed your, umm . . . ."

"This?" He glanced down, acknowledging the name tag, but not the name. "We all wear *this*. Only tag in the store."

"How democratic. So, your solution to the crime?"

"Gotta be somebody from Farclas. Bunch of sickos. Did you hear about that guy who tried to kill the bookstore clerk? You gotta be queer anyways to work in a place like that, but really, eh."

Chellis suddenly found himself at the door. "Must be on my way, no rest for the wicked. Bodies are littering the streets even as we speak. *Ciao*, Suzie." Queen-for-a-Day.

He almost made it through the door, too, before hearing the deal-concluding curse of the service industry, "Enjoy!"

Enjoy? *I don't think so.* Not knowing that Mrs. Havlock was . . . what? What *was* she doing hanging out with Dick Major, and what did the two of them have to celebrate? Curious choice of beverage, the Widow Cliquot's intoxicating invention (and why couldn't Elaine invent something like that?). Chellis motored out of Claymore and back onto the main road, very much in a mulling mood. If the afternoon hadn't been so far advanced, he might have driven downtown to ogle the crime scene for himself, perhaps even drop in on Dyer Nutt Maroon for a beer and a fix of legal expertise, or to see if the firm even existed. (Mr. Maroon? A dyed-in-the-wool relative of Mr. Pink? Come *on.*) Fiction filtered so surreptitiously into everyday life that you had to keep your eye on it. But not banish it altogether. That would be too *too* boring. Besides, it was so useful.

Fact: Elaine's friend Melissa Thoms had died while out with Dick on the night of a Sadie Hawkins high-school dance. She had invited him.

Fact: She should not have. Although ancillary to the group, Plutonic in the distance of his orbit and non-planetary status, Chellis had caught the roguish wink Dick had aimed at the boys.

The tragedy had been the town's own Chappaquidick in the view of some, Elaine in particular. In Chellis's view it was an even greater tragedy to place it in the same context, making it a diminished popular culture knock-off. Driving back in the small hours from a lovers' lane session on some country road outside of Farclas, Dick's car had swerved on loose gravel moments before crossing the town bridge. His car spun through the guardrails and flipped into the river. Dick managed to escape, and Mel didn't.

Fact: Dick's father was one of the town's prominent businessmen. No autopsy was deemed necessary for Mel.

Fiction: Dick hadn't "touched a drop" that night.

Fact: Date rape was a term not in use then, being largely an unacknowledged recreational activity.

Fiction: Dick had done "everything he could to save her." He'd been "devastated" by her death and would "never get over it."

Mrs. H would be very annoyed with Chellis for using the term fiction interchangeably with that of falsehood, because fiction *conveyed deeper truths*. Okay, fine, he bought that, why not, but with the purchase he also wanted conveyance to some immediate truths. He began to wonder if his employer had done something that required the services of a Reputation Management specialist, a career that for Dick had begun in high school. Writers committed crimes aplenty, but these usually involved punctuation, vanity, absurd optimism, and self-pity. None of which were Athena's failings. They also wrote savage reviews of their contemporaries' work, dissed their publishers and agents, diddled with their friends' wives/husbands, and slipped knives into unwary backs, but not literally. They were criminals of the figurative. Usually. What would propel a writer to commit an actual murder? Serious plagiarism found out? A vicious rejection (editorial boards being the favoured haunt of sadists)? The extremes of publicity? Sinister, out-of-control research? Or the standard motives that drove even normal people around the twist: love, money, revenge. Writers happily waded in fictional buckets of blood, splashed it around liberally, killed off characters by the score, and even settled a few personal scores in the process. But the type was too squeamish and sane and cowardly – and principled, don't forget – to wander into the genuine dark side where real horrors lurked. Writing about murder didn't accustom one to the actual deed surely, didn't tempt one to cross that most forbidding of moral boundary lines. Although any provocation could take a disturbed mind there. Injury, invention, zealous belief. An over-cooked mind could justify to itself any perfidy in whatever screwed-up way. If justification came into it at all.

Still, he couldn't see Mrs Havlock doing anything truly nasty. Whereas Dick? No question.

It might not have been her in the car, of course. Dick may have developed a taste for the mature, well-seasoned female. Could have been his own mother with him. Did Dick have a mother? Mothers did seem to be in short supply, although one might have come with the car, an upmarket human accessory who reminded you to flick on your turn signal or nagged you about driving too fast.

Accessory to the crime.

Vis-à-vis tricky plot situations, Mrs. H had on occasion asked Chellis what Marcel Lazar would think. *Think?* he had always wanted to reply, and would have if Athena weren't so enamoured of her creation. Lazar's brain was made of paper, his vitals nothing more than squiggles of black ink! He could have a whole *Dummies* series written for him alone. He was a flat man, a dead man, inflate him with your imagination, dear reader. But now, glancing in the rearview mirror and noticing not for the first time since he'd left Claymore that he was being followed, he found himself wondering, *What would Lazar do?*

Hit the gas, that's what.

As he bore down on the accelerator, his car made a sluggish, albeit earnest effort to pick up speed. It voiced a few economy car zoom-zoom noises, fooling no one except Uncle Bob in the back, who slid silently to the floor.

"C'mon baby," urged Chellis, and baby was doing her best, but the shadowing vehicle was gaining ground. He glanced around nervously, assessing the terrain for portals to alternate realities. He zoomed along like a Sunday driver through this dingier, ungroomed stretch of the province. The very source, he assumed, of its literary gothic reputation. Wealth, if it had ever graced this locale, had long ago packed up its booty and moved to the city. The houses were quietly derelict on the outside and ragingly oppressive within. Of this he was aware because he could almost see the desperation, generations-deep, pouring out of the windows like smoke. Romantic if you had a means of escape or thrilled to the sight of unhinged shutters, cracked brick, junked cars in the front yard, and stands of overgrown lilac bushes originally planted to absorb the smell from the crapper out back. These houses were upright rectangular containers for no-fun Presbyterianism, incest, and dads wearing green work pants, pilled cardigans buttoned in the wrong holes, and thin nylon socks twisted at the ankle, heels sticking out like teddy bear ears. The Sears catalogue the only reading matter in sight . . . .

His pursuer was almost on him and signalling Chellis to stop. *Shit on a shingle*, it was the fuzz.

If placed under duress, he might have to admit to being snotty and unfair to the residents of this economically embarrassed stretch of wherever.

Chellis pulled over and cut the engine, causing his car to *tick tick tick*, winding down as if it were about to relax on the road like one of Dali's molten clocks. He rolled down the window and smiled winningly at the approaching figure, even though he didn't approve of the forest ranger style of the newish O.P.P. uniforms – so Smokey. And since he was privately grousing, he also didn't approve of the way the news announcers on the CBC had adopted the American pronunciation of the word "missile." Let's keep our military argot distinct, as well as our overseas operations. He wouldn't bring that up now, but he might if things got contentious.

"Afternoon, sir," the cop said.

"Officer." A pup, which promised easy intimidation. Child labour in the Western World, that's how it seemed the older he got. Doctors, plumbers, and other figures of authority – all children.

"You in a hurry?"

"Funeral. I'm late."

"Uh-huh. What's wrong with your head?"

Interesting. Here was a question Elaine herself had often posed, and for once he had an answer. He touched one of his ailing, bandaged temples. "I have complexion issues."

"I see. I have quota issues. You were going one kilometre over the speed limit."

"Seriously? You'd give me a ticket for that?"

"Mind if I have a look in your trunk?"

Yes. "Not at all."

Chellis removed the key from the ignition and hopped out, taking care not to knock the officer on his arse by opening the door with an overabundance of cooperation. They both walked to the back of the car, Chellis noting with much satisfaction that the cop was shorter than he was. That too had changed, the O.P.P height requirements, allowing women and minorities, elves for example, into the force.

"You think I have a body stowed in here?" Chellis asked breezily.

The cop gave him a look that said plenty, and none of it reflecting well on Chellis's character. He opened the trunk to reveal a cache of homemade crosses, plastic ferns and flowers, the Raggedy Ann doll, and other maudlin memorabilia of the highway departed.

"What's this crap?" Obviously a dead body would have been a less offensive sight.

"Um, I *did* say that I was going to a funeral."

"You stole this stuff?" The officer took a step backward and eyed Chellis with . . . horror? Perplexity? Admiration? Don't ask.

He reached into the breast pocket of his jacket and pulled out a pad and pen.

"What, you're giving me a ticket for cleaning up the road?"

"Nope."

"For speeding? In this thing?" He gave his car a kick, adding injury to insult – the bootlace that had been holding up the tailpipe broke and clattered noisily onto the road. "You haven't even asked for my licence." Then he thought, *Bugger, did I bring it?*

"Right, that reminds me." The officer dug into his back pocket and pulled out a wallet, which he handed to Chellis.

Generous!

"You left it at the liquor store."

"I did? Geez, thanks."

"That's why I was following you, to give it back. And to check for a body in the trunk. Suzie said you were acting suspicious. Impersonating a detective, for one thing."

The little prick. "I *was* suspicious, I'll be wanting to count my cash. Or do you mean, suspicious*ly*?" Save the Adverb. "I do sometimes act that way. Girls like it."

"Yeah?" The cop smiled. "I was hoping you could do me a favour?" He scribbled something in the notebook, tore off the sheet, folded it, and handed it to Chellis.

"You *do* have quota issues?"

"Nah. If you could give this to Cindy, she's a waitress at the coffee shop in Kinchie, I'd really appreciate it."

"Why, sure. Be happy to." Kinchie *was* next up, so it's not as though his itinerary was common knowledge. "Which coffee shop?"

"Only one in town, can't miss it." He walked back to his car and got in, calling out, "Have a nice funeral."

"I will." Chellis waved as the officer did a U-ey and drove off. But when he bent down to tie the tailpipe back on, he thought, *I will?*

10

Body Burden

UNDENIABLY, hard things come at you through your soft life. Surprise existential meteors blaze into your charmed atmosphere and a glowing corona of good fortune is no protection. At the moment of impact you may even be snarled in the strictures of complaint, although honestly what's there to complain about if one is sufficiently hydrated and moisturized, well-fed, comfortably and stylishly clothed, psychologically healthy (more or less), ditto physically, relatively debt-free, and young enough? You may *even* be shod in a pair of hip Beatle boots and staring down at their splendid, time-prinking toe caps, trying not to splatter them as you take a leak on the grassy mound of a vintage corpse (1918, a very good year) in the Kinchie graveyard. Golden showers for the deceased, voiding into the void.

You, no not *you* . . . *Chellis* could take this opportunity before the hard thing arrives to count his blessings, to appreciate the wonder of life itself, to consider that he has been spared disability, disease, poverty, and random violence (for the next few seconds anyway). Instead, he was grooving in a piss-meditation (it had been a long trip) and wondering what it might be like to marry and settle down with Cindy, the waitress at the Kinchie coffee shop. He had not yet clapped eyes upon Cindy, but has managed nonetheless to come up with an image, a composite of all the waitresses he has ever encountered in small towns (sensibly excluding Bev from The Age Spot). She's a comely enough girl, a bit husky of build, the hair a bit too crisp from over-bleaching, the rose/fairy/teardrop tattoo on her ankle or on the cusp of her right buttock a bit too predictable, the tongue a bit too sharp, but all the better for slicing off her g's and droppin' them like so much mealy-mouthed verbiage. Still. She might do. Little white clapboard house on one of the side streets, linoleum

flooring, furniture constructed from wood product, leftover instant scalloped potatoes in the fridge, a lilac polyester comforter with an abstract design on the bed, an indefinable whitish splat on the speaker mesh of the clock radio . . . Friday nights at the Legion, curling bonspiels, annual hunting trip up north, bake sales, road hockey with the two boys . . . the dog running off with the tennis ball. *Hey, come back here with that,* ahh . . . what's the dog's name? Nietzsche? *No.* No Nietzsches allowed. Chellis would have to put up a sign to that effect. Duct-tape it to the front window.

Naturally he had read the note the cop had asked him to deliver. Read it quicker than you can say, "MARRY ME." Which is exactly what the note did say. Only that. If Chellis handed it over as promised, wouldn't that put him in a ticklish position? Cindy would take one look at the note, then at him, see what she was getting, and despite their utterly brief acquaintance, would exclaim, *Yes, yes, oh yes!*

Too bad for Elaine. Tough beans, rough rocks. Yep, he'd drive his truck into Farclas once in awhile, go to the big box hardware store, pass Elaine in her Smartypants Car, give her a one-finger wave, maybe two. Better things on his mind . . . (nor would he waste time peppering his thoughts with superfluous ellipses, the serial dribble of grammatical shot) . . . wrenches, a Robertson screwdriver, male and female plugs. Him, a tight-lipped, minimally-smiling country boy in a faded blue-check flannel shirt, sleeves rolled up, golden hairs provocatively mussed on his tanned and muscled forearms. (He'd still secretly vote NDP or Green, despite saving a few bucks at the anti-union, screw-the-little-guy big box.)

Finishing up, the mound well-watered, Chellis was reminded of a couple of Elaine's proto-inventions for the forgetful male. Very clever, he had to admit, but problematic all the same. The "Flycatcher" was to be a tiny security system intended for implantation in the crotch of a man's pants, its purpose being to alert him when he neglects to zip up. Chellis could see how such a device might come in handy, especially for your thinking man, your absent-minded professor type, but there were romantic occasions when an alarm, however muted, would definitely be a spoiler. Which he had helpfully brought to her attention.

"Romantic occasions? When do you have those?" Elaine had retorted. "Although I see your point."

"My love life is robust, thank you very much, and don't say it's on my head."

"The point? Only you would say something like that, Chel. I'm much nicer."

"No you're not."

The other fledgling device was a remote control auto-zip for those who discover themselves to be gaping (down there) whilst in public. You simply reach into your pocket to hit the remote, or touch a disguised button on your tie pin, and up goes your zipper, crawling as surreptitiously as a real fly, or zooming up with real *zzzzzzip*.

"Okay, great, wonderful," had been his assessment of this one. "What if it malfunctions? Guy gets trapped in his pants or caught in the zipper, *yow*. Or severed, nipped in the bud? Don't you think these ideas through, Laney? I suppose you *could* use the remote to undo other people's zippers at a board meeting or a party. Now that would be fun, kids would love it."

"*Damn*, you're right. Ruin my life, will you."

"Doing my best."

In envisioning Elaine's wholesome, lovely, exasperated face, his Cindy simulation was entirely eclipsed. He grinned, thinking about the Home Psychiatry Kit, reached down to zip up, and then crumpled, felled by the sudden (to him) arrival of the hard thing. His body, with its freight of pollutants and cellular deposits of mercury, lead, formaldehyde, DDT, and bisphenol A hit the ground like a bag of wet crap. His mouth, opened in shock, took in a sampler of Kinchie soil, compact as Christmas cake with loamy corpse-enriched earth, stones the sizes of raisins, snails, friendly bacteria and not-so-friendly weed killer. A tincture of his precious bodily fluids – eight parts water, and two parts alcohol – leaked out of his eyes. He knew he wasn't unconscious because he heard the *swish-swish* sound of someone running through the cemetery. Unless that was the sound of the blood in his head making a rapid retreat from the disaster zone in his occipital region.

The sound was gone. All sounds were gone, except for a gull keening in the distance. He didn't think he was dying, but it was a fantastic idea and the setting was perfect. As an iota of bent reflection remained possible, he took advantage of the opportunity by recalling that Marcel Lazar was always getting cracked on the bean, beaten-up, kicked in the groin. Chellis hugely enjoyed those parts of Mrs. Havlock's books, and he suspected that she did, too – slapping the guy around. No harm in that, it was a feature of the genre. Literature. Life. It really didn't do to let one bleed into the other, he now decided. Let the unfeeling Lazar take the hard knocks. Chellis was going to have to guard the borders with a great deal more vigilance, like a kid keeping everything separate on his dinner plate. What time was it anyway? Dinner time, Mr. Wolf. The grass here didn't taste that bad, especially lightly dressed in his own urine (nectar of the celebs), better than Laney's idea of greens.

Chellis heard footsteps again, someone hastily approaching. Seeing as a deceased individual lay in the earth directly beneath him, missionary position, there was a good chance that his new arrival was a furious descendant come to finish him off. *Piss on my grandad, will you!* He blinked a couple of times and inclining his head slightly caught sight of two objects resting about a yard, metre, cubit, or verge away . . . it was a smorgasbord of short distance, his cerebral storage bins having tipped over. One of these objects was a cherub's stone head, the size of a Sicilian blood orange, and the other was a golf ball. Choose your weapon.

"Omigod, are you all right? I mean, oh hell, I'm sorry!"

A pair of brand new, blindingly white sneakers came into view. Chellis raised his chin, upon which was decoratively affixed a yellowed willow leaf, and directly under his bottom lip, wriggling like an electric soul patch, was a centipede. A pair of large fingers reached down, picked the centipede off, and sent it back to its job of making the world a better place (every little bit helps). This was not the bloody-minded assailant, then. But rather, as it turned out, one Robert Burns, a recently retired high-school history teacher who had been out on the golf course next to the graveyard, despairing and knocking golf balls into deep space.

Chellis sat up and spat out a wad of saliva mixed with blood and dirt. "Couldn't be better," he said. Jaunty Lazar-speak. He was annoyed to hear it issuing from his own mouth.

"I can't believe I hit you. Half the time I can't even hit the damn ball." Robert helped him to his feet. "You crack your head on the stone? You feeling dizzy? Look, we better get you to Emergency."

"I'm fine, thanks." Chellis touched the back of his head where a dinosaur egg was forming. "Could use a drink, though."

Robert reached into his windbreaker pocket and produced a silver flask upon which his initials were inscribed in a lavish, swirly typeface. "Retirement present, and the best thing about golf." He unscrewed the cap and handed it to Chellis. "Ditto fishing, woodworking, and sitting on your fanny reading old *Reader's Digest*s."

Chellis took a long, grateful pull. "That's better. *Usque beatha*, water of life." He took another, more discerning sip. "An eighteen-year-old Talisker. Even better than an eighteen-year-old."

"I guess you haven't met Cindy."

Chellis took another sip. "Cindy of the coffee shop? Not yet." He handed the flask back. "She's something, is she?" He walked over to the cherub's head and scooped it up. Holding it cupped in his hand, he surveyed the crime scene, while its blank stone eyes stared up at him. There did not appear to be any decapitated statuary within view.

"Sure is."

Chellis next picked up the golf ball and tossed it to Robert. "You like high-class Euro- hooch? I think maybe we could liven this place up some."

*

By the time Chellis pulled into the Kinchie Coffee Nook, he was feeling *much* better and had learned an encyclopaedic amount about the wee town and its residents. Live here? No friggin way. It was like any small town, serene and pretty on the surface, with tangled, boggy depths below into which you did not want to peer. Unless Robert Burns, his imagination overstimulated by boredom, plus two fine bottles of wine (two dead soldiers now laid to rest in the Kinchie boneyard) was simply an outstanding storyteller.

The moment Chellis passed through the door into the Nook, all conversation, which had been lively, ceased. No matter. He marched boldly through the pin-drop silence to the only seat available at the counter, and while inserting himself between a burly trucker-type and a stocky farmer-type, he handed the policeman's missive to the stunning, dark-haired young woman who was stationed in front of the coffee machine, already pouring him a cup. A low, but audible groan emanated from the Nook's clientele.

Cindy slid his coffee into place, glanced at the note, smiled sweetly, then slipped it into her apron pocket, where it teamed up with a pack of fellow-notes, thick as a deck of cards. No doubt *everyone* wanted to marry her, but Chellis had gotten over her already. Amazing how quickly a crack on the head will bring you to your senses. He had what he needed from Kinchie – more than he wanted – and his only wedding plan at present was to fuel up, get mildly sober, drive home and reunite with his fabulously comfortable, safe, and secluded bed.

"Don't do it, Cindy," a guy sitting by the window called out.

"Yeah, don't let him wear you down," someone else agreed.

Several others chorused this sentiment.

The trucker-type turned to Chellis, "Seventh proposal from that cop today. I brung one in myself."

"Ah," said Chellis.

"Drink up, pal. You look like shit. Walk into a wall or sumpthin?"

"Defence wounds." Chellis sipped his coffee daintily.

"No kiddin? Wouldna guessed you was the type."

"Marriage." Cindy was gazing squarely at Chellis. "Isn't that the purpose of life, though? To give love, and to receive it. To be capable of doing both? To be strong enough."

"Umm . . . well." Obviously Cindy had been dipping into the Harlequins.

"Cindy's been reading Annie Dillard," the farmer-type spoke up.

"That's a fact," agreed the trucker-type.

"Way to go, Cindy," a guy in the back called out.

"Outa the mouths of babes," someone else shouted.

"True, I have," admitted Cindy, still eyeing Chellis. "But my observation is more general. I could be referring to any number of writers' works, couldn't I? I mean, isn't that the theme of most literature when you come right down to it?"

"Er," said Chellis.

"More coffee?"

"Please." He pushed his cup forward and cleared his throat. "Does this mean you're going to marry him?"

"Would you?"

Chellis shrugged. "He's honest." (He's short.) "He followed me for miles to return my lost wallet. See here." He retrieved the wallet from his back pocket by way of proof and held it up. "Wait a minute, this isn't my wallet." He flipped it open. "Mine had plastic surgery weeks ago and . . . *good gravy*, can this be right? Get a load of the Robert Borden clones, the MacKenzie Kings." Dead white guys (tinged with colour) with too much denominational class to visit his own working-man's wallet in such numbers. "Okay Cindy, dessert's on me, everyone hear that? Eat up, have seconds, thirds, go ahead fill your boots, pie for all!"

"That's nice," said Cindy. "I should marry you instead."

"Nah," said the trucker. "He's not the marrying type." The farmer nodded in agreement.

"Too bad," Cindy smiled again, and turned away to serve out slabs of Boston cream and lemon meringue pie, laying waste her whole fan club with lard, white death, and yellow food dye #5.

"So what type *am* I?" Chellis said huffily.

"Wuss, I mighta said, but since yer buyin . . ."

"Tell us," said the farmer. "What brings you to town?"

"Genealogy."

"We've had a few of those in the last while. Nothing better to do, I guess."

"It's for a friend. She's curious, can't blame her. Her past is a mystery."

"A blessing if you want my opinion. You know what Nietzsche said?"

"Woof, woof?" offered Chellis.

"Mm, more or less. But more specifically, he said we spend far too much time labouring in the shadows of the past. That our personal and collective inheritance stands in the way of our enjoyment of life."

"You're pretty knowledgeable for a man of the soil."

"Who said I was a man of the soil? Although I suppose I am in a way. I'm the county coroner."

"Holy, what brings *you* to town?" Chellis asked.

"The usual."

"You wanna know a little secret?" the trucker cut in.

"Let me guess," Chellis said. "You don't really drive a transport, but operate a boutique in town called Intelligent Design that sells Alfred Prufrock coffee spoons and Jackson Pollock wallpaper?"

"More candy-asses, huh? Nope, I drive a truck all right, but what I wanna tell ya – "

Chellis didn't find out, at least not immediately. Someone's cell started to play *Funky Butt*, a blues tune he liked, and turning to check who was going to answer the ringtone, he was surprised to see a Mennonite in traditional togs cup the phone to his ear. "Yo," the Mennonite said, or it might have been, "Ja?" It was difficult to hear over the resonant clamour of forks scraping pie off restaurant crockery. The Mennonite looked up, nodded curtly at Chellis, and waggling the phone, called out, "It's for you, man."

"Me?"

"Here," he tossed the phone.

Chellis made a grab and caught it. "Hello?" he said tentatively, thinking maybe it was Robert Burns, his raconteur, last seen weaving into a grey brick bungalow with a darkened, oversized picture window that made his house look about as inviting as a black hole, poor bugger.

"Chelly, is that you?"

"Moe? Is that *you*? How did you know I was . . . *how* did you find me?"

"Heck, it wasn't that hard. But Chel, um, Hunt is having a cardiac event."

"Great, am I invited?"

"Ha, ha, you're so *funny*. But no, what I want to say is . . . is . . . he's dying."

"What? *What?!*"

"I'm at the hospital, could you . . . could you, please, Chelly?"

God. "Right away, Moe, I'm leaving immediately, this *very* instant." Not Hunt, *not Hunt*. "Hang in, I'll be there. It'll be fine, Moe, everything will be okay."

On the other end of the line her voice shivered, and broke.

Another complete silence now possessed the Coffee Nook.

"Hey, sorry," someone said quietly.

"Yeah."

"Yeah."

"And thanks, eh."

"Yeah, thanks."

The coroner touched his arm, gave it a squeeze.

The trucker, leaned toward him, and whispered, "What I wanted to tell ya, eh, you'll wanta know, is uhh, yer fly's down."

Cindy, gazing over all their heads through the Nook's front window at the gathering darkness, said only, "Horseman, pass by."

11

HEART, failure

CALL IT WHAT YOU WILL – a cardiac event, an arterial incident, a corporal malfunction – but it was only language pussyfooting around disaster and throwing up little white picket defences. Chellis whacked himself on the head with a rolled up magazine. Punning in the present circumstance was a *pun*ishable offence. He whacked himself again. The five others seated in the OR waiting room pretended not to notice, but their slack postures tightened ever so slightly and their eyelids faintly quivered as irises contracted in an attempt to block further disturbing data from entry. Chellis whacked himself one more time just for the hell of it, and because a pain in the head was preferable to a pain in the heart.

No one spoke. Not even Moe. She patted his hand reassuringly, the habit of cheeriness so deeply ingrained that she herself might require an operation to have it removed. Death would surely arrange that.

Chellis unfurled the magazine, a sadly mauled *Time* from the previous century, and tried to read an article on stem cell research. He failed. The columns in the magazine consisted of indecipherable slabs of wordage. He was experiencing an illiterate incident, possibly related to cranial trauma.

"I can't read," he whispered to Moe.

"Neither can I," she whispered back.

"I mean, I've forgotten how."

"No you haven't, Chelly. You learned in grade three. You were a slow learner, but once you got started, boy oh boy."

"Who told you that?"

"Hunt."

"Hunt," Chellis nodded. "You talked to his folks? When are they getting here?"

"Can't make it," Moe said. "But they're sending a fish."

"A fish?"

"Very good for the heart."

"A fish."

"For Christmas last year they gave us gift certificates for colonic irrigation."

"Thoughtful."

"Yeah."

Chellis tackled another article, and although his reading skills had been restored, he found the writing repulsive, the prose bone-thin and expiring before his eyes. It made him feel ill. More ill. He tossed the magazine aside and smelled his hands. He seemed to be the bearer, on his skin, under his nails, of a subterranean, graveyard taint. Not only was he bad luck and bad news, but he'd gone bad.

"I stink," he said.

Moe leaned toward him and sniffed, while everyone else in the room leaned farther away.

"French fries," she declared. "That's not so bad."

"Dammit, I bet it was The Age Spot. That's what did it to him."

"You can't die from one of those, can you?"

"God, I feel so porous."

"Chel?"

"So organic."

"Organic is good."

"I'm damaged tissue."

"I don't think so, that's an infarction."

"An infarction?"

"Myocardial infarction, what Hunt has. That's what Dr. Huh said. Hunt thought it was indigestion."

"Did you say Huh?"

"Dr. Huh, the specialist."

"We're entrusting Hunt's life to someone called *Huh*?"

"All doctors take the Hippocratic Oath, Chelly."

"Moe, *everyone* should take the Hippocratic Oath."

"That's so true! I hadn't thought of that." Then she did, blinking quickly a couple of times as she entertained a fleeting vision of global good manners and universal kindness. "But anyway, I didn't see how it could be indigestion because Hunt never seemed to eat much anymore. He was never hungry and yet he kept putting on weight."

"That *does* it! It *is* her fault. I'll kill her."

"Who?"

"Bev."

"Gosh Chel, was Hunt . . . are you telling me . . . be honest now, was he having, was there someone?"

"It was an affair of the stomach, Moe, that's all. You know how much he loves you. Loves you and loves you and – "

Moe gasped. Her hands flew up to her face, trembling hands, the reason she'd been clasping them so tightly, he now realized. This earned him a sideways, *way-to-go-pal* look from a Mafioso-type seated several chairs to the right. At least he hadn't said *he loves you to death.* Clichés could be so casually reckless, coolly plunging through the guardrails into cold, otherworldly waters: *I could have died! Look alive, will you. Dead on!* Or possibly it was only his own phrasing that kept pulling him into Pluto's realm.

Someone else in the room sighed in subdued condemnation, expelling exhaustion into this dread antechamber, this waiting and waiting and more waiting room. Well, it wasn't the first time Chellis had said the wrong thing (his average about one out of three), but his heart was in the right place. *Oh Christ.* Where was Hunt's heart this very moment? In the hands of Dr. *Duh*, getting reamed like the lemon it apparently was. What were his chances? Slim, Chellis understood. And if he lived, what kind of shape would he be in? Oxygen to the brain being the true elixir of life. *Get Rèal.* That was the catchy slogan on Hunt's business card. Chellis had been greatly amused when Hunt, on entering the realty game, had changed his first name from Humphry to this dashing little French syllable. *I'll never tease him again*, Chellis promised the overheated air in the room, the deep-fried *chi*, the overworked deity-intern on duty – *Was anyone or anything listening?!* Or perhaps that was the wrong tack. Rather, he'd tease him mercilessly, tease him back to health, galvanize him with electric wit. Get Rèal! It hadn't been intended as an invitation to the Reaper. The name was nothing more than innocent advertising, a bilingual jest, OK?

"Moe?" He placed his hand on her back, rubbed gently.

"Sorry, Chelly." She wiped her cheeks with her sleeve. "That was really very sweet of you. To say that."

"You know me, I say the darndest things." *Don't lose heart.*

"A coronary, though. A coronary? I was thinking, I know this sounds totally dumb, but doesn't it sound like it should mean something else, that word? Something better?"

"You mean like a crown?"

"Mm-hmm. Made with pretty yellow flowers."

"How about a rosary strung with corn kernels? Ideal for sending a few prayers to the god of corn, my personal representative in the heavens."

Moe smiled.

"You want anything, Moe? A coffee? I have to go make a quick call."

She shook her head, lowered her voice to a frightened, wisp of sound. "Is Hunt going to make it?"

A query aimed point blank. What to say?

"Yes," he said. Then bolted before she took note of the yellow streak on his back.

*

When Chellis returned from getting no caller satisfaction, his brow all-a-crinkle, and rolling a bandage from one of his destroyed temples consideringly between his thumb and forefinger, he discovered that Moe had company. Old girlfriend of his.

"Elaine!"

"Why, hello, Chel. I thought you were – "

His eyes widened in alarm. Elaine was usually more tactful, if not with him.

"Er, away," she continued. "On a trip. Vaughan said you'd be gone for months."

"The dork."

"He is *not*."

"Doink, then."

"Mnph!"

"Now, you two," scolded Moe. "Don't get started. Sometimes, I dunno, I swear you're brother and sister."

"Ick," said Elaine.

"I would never under any circumstances let my genetic material touch *hers*," Chellis countered. Well, mayyybe. "Any news?"

"Not yet." Moe bit her lip.

"What happened to your head?" said Elaine.

The question of the day! When he had roared into Emergency trying to locate Hunt's whereabouts, he'd had a devil of a time convincing the nurses not to haul him off on a stretcher. "I dislocated it."

"Surprise, surprise," she said. "Your head's always somewhere else."

"Why do I like you? Remind me, will you?"

"Got me." Elaine brushed a pencilshaving off the cuff of her baggy utility sweater. "But you do wear your heart on your sleeve, don't you?"

Chellis winced and Elaine bit *her* lip. But Moe didn't catch the gaff; she didn't seem to be listening.

"If you really and truly want to know, someone tried to bump me off. Someone other than you for a refreshing change."

"Give me a break," scoffed Elaine. "You've been reading too many of your employer's books."

"I'm so embarrassed," Moe blurted.

"That's okay," said Chellis. "I know you wouldn't try to bump me off, Moe." Now he bit *his* lip.

"I'd *never* do that! Not intentionally, anyway."

"Great. That's a relief. So what do you have to be embarrassed about?"

Moe made a face. "Hunt popped a button on his pants."

"Could happen to anyone," said Chellis. "But go on, I sense there's more to this."

Everyone in the room grew very attentive.

"I *should* have sewn it back on," Moe said.

"'I know not should.'" responded Chellis.

"That's for sure," said Elaine.

"It's a quote," hissed Chellis. "Hamlet."

"Another ditherer," said Elaine. "You don't have to be embarrassed about not sewing a button on your husband's pants, Moe. I mean, honestly. It would be more embarrassing to confess that you had."

"It's not about that, it's not a feminist thing. You see, I told him to use a twist-tie until he could fix it. So when we rushed him to Emergency, he had a twist-tie holding up his pants like some poor street person. Golly, I *cringe* when I think of it. The nurses probably thought it was a hoot, a big laugh. I turned the man I love into a laughingstock."

"But Moe, a twist-tie, that's quick thinking," said Elaine.

Several people in the room nodded.

Elaine patted her knee. "If Alexander McQueen got hold of that idea, twist-ties would soon be on all the catwalks of Paris."

"Please don't tell him," begged Moe.

"I'd get a patent for that idea if I were you," said Chellis, giving the now shrewdly pondering Elaine a warning look.

"My sister choked on a button and tried to give herself the Hiemlich Manoeuver." A member of the room's silent majority had spoken up. A middle-class, middle-aged woman with a worry-engraved face.

"No!" Moe turned to her. "What happened?"

With this, the therapy session was officially open. Moe's two friends were left on their own to gnaw at one another other, while the rest of the room erupted into spontaneous confession, causing formerly untapped springs of sympathy to flow.

"Give me some money, will you Chel," Elaine said.

"What? You've wrecked my life and now you're going to rob me."

"I haven't wrecked your life. You've done a perfectly good job of that yourself. I left home in such a rush, I forgot my purse. I'm starving. C'mon, don't be cheap, I'll bring you back something from the cafeteria."

Chellis sighed as he reached into his back pocket. "The rich get richer."

When he retrieved the wallet, she said, "When did you get that?"

"Today."

"You bought a new wallet? Never thought I'd see the day."

"It's not mine."

"What do you mean it's not yours?" The wallet was designer vintage, its leather smooth and rich as dark chocolate. "What have you been up to?"

"I haven't been *up* to anything. Mostly I've been flat out, munching on foreign turf. There was this mix-up at the, er, store I stopped at on my trip and I ended up with some other guy's wallet. Haven't had a chance to return it . . . to . . . to . . . ."

Chellis had flipped the wallet open and was staring at the name on a platinum credit card that he'd nudged out of its slot. There were any number of them slotted and overlapping like the shimmering scales of a dragon.

"What?" said Elaine. "I can buy the whole cafeteria?"

Chellis clutched his chest. His luck, Elaine finally makes a minor quip and he's in no shape to savour it. He was in the throes of his own cardiac event.

Bring in the clowns *and* the neurocardiologist.

Elaine leaned over and peeked at the card. He caught a reviving whiff of her standard perfume. Turpentine.

"*No,*" she said, confused. "No way. Where did you say you got this? I'm supposed to believe it was some sort of mix-up? This is one of your stupid, thoughtless gags, right?"

"If I ever find the asshole who did this . . . ." The Mafioso guy was taking a turn regaling the room with a sob story, telling the appalled group about his son's recent skin graft and how the kid now couldn't look at a bar of soap without breaking down and weeping.

"*Richard Major?* You just happen to have *his* wallet?" Elaine had heated up, her face gone blotchy. "That . . . that criminal."

A young nurse pushed through the waiting room door, OR side, and said, not unsympathetically, "Ms. Hunt? Dr. Huh would like to speak with you. If you could please come this way."

The room fell silent as Moe shakily got to her feet. She gave Chellis and Elaine a despairing glance, then turned and followed the nurse.

"Poor woman," someone said.

"He's a goner," someone else muttered.

Chellis uttered not a word. He didn't have to. His heart had developed a murmur and was saying something to him very softly but insistently, and he sure didn't like what he was hearing.

12

Call of the Gastropod

OKAY, so it wasn't the sleepover he had envisioned. But then, his whole life, given this opportunity to reflect upon it, wasn't the one he'd envisioned, either. Does anyone get to have that, besides Vaughan and his ilk? Does anyone get to have the fully realized, king-size package complete with all the hedonistic perks? (Vaughan's ilk, android-souled and smooth-faced, grazing in the fields of plenty.) *Tell me* (Chellis was most eager for the answer to this burning question), what kind of husband, when his wife calls him late at night to say that she's going to crash at her former boyfriend's place, says (a lilting, pussy-whipped falsetto the appropriate tone here), "Lovely sweetheart, glad you called. See you when you get home. Sleep tight."

¡Hola!

"Isn't he worried at all?" Chellis had needled Elaine, couldn't let it drop.

"About what?"

"About, *you know*. You spending the night here. With me."

"Why should he be?"

Chellis had been leaning against the door jamb of his room, watching Elaine strip the bed.

Watching with an accumulating combo of longing and irritation.

"Where's your vacuum?" had been her follow-up question.

"Vacuum? You're going to vacuum at this ungodly hour?"

"The mattress, yes. I've honestly never seen anything like it. You should send it to a natural history museum."

"My, but you're becoming quite the wit, aren't you? Forget it, vacuum's broken."

"No it isn't. You just don't know how to turn it on."

"Baby, I *know* how to turn it on."

"Jesus, Chel, give it a rest." She pushed past him to check out the broom closet. "And to answer your question, Vaughan trusts me. Completely. Anyway, he thinks you're gay."

"What! He thinks *what*?"

"Don't tell me you're homophobic?"

"I'm not telling *you* anything."

"Don't be mad. Where are you going?"

"To clad myself in leather. Good night!"

Chellis was still sulking hours later. Not only that, but he had fallen prey to the evils of deep night, the cerebral succubi that queued-up, waiting their turn to sit on his head like an array of novelty toques. This, despite having slipped Uncle Bob protectively over his jammies. His security detail. Imperturbable and tough as a cowboy's hide, Uncle Bob was all that remained of one of Rennie's old lovers, a decent enough lunk who'd hung around longer than most. So precipitous had been his departure, though, that he'd abandoned his roughed-up biker jacket on the kitchen floor. (The switchblade slash on Bob's left arm was of dubious provenance; the guy had not been overly valorous, to put it kindly.) Chellis had grown to like him, drawn by his surrogate father potential and his limp, but Rennie must have gotten fed up, or bored. Not that Chellis had it all figured at the time, a kid taking a kid's-eye-view. A stockpile of booze had fuelled the relationship, and the fights, nothing out of the ordinary. Chellis had been well accustomed to the drinks ritual (a bit too) and the rising sound level of *ardentia verba* that followed. Thing was Rennie could hurl a plate like an Olympian and she never took any guff. For all their differences, Rennie and Elaine were very much alike: confident, determined, self-possessed. Whereas he was a soft blob quivering on a lumpy couch in the dead of night. Not to mention wide awake and staring down a rathole of loneliness. Did absolutely *everyone* have to leave him?

Hunt, mercifully, was hanging in. He was connected yet to life by the merest, most delicate thread, a twist-tie of fate precariously secured. While his sutured and intubated carcass lay in intensive care hooked up to a factory's worth of machinery, Hunt himself, what really constituted the man, was stumbling through the underworld holding his wrecked heart in his hand like an extinguished lamp. Chellis felt his own heart racing and racing, trying to catch up, trying to reach his friend and lead him home.

And Mrs. Havlock, where in God's name was she? Not out joy-riding with Richard Major, he dearly hoped. For one thing, Chellis had the jerk's licence. He supposed he would have to courier the wallet to him, which was a good excuse to call him first, do a little sleuthing à la Lazar, and do it better. He'd flipped quickly through it at the hospital, while restraining Elaine from beating it to mush with her clenched fist . . . that girl had some unresolved issues. Outside of the usual, there was nothing much in Dick's wallet, other than the evidence of unlimited and undeserved wealth, plus a photo of Di in a string bikini that Chellis admittedly lingered over some.

"He married that whore?" had been Elaine's only comment, before removing herself to another seat.

But Mrs. H? She wasn't answering her phone, nor did she have the machine on. Normally, she'd let Chellis know if she was going to be away, touring or at her place in TO. Especially if he was in research mode, and he did have information for her, something he was sure she would find extremely interesting. Hard won info, too, considering the cherub's stone head some lunatic had beamed off his noggin. Who would do such a craven thing to an innocent, mild-mannered tourist? Some cantankerous local, or a feral child, or some misguided assassin with a Neanderthal's limited arsenal? Chellis couldn't think of any reason why someone would want to hurt him. So why did he feel so twitchy and apprehensive? Doomy, doomish, doomed? Free-floating, all-purpose anxiety was nothing – one's daily bread – but this was more insidious and particular. A specialty anxiety that made him want to compact himself into a furry ball and roll away.

Chellis wondered if he should be worried about that book clerk's Mafioso dad? Nah, that had been nothing but loose talk. He was grateful nonetheless that Laney hadn't begun badgering him about her soap's test results while in the OR waiting room. Laney. Was she asleep? Deeply asleep? He could maybe . . . maybe *very* quietly slip into the bed beside her. For a little human comfort, that's all. To bask in the warmth of her essence. This, he imagined, would come tearing off her like the flame from a blowtorch. If he were caught? Curtains for him. He'd be excommunicated, drawn and quartered, his skin tanned and turned into wallets of the very kind that Dick, and doubt-less Vaughan, carried in their back pockets, snug against their taut, manly buttocks. See, see! He'd conjured up a pair of pampered and hairy male gluteals and it hadn't done a thing for him.

He *could* sneak into the bedroom and simply gaze at her, wist-fully, even if she were sawing logs, raw material for some dream-invention, her mouth hanging open, fillings exposed (the sins of her low-income childhood), dribble on her chin. She'd certainly been making enough racket earlier, shortly after he'd stomped off in a snit.

"You renovating my room, or what?" he'd shouted through the door on his way to the bathroom. This provocation had resulted in no let-up of the noise. On the way back, he'd tried, "Having difficulty getting into your chastity belt?"

No response.

"Keep doing those Kegels," was his parting piece of advice. "Yeah, sleep *tight!*"

Nothing.

Hell, he still loved her, didn't matter what she didn't say. After all, they had the very same fillings acquired from the very same cut-rate, sadistic dentist. They had suffered together; they were as one.

"Doesn't this remind you of old times?" he'd said even earlier, as they shared a post-OR beer in the kitchen before getting ready for bed.

Elaine had lightly touched his hand, saying, "Chel, our old times occurred mostly in your head. By the way, I have some salve at home if you'd like to try it on your temples, they look sore."

"They are, they're festering. But no thanks, and what was 'mostly in my head'?"

"We've never even slept together."

"We haven't? I could have sworn that was you."

"Not properly."

"Properly? Silly me, I thought passionate was more the idea. Dirty even, but hey, I can do properly. I can be a perfect gentleman, if not Herr Perfecto himself."

"Give up," she'd said softly. "It's not going to happen. You're only hanging onto me because I'm the female equivalent of your biker jacket. Grow up, send that ratty old thing to the Goodwill. Find a girlfriend."

The nerve!

As he lay *dying*. Practically. Fretting himself away to a nub, the star performer and central ingredient in an insomniac stew. Fidgeting, tossing and turning, *worrying*, generating enough cortisol in his system to fuel a whole army of deserters, he thought *screw that*. Grow up? It wasn't that simple. He wasn't that simple, despite evidence to the contrary whenever he opened his mouth. He had a serious and sensitive core that he kept private and shielded from mockers, naysayers and female impersonators like Elaine. If he *had* a Peter Pan complex he'd fly out the geezly window and bugger off. *No . . . no buggering*.

Chellis hugged himself, thereby burrowing deeper into Uncle Bob's embrace. A soft, leathery warmth enveloped him. Dump Bob at the Goodwill? He'd rather have him grafted onto his body, and should do, just to spite her. He'd always wanted arms with zippers, some decent corporal hardware. Black *is* beautiful. Black *and* white, social progress. With the exception of Michael Jacket . . . Jacketson . . . ? *Fuck it*. His head throbbed. His whole body throbbed, but not in romance novel fashion. *He entered her*. Somehow that always makes the her in question sound like a concert hall. What's worse than bad writing? Plenty. Child molesters. Mind molesters. Celebrities. Theocrats. *Swell*, he thought, ramp up the stress, *precisely what I need*. Let's slaughter the sheep on their way over the fence, why don't we? Estrogen in the drinking water, endless war, factory farming, species extinction, *Clostridium difficile*, Elaine *difficile* . . . .

Thus aggrieved and despairing, Chellis spiralled into a profound and peaceful sleep, unattended by menacing dreams, outside of a few ill-defined coalescences (with tails) that scurried up from his subconscious and fled out of his mouth, vanishing into the boundless dark.

*

"Sleep well?" Elaine asked.

"Not a wink."

"Go on, I heard you snoring."

"You were the one snoring. Can't believe I still have a roof on the house. No wonder Vonnie was thrilled you were staying here."

"He wasn't 'thrilled'. He was being mature, unlike someone else I could name."

"That again? What if *he* has a girlfriend? A sexy little bit on the side. What if he spent the night with his minuscule grastropod buried in the old – "

"Chellis! I'm warning you." She had snatched up a fork and was aiming it at his forehead.

"Please, please." He held up his hands. "No domestic violence, I'm healing. What would you like for breakfast?"

"What do you have?"

"Beer."

"What else?"

"Salt."

"Nev-er mind." She jumped up from the table and headed toward the front door.

"Where are you going? You're spurning my hospitality? As well as stealing the silverware?"

"It's plastic."

"So I exist on a much lower socio-economic rung than you. Don't rub it in."

"Chel, do me a favour and shut up. I'm going home. To have a nice hot shower."

"I have indoor facilities."

"Might as well be outdoors. Your bathroom's disgusting."

"Unfair. I cleaned the tub only the month before last. Pulled a whole hairdo out of the plughole, all black and slimy. Who knew I had a heavy metal rocker lodging in my drain? It did look remarkably like a shrunken head, the sort of trophy one might pin to one's sash if one were an ancient Celt."

"Fascinating."

"Isn't it, though? Research, my dear. So, when would you like me to pick you up?"

"I beg your pardon?"

"That's my girl, beg for it. Wait, *wait*, don't go . . . what time?"

"What time?"

"Hmm, let's see. I can be ready in about five minutes. Once I've had breakfast."

"A liquid breakfast."

"You had your chance."

"I can't make it to the hospital until later. You take the first shift."

"I will. Then I'll pick you up and we'll go for a drive."

"You don't say. Where?"

"Havlock House."

"Get lost."

"I'm serious, you have to come."

"And why is that?"

She moved over to the kitchen counter, leaned up against it, and crossed her arms. Chellis hoped she wouldn't get stuck to any spillage from days of yore, as then she'd be even less amenable than usual.

"I don't want to go out there on my own. Something weird is going on. I think Mrs. H has vanished."

"So? Happens to writers all the time."

"A different kind of vanished. Also, someone's trying to kill me."

"No they're *not*. You're just being your neurotic self."

"Me, neurotic? Hang on, did you hear *that*?" Chellis strained to listen.

"I did, yes. Someone's knocking on your front door."

"The killer."

"Probably. Why don't you go see?"

"In case I don't return, I want you to know that I'm leaving you Uncle Bob here in my will."

"Marvellous."

He gave Bob a little tug, pulling him closer, then sauntered off to answer the door. No point in delaying the inevitable, but he didn't want to blow his cool.

A police officer was standing on the front stoop with a chary look on his face and a wallet in his hand. *More* socializing with the fuzz, what was this?

"Sorry, officer, I don't accept bribes," Chellis said.

"Commendable. Wish I could say the same."

"Ha."

"I'm looking for a Mr. Chellis Beith. That you?"

"It is, everyman honorific and all."

"Can you prove it?"

"Who else would answer the door wearing Ninja Turtle PJs?"

"No one over ten." He handed Chellis the wallet. "Someone dropped this off at the shop."

"Cowabunga. My lucky day, thanks." He opened it up, counted the bills, primary numeracy all that was required where his finances were concerned. "Cash intact. I'm heartened, Good Samaritans still do exist. But you don't usually do home delivery, do you?"

"Not usually. Had to come by anyway. Your neighbours have lodged a complaint against you."

"That's not very neighbourly. What for?"

"Harassment."

"Harassment? What utter and complete molluscs. What did I do, make some style faux pas? Tie my shoelaces the wrong way?"

"You're not wearing shoelaces."

"No, otherwise I might hang myself."

"Anyway, here. " The cop reached into his pocket and yanked out the impossible-to-get-rid-of bar of soap, Laney's only invention so far that was installed with boomerang genes (it *was* slightly curved, an overly-accommodating feature). He wrenched the bar off his leather glove with a ripping noise that sounded like an industrial-strength strip of velcro letting go. "Practical joker, eh? This stuff took a whacking great chunk of plaster off their wall, they showed me the hole. They'd only finished redoing it."

"They weren't supposed to wash the walls with it." Chellis stretched open Uncle Bob's pocket and pointed to it. With some effort, the cop managed to get the bar in, making the transaction seem like some comically inept drug deal. "Isn't it demeaning, officer? Answering petty nuisance complaints like this? I can't believe you even bothered. I mean, a bar of *soap?*"

"Slow day. What we need in this town is a good murder. Claymore has all the luck."

"I'll see what I can do." Chellis patted his pocket.

"Great. Make it a double while you're at it." He gave a nod and turned to go. The finger pads of his gloves were missing.

When Chellis returned to the kitchen, he was disappointed to find no new labour-saving devices in place. The leaky tap wasn't even fixed. *Drip, drip, drip*, enough to drive a guy crazy. Although Elaine herself, leaning up against the counter and lost in dreamy speculation about Gorilla glue, or some such improvement for her soap, was more than enough to do that.

"Take off your pants," he ordered.

"Why, what's wrong with them?" She glanced down at her perfectly pleated slacks. Evidently, the husband also ironed.

"Nothing. I require glandular relief."

She actually laughed. "Your male prerogative?"

"You got it, sister."

"Touch me and I'll scream."

He didn't, but she screamed anyway. A surprised shriek when she discovered that she was stuck fast to the counter, as he had feared. His house had turned into human flypaper.

He rubbed his hands together. "Now I've got you where I want you."

Incredibly, she laughed again. "All right, you villain, I'll go with you. But you have to buy me breakfast first."

"Breakfast? You talking about those square, buttered, wheaten objects?"

"That's right. Remember, you always bite off the bottom corners first so that they look like a pair of briefs."

"A guy has to have some fun."

"Sad fun, Chel. You do it because you're sexually repressed."

"Well, whose fault is *that?*"

116

13

Let's Call the Whole Thing Off

IN AN ATTEMPT to protect his vehicle from verbal abuse, Chellis flicked on the radio, catching some castrato in mid-opera, possibly even mid-operation, wailing away. He flicked it off, ending the torture for all concerned.

"What's that rattling noise?" asked Elaine.

"What rattling noise?"

"Your car, what's causing it?"

"You mean that mellifluous *clunk clunk clunk* sound? That's how it works. If it didn't do that it wouldn't move, you see, that's the beauty of it. There's this clever whirligig thingy under the hood."

"I didn't know you'd taken a course in powder-puff mechanics."

"Don't be mean."

"We'll be lucky to make it to her place. So much for being unnoticed. Might as well roar down the driveway leaning on the horn."

"Horn doesn't work."

Elaine groaned and gave over to staring out the window. They drove past a gardening store with a mob of cement and plaster lawn ornaments on display: nymphs, coyly clad in diaphanous hard wear, gnomes (the usual suspects), giant fish, triceratops, Aslans, pigs, big Bambis, and life-size courtiers of a vaguely Renaissance persuasion. There was such a crowd of them that they gave an impression of a population explosion, the fantastical insensate breeding like rabbits.

Or rather, like humans. "Did you know that there are over six billion people in the world and at least one billion of them are writing novels?" Chellis said.

"I got that impression." Elaine plucked the cherub's head off the dashboard, placed where Chellis could keep an eye on it. She weighed it in her hand, ran a finger over its gritty, pocked face. "Where did you say you got this?"

"Secret admirer. Came special delivery." Talk about getting an impression.

Elaine slid the head back onto the dash. "What are you expecting to find at her place, anyway?"

"Dunno. Her corpse?"

"Chelly, don't say that." Elaine shivered. "Wasn't there some book of hers where a writer character – ?"

"Gets it in the neck? Yup. I don't think she much cares for other writers. Can't remember which one. *Death Notices? Dead Lines? Hit List?* They all begin to blur together after awhile."

"Some sort of blackmail plot, wasn't it? Lazar becomes involved in the investigation and then gets fingered for the crime."

"The fool."

"Let's turn around."

"Can't. Car only goes in one direction."

"Be serious, will you."

"Always am, deep down. Tell me again what Vaughan said. What he heard when he was at the vet's getting Noir deballed."

"Fixed."

"In my line of work we call that a euphemism."

"Work? Right."

"Let's not go there, okay?"

"Let's not go where we're going."

"Ah, but we're almost there. So tell me."

"I already did."

"You might have left something out. Old investigative technique, eh."

Elaine sighed so theatrically that her exhaled breath lifted the bangs from her forehead. "The receptionist . . . Ewan? I think that's his name. He's been trying to get in touch with Mrs. Havlock, but no luck. Her precious doggies have been terrorizing the place. That's it. End of report."

"The little devils, good for them. Sounds like they're back on the job. But where's Mummy?"

"Chel, if you think there's something funny going on call the police."

"No thanks, I'm practically going steady with those guys as it is. And don't tell darling Vaughan that. What if there's nothing going on? I'd look like a doofus. She might be caught up in an inspirational whirlwind, writing her brains out, temporarily lost to the daily round."

"I doubt it."

"Me too. It's more the sort of thing you would do. C'mon, let's change the subject. Heard from your folks lately?"

"Postcard. Alcatraz."

"Cool. Must be nice to have parents."

"No it's not."

"Maybe not *your* parents."

"You romanticize family too much."

"I'm a romantic guy." Chellis began to sing, "You saaay tomato . . . and I say tomato."

"It's towmawtow."

"Tomato."

"Stop it."

"You say psychopath . . . and I saaay sociopath . . . let's call the whole thing . . . oops, we're here!"

"No we're *not.*"

"Can't you agree on anything?"

"Well we're not."

"Shortcut." Chellis had pulled off the highway onto a side road and was delighting in the sound of gravel crunching under the tires, pinging away into the ditch. It gave him an illusion of speed and power and . . . what else was it that men were supposed to want? Respect, that was it. Never fear, that would be arriving soon. "Don't you love these country roads?" he said. "They're like a labyrinth."

"Wrong. They're set out in a grid pattern."

"Go ahead, wreck my metaphor. If we meet the Minotaur, you'll have to recant."

"It was a simile."

"*Same* thing. And pedantic is my territory, don't you be poaching."

Chellis turned onto an even smaller road, no more than a rutted track that vanished into a wooded area. The car bounced up and down, long grass brushing against the underside. Another delightful sound, interrupted shortly by an abrupt scraping noise. As the engine sputtered and died, he said, "That was convenient. Upon this rock I shall park my car."

"Brilliant."

Respect, *yes*, finally. "Time for walkies, anyway. Her place is beyond those trees there."

"You're sure of that? Something tells me you don't have a clue."

"Laney, you forfeited your woman's intuition years ago, remember? Whereas I am in touch with my inner navigator. Besides which, I checked with an ordinance map before picking you up. Believe you me, I know every trembling leaf and quivering blade of grass in the immediate environment."

"And every rock."

"Getting better acquainted by the moment. Let's shake a leg."

*

When they emerged from the woods *quite* some time later, Chellis's self-respect was still attached by a filament at least.

"Do you always carry one of those GPS things in your purse?" he asked testily.

"Only when I'm with you." Elaine gazed up at Havlock House, rear view. "So now what, we sneak in through the servant's quarters?"

He methodically began to pick a scattershot sampling of beggars' ticks off the sleeve of his denim shirt, thereby removing all evidence of the sexual attack he'd endured while ambling through the flora. Vegetation apparently couldn't resist him. He'd been leafily embraced and tumbled, poked, pollinated, and almost grafted – wed to a massive oak that had practically leapt in front of him. "It's a wonder I don't burst into bloom on the spot," he said. Then added, "First we peek through the windows."

"And second?"

"We leave."

"You're kidding."

"Nope. There was an extremely low percentage of kidding in that comment. About .005% would be my estimate."

"Why, *why*, do I let myself get talked into these things?"

"Self-reflection is good, Laney, and about time, I'd say. If you'd indulged more often, it might have saved you from some serious miscalculation in your love life. But as regards Mrs. Havlock's, I only want to see if anything seems suspicious. Whereas, what? You want to break the door down?"

"We could try knocking, if that hadn't occurred to you. She might be in there having a fit because a couple of prowlers are skulking around in her backyard."

"I don't think so."

"Let's see."

"*Elaine*, no." But would the woman listen to him? Never. Too bullheaded – she could be the Minotaur's wife. Hands on hips, he watched her charge like Mrs. Minotaur across Athena's precisely trimmed lawn, past burgeoning perennial beds and robustly flowering bushes. Someone here was keeping appearances up. He took in the verdant scene, spotted a Flowering Judas. It was easily identifiable, seeing as a poor cousin to this one had staked a claim in his own postage stamp of a yard, planted by Rennie in a one-day gardening blitz, thereafter to be neglected forever. What remained of it were a few malnourished and balding twigs determinedly eking out an existence in a depleted patch of soil like an old-timer in a nursing home. He walked over to this more privileged plant, which for some reason reminded him of Wayne Gretzky. A bunny magnet, maybe that was it. Truly, it was a mystery how the mind works, his anyway. Despite all the cranial distress he'd endured, he did recall that this was the setting Mrs. H had used for her non-compliant corpse, her turgid bit of starter material for the new book.

While Elaine was politely but firmly *tap-tap-tapping* on the back door, successfully rendering pointless their cloak-and-dagger work thus far, he crouched down to take a closer look at the ground beneath the bush. Disturbed. It was and he was. Someone could have easily been stretched out here, given the flattened grass, the uprooted spurge, the *button* nestled so conveniently in a tuffet of moss and winking at him like a wayward metallic eye. He picked it up, fingered it, a small two-holer, fallen off a cuff perhaps. Male or female apparel, hard to say. His boss might have taken a turn under the bush herself as an imaginative stimulant. Who knows, she may have conducted her own research for some realistic detail he hadn't been asked to provide: the exact feel of the bone-chilling damp beneath her back, the intoxicating freshness of the foliage, the up-ended world view from the underside of the Judas. Some authors did go to extreme measures for authenticity, for the real dirt. Some even travelled extreme distances on ambience safaris, hunting for local detail, local wine, and other interesting commodities, spending tor-mented, but *essential* days away from the desk, all the better for pumping padding into novels as fat as the average North American. Research, research, it had its allure. It was his personal theory that the Sirens had tried to distract Odysseus with particulars, not song. They had called out to him the ancient and seductive equivalent of baseball stats, the endless trivia generated by divine superstars, the infinitesimal constituents of the hitherto unknown.

Elaine?

Chellis quickly looked toward the house and caught sight of the back door closing. She was not on this side of it. *Christ.*

He rushed over in case immediate heroics were required, and entered the house as quietly as possible only to hear Elaine's hard-heeled loafers *clack-clacking* across the hardwood, while she simulta-neously called out Mrs. Havlock's name. Called into an unresponsive churchy silence.

"Not here," she announced from the far end of the hall.

"Geez Laney, it's too bad you left your megaphone at home."

She ignored him, a practice with which he was all too familiar, and ducked into a room on her right. "God!" he heard her gasp.

"What? *What* is it?"

An icy stiletto of fear slid in under his ribs.

When he caught up with her, though, he found that the crime scene was missing a few essential elements. The dining room, yet not a single speck of gore was being served up. Nor had the gold, tasselled holdbacks on the heavy silk curtains obviously garroted anyone of late. The reproduction artwork was criminally bland, but blameless as far as he could see. "Okay, I give up." Not only was the room missing a dead body, but there wasn't even any dust. No one had decomposed here in at least the last hundred years.

Elaine was staring at one of the walls and shaking her head. "How could she? That colour? It's hideous."

So. The worst kind of misdemeanour: bad taste. Or taste that was not Elaine's. The walls were painted a sanguinary red, which admittedly was intense. Chellis felt as if he were standing inside a corpuscle. The dining wound.

"You're out of touch, sweetheart," he said. "Don't you read *House & Home?* This is the latest from the Serial Killer palette. Ripper Red, Slasher Scarlet – "

"Do you *have* to say that?"

"Yes. Perversity is psychologically nourishing, a healthy habit. Consider how many proto-cancer cells withered the moment I formulated my witticism. And did you know, by the way, that the decks of warships used to be painted exactly this colour so that subsequent carnage wouldn't unnerve the sailors?"

"Useless information."

"You think? There could be blood splattered all over these walls and we wouldn't be able to tell unless we looked more closely."

Elaine turned on her hard heel and marched out of the room.

He followed her out, then continued to trail behind her as she pushed open half-closed doors and vetted several tidy, unrevealing rooms. In the kitchen, she was momentarily distracted by a postmodern pepper mill the size of a fire hydrant, while Chellis checked the fridge and found a sorry, wilted head of lettuce, but no other decapitations. The house secrets, if there were any, were all stashed well out of sight.

"I wonder who cleans this place," Elaine mused, wandering back down the hall.

"Who cleans your place? And please don't say – "

"Vaughan."

"He does not. Give me a break."

"Nothing but the truth. He doesn't believe in making other people do the grunt work. He feels that everyone should be responsible for cleaning up after themselves. Besides, he enjoys hands-on labour, doing simple things."

"'Tis a gift to be simple," observed Chellis, smirking into the stairwell. "We'd better check upstairs, too."

"Fine. You go."

"You're not coming?"

"No."

"Why not?"

"Because I'm out of here. This has been a colossal waste of time."

"Come *on*, Laney. Why are you being so . . . so . . . passive-aggressive?"

"That wasn't being passive-aggressive. It was being sensible. Which is better than being passive-passive."

"You're not implying that I'm that, I trust?"

"No. I'm *saying* you're that."

"Oo-la-la, *quelle chienne*," he muttered to himself.

This earned him a sharp, phlegm-clearing elbow in the vicinity of his left lung. "Say that again and there *will* be a body on the floor."

He clutched his chest, and coughed. "Now you're being aggressive-aggressive. I can't take you anywhere." Although the thought of taking her was pretty thrilling. Better not mention it, though, and shorten his life even more.

"Is this her office?" With the toe of her shoe, Elaine nudged open the door of a sanctuary that Chellis had on occasion been allowed to visit. "Wow, how can she work in such a mess, papers and stuff everywhere? The rest of the house is so orderly, too. I'd never be able to concentrate, but some people need this sort of ferment, I guess."

Glancing over her shoulder and taking in the room's staggering disarray, he said softly in Elaine's ear, "*Bingo.*"

14

Manual Labour

CHELLIS WAS STARING at his hands, surprised, as though they had turned up unexpectedly after having been missing for several weeks. Or years, for they had changed had they not since his last close inspection? Their complexion had acquired more character, which is to say, more freckles, the odd brownish splotch, extra knuckle-crinkles, a wart (!), more prominent veins, deeper lines in the palms. His hands were aging in advance of him, possibly in their efforts to hold the future at bay, reaching out protectively, blocking further harm like flesh shields.

Harm, he thought, and here he was seated in one of the more dangerous places in the Western world – a hospital. He could almost hear bacterial novelties mating, hybridising, seething as they dripped off the walls like swaths of Spanish moss or virulent macramé wall-hangings from the sixties. Consider the operating theatre itself, where the moral of the performance was all too often the old sad truth that *to err is human*. He fully expected the patients that passed him in the halls to clank as they ambled by given all the medical hardware that was sewn up inside them, tools forgotten at a work site.

On entering the hospital, Chellis had scrubbed his hands with so much of the anti-bacterial gunk on offer it was a wonder they had any identifying features left. Mannequin hands, like Vaughan's, those smooth, long-fingered rakes that scooped up life's gifts and pleasures (simple pleasures!) as they tumbled his way.

Was Chellis bitter? Am I, he asked? Naw, only bored. (Bitter was for pills.) Hence the hand reading. He'd forgotten to bring a book with him, but hadn't been able to delve into the matriarchy of litera-ture that Moe had compiled on Hunt's bedside table, even though, unlike most males, he was an equal opportunity reader. He eyed the book pile. Paper progeny was perhaps a more accurate descriptive, as there was an identifiable theme at work here: *Desirable Daughters; The Optimist's Daughter; Not Without My Daughter; The Daughter of Time, A Family Daughter etc.* All for Moe's own edification and entertainment certainly, since Hunt had not yet returned from his soul-journey. But his return *was* expected, and for this miracle Chellis knew he should retract his hospitalist sentiments. Hunt was hooked up in the bed beside him, the machinery burbling away like an old-fashioned percolator, and where there's coffee, there's life. Even though Hunt didn't look so hot himself, more like a blancmange, unnaturally white and puffy, the IV having pumped him full of fluids.

Harm, he thought again, remembering how a friend of Rennie's had read her palm once for a lark, predicting among other far-fetched improbabilities that she would lose her adopted son, that a tall, dark, and beautiful stranger would spirit him away. How was Rennie to know that Elaine would transform herself into Ms. Universe, his whole world? Instead of laughing along at this bit of joshing, Rennie had slapped her friend hard across the face, knocking the friendship right out of her. True, it hadn't been much of a jest. It had been more of a dig for the love she bore him, her found mutt. Before this uncharacteristic, hair-trigger response, he hadn't realized that there were aspects of her motherly self that were unprotected by her own wall-to-wall (and off it) sense of humour. Humour, armour, amour – a revealing declension. Well, love was a funny business all round. Rennie's hands had been small and rough, she hadn't been one for kneading emollients into them. He could almost feel them still, fingers grazing his forehead, brushing back his hair, but lightly, tenderly. No sucker punches for him. Not from that source.

Elaine had mathematician's hands, fingers slightly square-tipped at the ends. Hands that were rarely empty or at rest. She'd twitch them away if you tried to hold them. He suspected that not even Vaughan had any luck there. Her hands were not a propitious breeding ground for idle-worms, which in former times was an affliction dreamt up to intimidate servants who were deemed lazy. A laziness that presumably could strike at any time in the course of an endless, brutish work life. (His own unknown ancestors likely *were* lazy sods.) Did they fall for such medical malarkey, the credulous, indentured masses? But then, why wouldn't they? Their modern equivalents – anyone who wasn't a CEO – had also been goaded into the 24 hour workday. No millions socked away for retirement? No RRSP's? No investment properties, no Hummer, no designer sneakers . . . get to work you *idle worm!*

Chellis brought his hands together and cupped them, creating an empty bowl worthy of contemplation.

An Intensive Care nurse whispered over to Hunt's bedside to check on him and twiddle with the machinery. She smiled at Chellis as he sat staring down into his fingerbowl of nothing.

He glanced up, and returning her smile, asked, "Do you have an RRSP?"

"Sure," she said.

"May I be your beneficiary?"

This netted him a bigger smile. Great, he was earning some interest.

"I'll think about it," she said. "You might have to marry me first, though."

"Bring on the chaplain."

"I'll have him paged."

"Tell him it's an emergency."

"I will," she laughed, and moved to the next bed, where a child lay in a coma, the victim of a hit and run. Humour drained instantly from her features as she checked the heart monitor, adjusted the IV. No idle-worms writhing on her fingers.

Later, he overheard her say to another nurse, "Rèal Hunt's brother? He's sweet, isn't he?"

"Really, eh. Been here for hours. I'd be lucky if my brother bothered to come to my funeral."

"They must come from a wonderful family. Both have such neat names, too."

"Yeah, class. A name's a dead giveaway. That's why I called my daughter Krystal."

As in meth? Chellis reflected, not so sweetly. His forename was rather swish, wasn't it? Pretentious some might say, and had said. He tolerated it, his name, but was too accustomed to it to hate it. Rennie had discovered it while standing in line at a Loblaw's checkout and flipping through a *Cosmopolitan* magazine. (And *why* did the significant moments in his life have to occur in a grocery store?) The intensive care unit was restricted to family, so Moe had come up with the fib about him being a brother, which was all but literally true. He was happy to claim bro-hood with Hunt, and it was a refreshing change to have a last name that was a verb and not an arrested state, like *Beith*. Chellis's only fear was that this new, if invented, relationship would doom his friend, since he seemed to be a family-repellant, the very fact of his existence blew his relations away.

He opened his cupped hands and let his woolgathering spill into his lap. If he stared at his palms straight through to the bone, he'd still not be able to read them. Heck, since he was here, maybe an X-ray was in order, some revealing medical palmistry. But what if there was absolutely nothing to discover: hollow man, hollow bones? No discernable future. He certainly didn't seem to have an employer at present; he was as empty-handed in that regard as he had been at Havlock House after searching Mrs. H's office. Something significant *was* there, of that he was certain. Or had been there. Whoever had been hunting and gathering before them could have already taken it. The elusive, indefinable *it*, to which Elaine had not given much credence.

"So she messed up her office," she had concluded. "She was rushing to catch a flight to some writer-gig and couldn't find her specs."

"Ransacked is not her standard *modus operandi*." Filing cabinets had been left open, contents yanked out, papers and old proofs littered the floor, as did books, disgracefully splayed and exposed, pages a vulnerable, dog-belly white. "Why are you resisting the obvious?"

"Okay, fine. She killed him and has gone into hiding."

"Pardon me? Who are we talking about?"

"That guy they found in Claymore, what was his name?"

"Jude Thomas. And exactly how do you deduce this?"

"All this . . ." Elaine had been hovering over a pile of newspaper clippings on the desk that had been left undisturbed by the recent raid. "She collected everything even remotely related to the murder."

"Murder's her business. As in, her subject. She's simply panning for gold, a new take, a captivating detail."

"How can you be sure?"

"Trust me. I know how she operates."

"So you really think something's happened to her?"

"I do."

"Then go to the police, Chel. File a missing persons report. This is damning enough." She'd swept her hand around the room. "Unless she did it herself to make it seem like she's in trouble."

"I will."

"You won't."

"I *will.*"

"No, you won't, I *will.*"

"Tomato. Hah!"

"What?"

Would she? Chellis wondered. Not likely, she was simply using Laney slychology. She knew that he knew he shouldn't leave it (*it!*) in her hands. Nor would he (would he?). He vowed to go to the cop-shop as soon as Moe returned from getting her nails done. A seemingly frivolous mission under the circumstances, but therapeutic, and she could use that. Given the time it had taken, he guessed that she'd worked in a soothing round of shopping, too. Loyal Moe had logged in hours and hours at Hunt's bedside, healing him with her reliability, her irrepressible optimism, her touch.

Chellis thought about Moe's hands, which were pretty, soft and dainty. Unfortunately her handshakes were of the alarmingly limp variety; she could as easily be handing you an empty angora mitten. Or a dead vole. Whereas Elaine could wrench your arm off. *Her* hands were dextrous and patient in invention, but much less so when it came to some of the 'womanly' arts, if one dare even think in those terms. Sewing, for example. Her method of re-attaching missing buttons involved either a stapler or wire. Watching her 'put on her face' was unfailingly entertaining. Not that she needed makeup, but like every female gazing critically into a mirror – which is to say, every time a gazing occurred – she felt that improvements were required, that *something* needed to be done. The ritual never varied. First she would briskly pencil on some eyeliner like a copy editor fiercely marking an error, then rub most of it off with her finger, concerned about overdoing it. Next, she'd dab on some reddish-brown lipstick, which vanished into a tissue when she blotted her lips, and then came the blusher applied in a flurry of pink dust. In the moment of doubt that inevitably followed, she'd wipe this off on her palms. *There*, done! When she turned to him (and she *had*, no fantasy this) with a small, endearing smile, she looked exactly the same as she had before initiating the beautification project. But she felt better.

"Let me see," he'd said once, taking her hands in his own, and turning them palms up.

"They're blushing, you must like me. Caught you red-handed, didn't I?"

His rosy-fingered girlfriend? Make that girl friend. And what a heartbreaking and unbridgeable chasm lay between those two words. The tiny space between them defined a breach as wide as the continental drift.

Chellis drummed his own pale fingers on his kneecaps, then brought his palms together in a prayerful salute, then crossed his arms, tucking his hands under his pits. Now that he'd taken notice of his hands he couldn't stop noticing them, they kept crawling or leaping into view. Hands *are* expressive, but his seemed to be involved in some sort of theatre-of-the-absurd dumb show. Wasn't there a condition where one's hands couldn't be controlled? Alien Hand Syndrome, that was it. A rare affliction, although not as rare as idle-worms. It was a neurological condition in which one's hands refused to obey orders from brain-central, rebelliously following an agenda of their own. In the case he'd read about, a woman pinched her own nipples uncontrollably. Self sexual harassment. *If thy hand offends thee, cut it off.* Chellis clamped his upper arms more tightly against his sides so as not to attract the attention of a sawbones who had swanned into the Unit and was flirting with the nurses. Including his intended! Physicians used to carry dead men's hands in their bag of tricks. Stroke a tumour nine times with a hand that had been lopped off, fresh from the gallows, and *voilà*, the horrified patient's tumour remains intact, but if he pays up for the treatment he at least has a decent chance of getting rid of the doctor.

Chellis hid his hands by sitting on them, risking molestation, and thought about the recent publishing trend in book covers: photographs of hands holding eggs, or flowers, or fire, or hands that were beseechingly empty and appeared to be offering more ineffable produce to the potential reader. Either that or the hands were simply begging the hard-hearted book buyer: *Buddy, can you spare a dime? That's all my 2% royalties amount to.* Mouths were popular for awhile, and feet, usually shod. Big red lips plugged with roses or oozing caviar, but as far as he knew there were no book covers that featured the foot-in-mouth option, which would optimize both fads. He would have to mention this unexploited anatomy angle to Mrs. Havlock . . . dear Mrs. H . . . it's not as though he wasn't worried about her. He was worried sick, but given the present environment didn't want anyone to notice. He'd prefer to get out of this place alive.

My Hands, Your Death. Jesus! Or was it, *Your Hands, My Death?*

He held out his hands again, which had fallen asleep while his thoughts had maundered on, and began waving them around and flexing his fingers.

Moe pushed through the door and hurried over to the bed.

"Hi Chel, I'm back. Sorry if I was a teensy bit long. What are you doing?"

"Playing."

"Aww."

"Actually, it's a new technique I've been trying out. I've been massaging the molecular force field around Hunt."

"Chelly, you're such a good person. Hunt looks better, he *does.*"

Instantly and painfully, Chellis became aware of why the Supreme Being had bothered to give hands to humans. They were the required appendages for hiding one's face in shame.

"No I'm not." He sighed and attempted jerk reparation. "Your nails, Moe, they're sexsational. Truly. And is that a new dress? Colourful, jazzy! I had no idea muumuus were back in style."

"This is a *maternity* dress, Chel."

"A . . . no way! Are you serious? I . . . holy cow, Hunt never said you guys were thinking about starting a family. Why would he, but, I mean, we're pretty close, and, my God, I'm going to be an *uncle*, how fantastic is that, I – "

Moe had raised a hand, enough with the julienned congratulations. "I'm not pregnant *yet*." She dropped the hand to pat Hunt's inert blanketed leg. "But I have plans."

"Uh, yeah? You know, it might be a while before Hunt can, uhh, contribute."

131

"Not that long."

"Love is very bad for the heart. And most other major organs now that I come to think of it."

"Life is precious, Chel. I don't want to waste any more of it."

"So you're saying where there's a willie there's a way?"

Moe giggled. When was the last time he'd made a female giggle? Grade school?

"Chelly, you *are* a good person. Please take care of yourself."

"I'll try, Moe. Here comes a nurse right now to give me an immortality transfusion."

It was the nurse he'd spoken to earlier, and by her worried expression he could tell she was having some doubts about the engagement.

"I'm sorry to interrupt," she said, sounding perplexed. "There's a police officer in the hall outside the Unit and I think he's looking for you, Mr. Hunt." Her smile wavered. "But he used a different last name."

The fuzz again? He honestly didn't need any more wallets. His needs were simple, like Vaughan's. They were exactly like Vaughan's.

"My pseudonym," he explained.

"Gee, you're a writer?"

For a mere second longer, he held onto her interest. But then he had to let go. "Not me." He offered her an open-handed, Jesus-gesture. "Truth to tell, I'm just an ordinary liar."

15

Missing

"WE MEET AGAIN."

"An unexpected pleasure, I'm sure." Chellis was going for suave. "But preferable under different circumstances." He gave his opponent the eye. "I see you've been promoted. In record time, too. From cop on the beat to detective in what, a day, a couple of hours?"

"We're short-staffed."

"Right, it's those new rules."

"Come again."

"Short staff."

"I don't follow."

"Never mind." Chellis had to remember that he was among the humour-deprived. "I guess that's why you guys haven't solved that Claymore case yet."

"Not our call, as you know. Unless *you* can tell me something about it."

"Not me. May I go now? Being dragged in here is doing untold damage to my reputation."

"You have one?"

In truth, Chellis was secretly thrilled to find himself in an interview room at the police station. He'd worked up descriptions of such rooms for Mrs. Havlock without an iota of actual or imaginative exertion, and this room did not disappoint. It was as windowless, underfurnished and anti-ambient as one could wish for, if one's wishes ran along particularly bleak lines and included hideous synthetic carpeting. The only feature he would not have thought to summon up was an oil painting that was hanging crookedly on the wall to his left, a concrete wall, ideal for smacking uncooperative heads against. The painting's purpose may indeed have been to conceal an embedded smattering of blood and hair, but it was doing a masterful job all on its own as an advertisement for violence. In colour and content it was painfully lurid and busy, like one of his more hectic and overpopulated nightmares, an extravaganza of interbred Jungian archetypes on the rampage. He hoped that the artist had been apprehended and sent straight to solitary confinement.

Taking in Chellis's disapproving appraisal, the detective got up from his chair and straightened the painting. As soon as he sat back down, it dipped out of alignment again, which made Chellis smile. Not only a bad painting, but a bad attitude.

"A fine example of *horror vacui*," Chellis said.

"Which is?"

"And I quote, 'A fear or dislike of leaving empty spaces in an artist's composition.' *Oxford English Dictionary*. Not only a good book but *the* good book, and I believe every word of it. Can't wait for the movie," he added, so as not to sound too earnest.

"Be a scream."

They stared at one another. Chellis noted that the detective was large enough to have good and bad cop incorporated as one. There may have been cutbacks in the force, but not in the donut supply.

"Name's Inspector Arthur Foote."

Damn. He wished that the man hadn't introduced himself. A named minor character usually turned up again, or so a lifetime of reading had taught him. But then, a body part last name, that was noteworthy. At one time Chellis had been a collector of those and had accumulated quite an extensive list. He'd seen it as a kind of informal, nominal-anatomical survey to see if the whole range of available body parts were being put to good use. Like verbal prostheses. But for all the John Bones, Roberta Heads, Mark Legges, and Sally Hands he'd discovered, as well as the physical unmentionables – the Groins, Bladders, and Butts – his Holy Grail, Anita Vagina, was still out there somewhere in the badlands, unrecorded and running wild. Or monologuing on some theatrical stage, God help us.

"Chellis Beith," he offered. *His* name merely a decorative piece of fakery, nothing so incarnate and gutsy as Bill Ball or Nancy Perineum. (Okay, so he made that one up.)

"I know."

"Right, the neighbours. I suppose they're having me arrested for not spraying poison on the crabgrass and depriving their future offspring of toxic H_2O cocktails?"

"Negative. Although they weren't too thrilled about all that morbid garbage you dumped on their front lawn."

"What, do they send in a daily report on my activities? I thought the plastic flowers and Styrofoam crosses looked fashionably goth. They *did* place two Etruscan urn knock-offs outside their front door, so anyone who knows anything would assume they were into funerary lawn decor."

"Uh-huh. Well, they're spooked. They think you're Sicilian."

"Seriously? I *could* give them a finger, but I wouldn't want to cut it off first. I don't like them that much."

"Who are your people anyway?"

Small town question, but a significant one.

"My people? I don't have people." He couldn't help but picture a cage with rodent-sized relatives within, scrambling on hamster wheels and gnawing on stale kibble. "Unless you mean my PR. Or is having people some sort of disease, like scabies?"

"A real joker, eh?"

"The genuine article." He considered a grammarian-style sally here, but wisely, and with a prickle of regret, let it go. "Only trying in my humble way to make the world a happier place."

"Does making the world a happier place involve taking out some of the people who are in it?"

"Inspector, that doesn't sound like a very nice question."

"*I* was only joking, Mr. Beith, when I said we could use a murder in town."

"And a fine quip it was, too. For someone in your profession. A worthy effort, anyway."

Arthur Foote was giving him the stoneface treatment.

"*Has* someone been murdered?"

"What do you think?"

"*Moi?* I'd say no. I'm sure you're familiar with the worn, although not unreasonable phrase, 'It can't happen here.' Why do you ask?"

His interrogator reached into an open briefcase on the floor and pulled out a baggie that contained what Chellis at first took to be a flattened brownie . . . or a slab of hash . . . or both. Alas, no. "Recognise this?" He dangled the plastic bag between them.

"Hang on." Chellis jumped up, slapped his back pockets, sat back down. Was this possible? Clearly he was going to have to rub some of Elaine's homicidal soap on his wallet and clap it permanently onto his rear.

"Twice?" he said. "What a hoot. Thanks for keeping it fresh, eh. Where did you find it?"

"In a forested area behind a house belonging to a woman named Athena Havlock. You know her?"

Chellis inclined his head toward the bagged wallet and narrowed his eyes. "It has teeth marks on it. What were you doing out there in the woods Inspector, scavenging for nuts and berries?"

"*Trevor* found your wallet."

"Trevor?"

"Canine unit."

"I see. Whatever happened to names like Sport and Champ?"

"Why don't you answer my question first?"

"Okay, yes, I know her." Elaine *hadn't* been bluffing about calling the cops, the minx.

"But wait, oh *Jesus*, you're not telling me . . . she isn't . . . ?"

"Dead?"

Chellis held his breath, eyes widening.

"Not that we know of."

He exhaled a stream of pent alarm. "You had me worried there."

"So you're an actor as well as a comedian? Could be you did away with her and buried her in the woods. Might be better to confess now and save us all a lot of trouble."

"Heck, I wouldn't want you guys to go to any trouble, but sorry, no confessions forthcoming. Not even about the jelly beans I nicked from the Five & Dime when I was a kid and for which I can't be blamed, since as we all know such petty thievery is a rite of passage into duplicitous and dishonest adulthood. That said, Mrs. Havlock is my employer. She funds my agreeably unstructured lifestyle, for which I am endlessly grateful, even though I can't believe I just used the word 'lifestyle.' Would you kill your own boss? Skip that, dumb question. What would be my motive? I scarcely have enough motivation most days to open a can of beans, let alone knock someone off. So she *is* missing?"

"We have good reason to believe so. Tell me what you were doing out there. And skip the lecture this time."

He did, infusing his recitation with as much boyish innocence as he could muster.

Arthur Foote listened with barely concealed skepticism, but Chellis knew that his was a standard information-gathering mode. When grilled about Athena's daily routine, he offered up what he could, but found for all their many meetings and work-related chats, that he didn't really know much about what she got up to when she wasn't working. What she did when she was at her city condo was as mysterious to him as the city itself. Toronto, he kept meaning to go there. Edgy shops, edgy art galleries, edgy restaurants (no Bev!), but what if he slit himself open on one of those edges? What if he had to get on the subway? The thought of zooming hellbent through the underworld in a fluorescent tube while pressed up against striving cosmopolitans, expressionless as stiffs, made him almost hyperventilate on the spot. Unless it was the formaldehyde and fire retardant radiating off the synthetic carpet that was getting up his nose.

He wondered if he should mention Richard Major hanging around Havlock House. Or, reportedly, driving around with an unidentified older woman in his car. Seeing as Dick's father was fast friends with the Chief of Police, he thought not, not yet. But by omitting his suspicions, biased as they were, was he endangering her further, if danger was what she was in?

"You'll find her?" This was more plea than question.

"She'll turn up. Lots of people disappear for awhile and don't think anything of it. Independent woman, no one she has to report to, might be off somewhere having a fling. Public person, too, could be she needs some R&R in an out-of-the-way place."

"Possibly." Can't get more out of the way than Farclas. "So do I get my wallet back?"

"Nope." Foote dropped it back into his briefcase.

"Doesn't matter," Chellis sighed. "I have another one at home anyway."

"Don't you be leaving town, Mr. Beith."

"Wouldn't dream of it. Before I go, Inspector Foote, I do have some practical advice to offer. If you slather some more acrylic on the right side of your painting, it'll hang better. It's unbalanced." In more ways than one.

"Yeah? How do you know I'm the artist?"

"*Horror vacui.* We're all afraid of something."

*

Driving home without a license felt daring, like not wearing underwear, which was about as much adventure and misdemeanour as his nerves could stand. And this was with knowing that both of those items, license and boxers, were presently residing in a secure, if not proper, place. How much excitement does a regular guy need? Albeit a sensitive guy with no more than a dash of paranoia in his half-glass. This, a squirt of psychological Tabasco, was all that was required to keep him alert and watchful.

As he motored along, the car purring like a kitten since Elaine, his sweet and sourpuss, had fixed it (parking on rocks evidently does nothing to improve a vehicle's more useful functions), he felt reassured about his immediate safety. No one had tampered with his brakes; no windshield-shattering steel rods had thus far 'accidentally' flown out of the sweaty grip of a roadside construction worker; no over-the-cliff sideswipes were being perpetrated by a shadowing fellow-driver who had fellowship far from his mind. All of the above were standard investigative disincentives that Marcel Lazar frequently had to survive before being allowed to wrap up a case. Or wrap his unbreakable mitts around a tumbler of Laphroaig while in some seedy bar brooding handsomely about the one niggling and elusive detail that would pull a mass of painstakingly accumulated evidence together. (Seeing as Chellis did most of the background accumulating, it was doubly galling that Lazar should be rewarded with *his* favourite drink, even if only on unpeaty paper. When he had once complained about this to Mrs. H, she had grinned at him with evident delight.)

Contemplating danger seemed to be giving Chellis an endorphin boost. Bonus. Thus, feeling expansive, he decided to take the long way home by cruising along the main drag. He saw that The Age Spot had a sandwich board leaning drunkenly out front advertising an All-You-Can-Eat-Or-Else buffet. This was tempting, in much the same suicidal way that gazing into an abyss from the roof of a high-rise is tempting. He didn't stop, also having noticed several over-satisfied customers staggering out the front door in search of the nearest vomitarium.

Wheeled sidewalk traffic was rolling along in sync with him. Little kids were being pushed in strollers by roller-skating parents, old folks were chugging along on scooters, a man on a unicycle was weaving in and around pedestrians. Chellis experienced a spasm of lyrical appreciation for his fellow travellers. He spotted a teenage girl in front of the drugstore, elbow raised and face pressed against her shoulder, nose twitching as she smelled her armpit. A sense of utter privacy, or indifference, while in a public place was one of the great advantages of self-absorption. Gormless youth was endearing in any event.

All in all, Chellis felt uplifted sightseeing in his own town. Everything seemed to be infused with a salutary glow. Why he should feel this way was beyond him, particularly under the present circumstances, but he knew he should accept it as a gift from nowhere. A gift that perhaps overlay and obscured a niggling detail of the sort that often eluded Lazar.

As he pulled into his driveway he did think, does Mrs. Hav expect *me*, her dauntless and indefatigable researcher, to find her, to actually research her whereabouts? Wouldn't put it past her.

Glancing over at his neighbour's place, he saw that their jacquard curtains – *window treatments* rather – were pulled shut. There also appeared to be a sign on the lawn that for a change didn't belong to a renovation company, but instead announced the installation of a security system. Well, good. It was decent of them to take on their share of the fear that seemed to be wafting through the air these days. Lessened his burden.

He took a deep breath on entering the house, gratefully inhaling the domestic and familiar, an olfactory concoction of his own making that not everyone (i.e. no one he could think of) would appreciate.

Oddly, taking in another lung-full, he detected a long lost odour in the mix. Not that he didn't welcome it back, but its sudden arrival was unsettling. A distinct but very faint sense of Rennie was in the air, that lily-of-the-valley, earthy smell of her skin. Her fragrance must have leached out of the walls, or out of her old tatty curtains and furniture, drawn by the heat of the day.

After a couple of stiff drinks, he got Elaine on the blower, surprised that he'd scared her up so easily.

"Why are you answering the phone?" he said.

"It rang."

"Where's Huckleberry Hound?"

"I haven't seen him for years, but if you mean Vaughan, he's at the veterinarian's."

"Did he decide to get fixed, too?"

"Ha, double ha. What do you want?"

"Don't be too friendly. I might get all hot and bothered." He registered her derisive snort. "I just wanted to say *thanks*, eh."

"You're welcome. What did I do, besides go with you on your moronic quest, save you from walking home, buy you lunch *and* breakfast, all of the many services for which you're usually not so grateful. Now if you don't mind, I have work to do."

"You could do some work on your social graces. I hate to tell you this Laney, but the Miss Congeniality title is going to elude you again this year. But getting back to my gratitude. The service you left off your *ta-da* list was calling the cops about my missing boss, which resulted in me getting hauled in for questioning. They think I did it."

"Did what? It'd be a miracle if you managed to clean your teeth in a day. Besides, I didn't call them."

"You didn't?"

"No."

"Well *who* did?"

"Don't ask me. Her publisher, her agent . . . ."

"She fired her agent."

"Okay, so maybe *he* bumped her off. Chel, listen to me for once. Stay out of this, don't get involved."

"I am involved."

"Good luck then."

"Thanks a load."

"As I said in the first place, you're *welcome*." And she hung up.

Fuck. He wandered into his bedroom to collect Dick's wallet. Might as well dig himself in deeper by making that call to the rep management specialist himself. All that cash (now minus a few bucks), plus his cards, Dick must be shitting himself, which was a gratifying thought. He'd be so grateful to get it back that he'd spill the beans about Mrs. H. Yep.

But the wallet wasn't on the dresser where he'd left it. He was positive he'd left it there, unless he was having a sudden sneak preview of dementia. He checked the drawers, delving beneath the mateless socks and T-shirts grey as dishwater. He got down on his hands and knees and gazed into the furred world beneath the dresser. He heard some sort of pounding racket, and realized that someone was knocking on the front door. The cops again? More likely some kid selling inedible chocolate bars for a school trip to Toronto where something horrible will happen to him that will mess him up for the rest of his life. Or something fantastic will happen, with the same result. Either way, Chellis felt that it would be morally reprehensible to buy the chocolate bar, but he couldn't fit himself under the dresser to hide. And since his car was in the driveway, it was obvious that he was home.

Or it might be Moe with good news. He hated it when people dropped by unannounced, but then, once they were in, giving him a hug or a peck on the cheek, then chatting and drinking and laughing . . . he loved it. Loved the unexpected company, the infusion of warmth in the house, the heightened and animated atmosphere. He got up to answer the door. Whoever it was, they weren't giving up.

As he reached for the doorknob, he had a disturbing thought. *A second body always turns up.* This was a reliable ingredient of the formula, and one to which Mrs. H adhered, although creatively, even deviously, so that the discovery came unexpectedly.

But hey, even if it was subliminally expected, the body wouldn't normally show up on one's own front doorstep. Would it?

16

Arrival of the Queen of Sheba

BOYS WILL BE BOYS, and he couldn't help but stare. The body was
a stunner . . . and fortunately alive. *And* said body appeared to have a
bagged bottle of hooch – aka corpse reviver – clasped in one hand.
Evidently the local missionaries were resorting to desperate, but more
delightful, measures. It was usually the bags themselves who appeared
on his doorstep, with a fervent gleam in their eyes and black purses
heavy as slabs clutched in their bony hands. This one was almost
tempting enough to make him want to invite her in to discuss the
worrying state of the world today. But better not.

"Sorry," he said. "I'm irredeemably irreligious."

She smiled. She was *very* pretty.

"Don't get me wrong," he said. "I'm a spiritual guy. I'm profoundly spiritual, I'm sure you can tell. But the whole religion thing,
it's not for me. I'm sure it's done some good in the world, but on average it's done more harm, wouldn't you say, inciting violence and
hatred and intolerance? And no matter the brand, it's usually headed
by some dickless, misogynistic power-hungry nut. Um, you're not a
Shriner are you, or a Shrinerette, I guess it would be? Of course
you're not wearing a fez and I can see you didn't park one of those
funny little cars in my driveway. You can't be a Girl Guide, too tall
and no obvious cookies, unless the Guides have gotten into bootleg-
ging, and you're far too comely for – "

"A sister?" she said.

"A Catholic! That explains the bottle. Well, well, so micks are
doing the old door-to-door now? The pews *must* really be emptying
out. So you're a nun? Wow." He surveyed her skin-tight black jeans,
her navel-revealing top decorated with the Stones trademark tongue
– unfurled and lolling as his was about to do – her wickedly pointy

green shoes. "I definitely approve of the more modern habit, but does the Pope know? His Fluffiness, he's a pretty conservative guy, eh, despite the nickname?"

Her smile widened. She had a beautiful mouth. He could hear the cells popping on the bubble wrap in which his heart was securely sealed (he'd been keeping it fresh for Elaine).

"You *are* Chellis Beith?"

He nodded. "'Fraid so."

"I read the obituary."

"So you've come to the wake?"

"I was shocked. But then I read it again more carefully and thought it was hilarious."

"*This* is a good review."

"I've been looking for you for a long time."

"*Me*?"

"You," she said, moving in and giving him a lightning-strike embrace. A one-armed hug because of the bottle she was holding, but still it was luscious, full-body contact, her warmth seeming to ignite his shirt. He was so enchanted he could have sworn he heard music welling up. Handel to be precise.

She stepped back, and raking her fingers through her long curly black hair, plucked out an ear bud. He hadn't realized that she was wired for sound. She tucked this into her back pocket along with the concealed MP3 Player, then she raised the bagged bottle and waggled it. "Let's celebrate!"

"Sure, wonderful, I'd love to. Although I hope it wasn't my obit that made you leave the convent. The world outside isn't really as amusing as I may have made it seem."

"Chellis, you still don't get it, do you? I'm your sister."

"You're saying that Nobodaddy has assigned a nun to me? Sort of like a spiritual personal assistant?"

"I'm saying we're related."

"No we're not."

"I'm your half-sister actually."

"Which half?" He gazed at her ruefully.

She laughed.

"This is a joke, right?" Who in his finite social circle would pull this kind of stunt? Both Hunt and Mrs. Havlock were experiencing their own bad jokes at the moment, although either might have set it up beforehand. Why, though? It wasn't Hunt's style, nor Mrs H's, he didn't think. That left Elaine, who wouldn't bother, or Vaughan? Not likely. Other various acquaintances didn't know him well enough for ribbing. Besides, the packaging of the jest might be gorgeous, but the intent was cruel, *n'est pas?*

"No joke," she said. "Here, why don't you take this." She handed him the bottle. "In case you think I mean to crack you on the bean and rob you."

"Why thanks, and no I wasn't thinking that. I've already been cracked on the bean and robbed. You wouldn't get anything."

"You're serious? That's terrible. I'm going to want to hear all about it, but I have the feeling I'd better vanish for awhile and let you digest the news. I know it must be overwhelming. It is for me." She gave him an ardent look. He tried not to wince. "I only found out a few days ago where you live and I should have sent you a letter or something, but I couldn't wait. I *had* to see you, meet you. *Finally.* But I understand, honestly I do." She started to turn away.

"Don't vanish," he said. "No, don't do that. I'll admit this is pretty wild. Totally amazing and . . . sorry, I'm a bit stunned. More than usual, that is, but come in, *come in*. Let's open this baby." He held up the bottle, stepped smartly aside, and using his free hand executed a gallant sweeping motion, welcoming her into his bachelor pad.

As he followed behind he was able to observe other fetching assets of hers. Not bad. For a sister.

So-called.

*

"You don't believe me, do you?"

Chellis sighed. Partly because of the Burgundy, which was heavenly, but mostly because of . . . "Bethany?"

"Bebe. I hardly ever get Bethany."

"Sounds Swedish."

"Funny, that's what Mother said. *She* always called me Bethany."

"Mother?"

"My mother, your mother."

"My mother's dead."

"Your adoptive mother. I'm so sorry, Chellis. You obviously loved her very much."

He shrugged, and pressed his lips together as though he were holding a dime between them. Who *was* this person, this lovely home invader?

"I want you to know that our mother loved you very much, too. She never forgave herself for abandoning you, which is why she kept me, I guess. But she was young, Chellis, far too young, and desperate. You were her big secret, until she became ill. That's when she told me about you. A brother! I couldn't believe it."

It *was* hard to swallow. Unlike the wine.

"She tried to find you. Ads in the papers. Sometimes she'd disappear for days, and I'm sure she was searching for you."

Hooey. He was radiating enough skepticism to strip the hardwood.

"It's true," she said simply.

"Where did she leave me?" Testing, testing.

"At a hot dog stand, I think she said. Here in Farclas, I forget the name."

"Lloyd's." An archival search of the local rag would have turned up that tidbit, his fifteen minutes of fame already expired by the time he was only a few weeks old.

"That's it. That's what she told me. Lloyd's."

He refilled her glass, then his. Sat back, crossed his legs, he liked a good story. "Tell me about her, Bebe." Bee-bee? He recalled the one that Hunt once planted with a soft *pock* in the calf of his leg. He still bore a faint scar. Hunt had been trying out the new air rifle Rennie had given Chellis as a grade eight graduation present. Both he and Hunt had packed in their outlaw ambitions after that. "You don't mind if I call you Bethany, do you?"

"I'd love that."

"All in the family, eh? Great. So what was she like? I don't even know her name." Out of the corner of his eye, he spotted a mouse tearing along the baseboard with a hoary snack clamped in its jaws, some artifact from the Ancien Regime, before there were any pre-tenders to the maternal title. Although, if this crock she was serving up, fishy as a bouillabaisse, had any truth in it, he might actually have to commit some vermin evictions, tidy the place up. Despite denying it for most of his life, he *had* always yearned for family, for an all-embracing, idiosyncratic network of siblings, grandparents, uncles, aunts, cousins. So why was he already beginning to feel put-upon?

"Fiona," she said. "Fiona Gordon." She leaned forward to place her drink on the coffee table, using an old sock of his as a coaster, and flashing a bit of harmless kin cleavage in the process. "It's weird. Some of your mannerisms are *so* like hers. "

"Nature not nurture?"

"In some respects, has to be. She herself never received much on the nurture side." Bethany then proceeded to tell him about his unsteadfast and unremarkable mater, exceptional only in that she was pure invention. Chellis couldn't help but think that if you were going to invent a whole person – as Elaine had obviously done with Vaughan, slapping him together in her workroom and installing a solar-powered enlivening device – why create someone so imperfect and depressing? A little sparkle and zip might have made her more credible, for she sounded more like the protagonist of some dreary, redemptive novel. But without the redemption, only cruel, unrelieved realism. A sob story so wet that even the punctuation damply sagged.

According to Bethany, their mother, knocked up with Chellis, had fled small town life, some barbarian outpost north of Claymore, and a repressive-controlling-abusive (what else?) family, stopping off in Farclas only long enough to drop and ditch baby number one, Bethany. Baby number two didn't arrive until several years later. Fiona had an unfortunate, B-movie attraction to cads and married men, and her second pregnancy may have been a bid to snag one of those. Or simply another mistake. Or the product of a longing for the baby she had given away. (Bethany sided with the last theory – "I probably owe my life to you, Chellis." "Oh, probably, lots of people do," he said.) Misfortune, the dominant and domineering theme of Fiona's life, had kept her firmly in place. Her only social mobility had been neither up nor down, but sideways, and involved, besides the flat-on-the-back feature of her rotten love life, moving from one minimum-wage job to another, and likewise from one basement apartment to another on the ugly, urban sprawly edges of Toronto. Death had been her escape, and she had taken up residence in the ultimate basement apartment at the age of fifty via an inoperable, metastasized uterine cancer.

At the conclusion of this uplifting bio, Chellis fled to the kitchen to hustle up another bottle and would have wept into the dishtowel if it weren't a microbe metropolis. He discovered a half-full bottle of gin in the cupboard behind a whiskered turnip and could have fallen on his knees in gratitude.

"Martinis," he said brightly on returning to the living room with the bottle and two smiley-face coffee mugs. "I make the best in town, better even than Hef, the ever-ready bunny boy himself. D'you think the makers of Viagra gave it that name because it rhymes with Niagara? Whoosh, you know." He gave the bottle a shake then glugged the gin into the mugs, filling them to the top. "Panty remover this stuff used to be called in my good old high-school days."

Bethany regarded him quizzically. He began to wonder if she was innuendo-proof, even lout-proof, for it didn't seem as if she'd be easily driven from her squatter's claim on his couch by brainless and lightly threatening commentary.

"Don't be nervous," she said kindly. "This *is* a shock, I realize that. In time, if you let me, you'll see that I'm telling the truth. I wish she'd had a better life, don't I ever, but she was as good to me as she could have been under the circumstances." She nodded toward her mug of gin. "Mother liked her drink, too. But I'm not about to blame her for that."

He sipped his gin, giving her a level look. Not only was she personable and quietly self-assured, embodying virtues he sadly lacked, but she also appeared to be fully ready to accept him, no matter how goofy. She was a genie who had come tale-bearing out of a bottle of Burgundy, easily (too easily?) granting him his long-held wish for relatedness. Here she was, improbably, in his very own living room offering to relieve him of the uncertainties that had forever dogged him. What had he missed in his other unrealized life? In the scenario as presented only a grim, deprived existence. His birth mother, if

Fiona Gordon was she, had done the best thing possible by abandoning him.

"And our fathers?" Who art in hell, he prayed.

"Took off, same old story."

"Which makes both of us the products of non-paternity events, as they say in the genealogy biz. Tell me about you," he said.

She shook her head. "Later."

"Sooner than, I hope?"

"I could drop by tomorrow if you like? But, you don't have to work or anything?" She surveyed the living room, brow fetchingly crinkled, as if seeing it for the first time.

"I do have a job, if that's what you're asking yourself." Maybe she really *was* his sister. As soon as they got cozy, the nagging would start. "My employer's out of town at the moment."

"Cat's away, huh? Lucky you." She stood up and hesitated for a shy, indecisive beat, before stepping over to him and bending down to give him a quick kiss on the forehead, her fingertips lingering briefly on his shoulders. "Time for me to go."

"Nice perfume," he said, breathing deeply, breathing her in, letting the fragrance lift him to his feet. "What is it, Lifebuoy? Irish Spring?"

"That's about all that fits my budget," she laughed.

"How refreshing, a girl who appreciates a guy's pitiful sense of humour." He followed her to the door.

"Oh, we gals are trained from birth to do that."

"I know one who isn't."

"Someone special, is she? I'll want to hear all about her, too."

"Say, Bethany, where are you staying?" It occurred to him that he was being inhospitable. Even if she was about as closely related to him as the starlet-of-the-day was – whoever that might be, he'd lost track – he could at least offer her a place to crash. Especially if she was short of funds. Especially since she was starlet quality herself.

"Place called the Caledonia. On Bruce Street."

"But that's a total dive. You can't stay there, it's not safe."

"That's what makes it fun, plenty going on. Don't worry, Chellis, I've stayed in worse. I've *lived* in worse. Adieu bro. Same time?"

"Same station," he nodded.

She fluttered her fingers at him, then turned and strode up his front walk.

After this, Chellis wandered around the house, checking for damage, a bomb had been dropped, after all. He went on a room-to-room tour, hands in his pockets. Walking and thinking, sibling activities suitable to the subject under consideration, the fantasy his visitor had spun out. Would it hurt to indulge it? It was a benign enough tale, and what if it were true? It might come to that peculiar pass: veracity. What if he really and truly had a sister? Too cool. *Hot*, actually, she was something else.

He ambled past the closed door of Rennie's bedroom and felt a stab of . . . a clutch of . . .a premonition of . . . fear? Hope? Emotions were such ill-defined creatures, it was sometimes difficult to tell one from the other. Love. Hate. Happiness? Would he recognize that if he saw it advancing down the road toward him with a big shit-eating grin on its face? He'd most likely cut and run. But then happiness was a state, not an emotion, wasn't it? If so, he'd let his passport to that elusive place lapse.

His journey, round trip, took him back to the living room, where he searched through his CD collection for some Water Music to go with the gin. *Solomon* he would have liked to hear, but he didn't have that one. He put on the Handel, which made him feel instantly intelligent, and sat down. He may not have been prepared to plumb the depths of his neediness, but he did begin to weigh the pros and cons of what he was being offered. Mostly cons? She was very well-spoken and had refined musical tastes for someone raised in a social substrata. Then again, this wasn't Victorian England or one of those countries where females never rise above the livestock in status. All one had to do here to crawl out from under one's birth burden was catch some education. Not easy, but not impossible. His upbringing hadn't been much different from Bethany's, only sunnier in its deprivations. And Rennie had been a class unto herself, *nobody* stepped on her.

The time may have come in any event to open up Rennie's room, clean it out, get rid of her closetful of cowboy boots and strappy high heels, her corny knick-knacks, her clothes. His overlong, grief-induced inertia had kept it in shrine stasis. Why not set it up as a guest room? New, unbleached, bamboo-derived sheets on the bed, matching virginal towels neatly folded on the dresser, a bar of olive oil soap resting on top (or some non-flaying soap product), sprigs of dried lavender in the drawer. The works. Just in case. Which didn't mean it would ever be occupied by anyone, say, who was as generously endowed as Bethany, with slender boyishh hips . . . .

Incest, he was beginning to see what all the excitement was about. God knows what talk shows and contemporary literature would do without it.

But wait, wasn't there something else he was supposed to be doing right now? Calling Dick to tell him that his missing wallet was missing? Elaine must have nabbed it when she'd stayed over. He *did* need a guest room, seeing as she'd practically wrecked his room try-ing to fix his broken bed frame. That must be it, Elaine had taken the wallet so she could stick pins in it, and not for the healing purpose of acupuncture, either. He'd call her, and then Moe to see if Hunt had surfaced yet, and what else? He jumped up, spotted Bethany's untouched mug of gin, and sat back down. What else? Find Mrs. Havlock, yes, mustn't forget. That too.

17

Fact

A WEEK LATER CHELLIS STOOD UP. Not that he'd been sitting around on his duff (or his withered laurels) the whole time. Procrastination simply wasn't what it used to be. These days, seven of them to be exact, he had been practising a more selective variety of indolence in between bouts of manic activity. The house was now middle-class clean, the fridge was stocked with an excess of broccoli – enough to club one's bad gustatory habits flat as a baby seal – and Rennie had been evicted from her bedroom. He hadn't seen Uncle Bob around for a couple of days and hoped he hadn't ended up in one of the green garbage bags into which his mother's worldly goods had been dumped and dragged out the door, rapidly, to avoid both separation anxiety and a disabling degree of guilt. After much badgering and suasion on his part, Bethany had given in . . . and moved in. He'd been worried about her staying at the Caledonia, a hot spot for the Farclas unsavoury – the desperate, the enraged, the cunning. The malfeasance conceived there by local bikers, druggies, and pimps, may have only been small-time, but was no less dangerous for that. He couldn't bear the thought that his sister, so recently and miraculously found, might get caught in a bad scene, whisked away. Lost.

She *was* his sister, their halves had bonded to make a whole, a family. She was his Eureka! the solution to his incomplete and fractional self. He had arrived at this conclusion after circling and circling the shaky evidence from what he considered to be an objective critical remove, like a hawk in a field zeroing in on its prey. And like a hawk he had finally pounced on a hitherto unknown and unassailable fact and devoured it. (And on the subject of prey species, while he had given Rennie the boot, he didn't have the heart to get rid of the mice.

What kind of son is that?) Before making his discovery, he was willing to allow that since the whole human race had evolved from the same crew who'd emerged out of Africa eons ago, then naturally he and Bethany were related. *I'm everyone's brother, man.* A heartwarming sentiment, if several millennia out of date.

This had been his position immediately after finishing off her abandoned mug of gin. Then, with nothing better to do, he had gone for another stroll in the house, less aimless than he realized at the time. Pausing by Rennie's door, he had put his ear against it, listening for . . . what? Who knows, the dust within might have pulled itself together, pulled up its socks (or hers), decided to live a little. Emboldened, he'd opened the door a crack and peeked in. His only discovery was that he'd been found out in a morbid cliché, that of giving the dead a long-term lease, not only in one's heart, but in one's house. Her room was as she had left it the morning she slipped chuckling out the front door in anticipation of her carefree bike ride. Bed unmade, dresser drawers hanging open, dropped bath towel dried into *rigor* on the floor, black bra flung across her radio, strap snagged on the volume dial.

He'd ventured in, poked around, uncapped the bottle of perfume that earlier, obviously going bonkers, he'd imagined smelling in the house. Cheap stuff, but intoxicating by association. He'd been tempted to take a swig of it, just for the sake of being stupid, but had twisted the cap back on and set it down. As a kid, he'd never been nosy or interested enough to snoop in her room when she was out. Certainly his interest in women's undies developed much later and was pretty much restricted to the lovelies who filled them, amply or no (he *did* feel that he had an all-round appreciation of the female physique). But way back when, if he had spent some time in Rennie's room searching for Christmas presents like a regular kid, or searching for secrets like an apprentice shit-disturber, he might have easily found one. A secret. It hadn't been all that well hidden, either, buried as it was in the bottom drawer beneath some sweaters, her old swimsuit, and the pair of pants that had gotten too tight at the waist, but were too good to throw out. Black, black, black. Her collected garb could have served as costuming for a low budget or snottily principled production of *Hamlet*. Rennie's favourite shade (and now she was his).

It was almost as if she'd been mourning herself in advance, a self-made widow.

And why had he been digging through her dark-wear like this? Because, unlikely as it might seem, he'd been looking for himself, and as unlikely as it might also seem, he found what he was looking for.

An envelope, square, probably left over from a birthday card long since tossed. The envelope's paper had aged to a faint yellow and it bore a human-seeming blemish, a splotch of brown in its upper right corner where a stamp would normally go, although its craggy profile was more hag than queen. Time had also given the hardened glue on the flap a lick, partially sealing the envelope, and Chellis had to tug gently to open it. Inside he found a small clipping from the personals section of an unidentified newspaper. The relevant bit appeared below an ad for a lost poodle named Gandalf and above one offering a free pair of nearly new Earth Shoes, size 13 – a worldly size. The ad sandwiched between these two, the one that still had riveting currency, read: BIRTH MOTHER SEEKING SON. His birth date, place of birth, and last name were cited, along with a request for any information concerning his whereabouts. A phone number and the contact, Fiona Gordon, rounded it off. It was brief, but in the way a knife slipped under the ribs is brief. He read it sixteen times, which should have killed him. He sank down onto the end of Rennie's bed holding the clipping on his palm like a sear leaf, one that had dropped from his ailing family tree years ago. He stared at it until he began to cry (no one was looking), but he was out of practise and this release didn't last long. He supposed he should thank Rennie for never giving him enough cause to get much teary exercise, but now she had.

Staring at this scant document, at once both mundane and devastating, Chellis had felt a torch flare up in his gut. Suddenly he was furious with her, angrier than he'd been when she'd left him without a word that sunny morning and rode merrily into her personal eclipse. It should have been *his* choice whether or not to respond to this ad. Right? *If* he'd made contact with his birth mother, it didn't follow that he would have abandoned Rennie. She should have known that. Presumably her motive for hiding the clipping had been self-protection. Sheer selfishness in other words. She sure hadn't been thinking about what might have been best for him. All those years! If nothing else, it would have been *helpful* to know where he came from, a relief, a defence against that sucking void at his back, that cold, untenanted black space. Son of nothing. People who had real families didn't understand this.

To be fair, Rennie *had* kept the clipping when she might have destroyed it. Could be that she had agonized over what to do. She may have even meant to tell him about it and then kept putting off the evil day, until she met the evil day herself head on.

And yet, she who had denied him so little had actually denied him this most essential revelation. She had stolen something vital from him and hadn't even bothered to hide it with any care.

Pissed off, he'd surveyed her room with eyes no longer softened with sentimentality. Time for a change, he had thought. Forget closure (odious term), he was instantly and ruthlessly ready to open things up and move things out. He was more than ready to make a leap of faith over the physically fragile fact of the clipping and into the arms of his sister.

So it had been an incredibly busy week in some respects, the ones that involved Bethany. The new family unit was small and tight, rather like her sartorial choices. They had to get to know one another, after all, and there had been scads to talk about, two whole lifetimes to merge. They were becoming bosom buddies, which was an extremely pleasant and cushiony experience for Chellis, as she liked to give him hugs (this is my *sister*, he kept reminding himself). Sibling rivalry never once reared its ugly head. What would they fight over anyway, a few maternal bones laid to rest? Besides, they'd been too busy shopping, cleaning, decorating, smoking up (the Caledonia had been useful after all), and bowling. She won every game and, unlike Elaine, hadn't gloated. Elaine?

"Call for you, sweetie." Bethany had shouted from the living room where she'd been packing up some of his boring old CD's for resale. Chellis had been in the kitchen whipping up a chicken curry. "Someone named Elaine."

"Tell her I'll call back," he'd shouted over the noise of the new Cuisinart pulverizing spices.

"Will do."

He didn't.

A day later there came a smart rapping on his front door, like machine-gun fire. Bethany was on her way out so she was the one who had answered the summons.

Elaine stood on the step, glowering. "Who are you?" she snapped.

"Who are *you?*" Bethany fired back.

"Elaine." She proceeded to give Bethany a CAT scan: the tousled hair, the skimpy tank top, the tart-tight jeans.

"The one who called?"

"The same."

"Friend of Chellis's then?"

"*Yes.*"

"Sorry, I'm afraid he hasn't mentioned you. But go on in, I think he's up. I have to run, I'll catch you later. My name's Bethany by the way."

Elaine had watched her skitter down the walk, heels clacking, tail wagging. Watched her hop into Chellis's car and start it up (no problem, *thanks* to Elaine), and watched her pull out of the driveway and take off. She had even watched the non-Bethany space created by her departure for a few ponderous moments, then had stalked into the house and found her negligent friend in the kitchen grinding coffee beans, an article he would have normally been grinding with his teeth.

"Well if it isn't *sweetie* himself."

"Elaine!"

"You didn't return my call."

"Gosh, *no.* Forgot. Want a coffee?"

"Why? What's wrong with beer?"

"Um, nothing, but it is only – "

"My God, what's happened to your kitchen? It looks like an operating room. Don't tell me that's a cappuccino machine?"

"It's – "

"Who is that slut I met at the door?"

"Hey, c'mon, that's my – "

"I have to hand it to you, Chel. I thought you were a slow mover. *Glacial*, in my experience. But a mere five days ago, *five*," she held up her fingers like a spray of firecrackers, "you were *sans* girlfriend, and now it would seem that you're shacked up with this babe. *Tell* me I'm wrong."

"You're wrong."

"No I'm not!"

My, how interesting, Chellis had thought, gazing with curiosity at his old flame, who indeed was crackling like one.

"Elaine, chill," he'd said. "I'll put the coffee on and let's go grab a chair in the living room. I have some fantastic news. I should have told you sooner, but it's, I don't know, somehow the days have just whizzed by."

*

Twenty minutes later, Elaine had been holding the newspaper clipping in her palm like a square of soiled toilet paper and staring at it with an expression that Chellis could only describe as *very* sour.

"I wonder where she got it."

"The *Star*?" he shrugged. "The *Mop N' Pail*? More likely the local rag. Rennie was never one for keeping up with the news. A friend might have seen it and given it to her."

"I don't mean Rennie."

"Sorry, I don't follow."

"Think about it, Chel. You're an intelligent person."

"Why, thank you. That's the sweetest thing you've said to me since we were kids and you begged me to lend you my new chemistry set. Which, it occurs to me, you never returned."

"It blew up." She tapped the clipping. "I don't mean Rennie. I mean Circe, your enchantress."

"Now you're calling me a pig?"

"I'm saying you've swallowed her story hook, line, and sinker."

"Now you're calling me a fish?"

"A sucker, more specifically."

"Laney, I'm *happy*. It's nice to have a sister, she's *nice*, give her a chance, will you?"

"And what about your employer?"

"What about her?"

"Has she turned up yet? I thought you were concerned."

"I am. What am I supposed to do, I'm not a detective. *You* were the one who told me not to get involved."

156

"You don't even look like her."

"Mrs. Havlock?"

"*No*, your pseudo-sibling."

"Do you look like Dwayne, your maximum-security bro?"

"God, no."

"See. Besides, she's my half-sister."

"And you're half in love. Or are you already head over heels?"

"My *sister*, Laney. I'm adhering to the well-established rules on that one. We're chums, that's all. What's it to you anyway, *Mrs. Champion*, if I may ask?"

"Chel, *I'm* your chum. I care about you."

"News to me."

"I don't want to see you getting hurt. Whoever she is, she's taking you for a ride. I hate this new couch by the way." She'd set the clipping on the sparkling glass-topped coffee table, and had begun to run her hand over the couch's nubby cotton seat cushion. "It's cheap."

"No it isn't, and wasn't."

"So you're paying for all this?" She'd swept her hand around the revamped room.

"I have savings."

"Not for long."

"Get off it, Laney. You're saying an adventuress waltzed in here out of the blue and is taking advantage of me by helping me buy some furniture I desperately needed?"

"Furniture isn't all, I bet."

"And tofu."

"You're eating *tofu*? Christ, you've really lost it. What else, 'fess up?"

"I'm helping her out a bit. She's out of work at the moment."

"Gee, I would have thought there'd be plenty of work for lap dancers."

A fraught pause.

"Elaine, do me a favour. Go away."

"I will. Gladly. But, Chel, take my advice and get some DNA testing done."

*

157

Two days later and Chellis was still smouldering, seeing as Elaine had set him on a slow burn. DNA testing! Did she expect him to run off to a lab with Bethany's toothbrush? Cheek swabs were tough to get on the sly. He sure as hell wasn't going to be jerk enough to suggest to her that they get it done. What would she think? It wouldn't be an honourable proposition. Wasn't trust something that families generated, families in good working order? Family members took you at your word, you didn't have to render proof. He was getting some unconditional love here and he didn't want to wreck it by making it conditional upon scientific verification. Verification of something that had already been established as fact. A *fact*. And not a factoid, which, as he knew (unlike most journalists), rested on a shaky speculative base.

Once Bethany cleaned out her digs in TO, there would be even more evidence of their bond: photos, papers, her birth certificate. She'd admitted to feeling foolish for not bringing any of that stuff with her.

"It's wonderful," Bethany had also said to him when she'd first stepped timorously over the threshold, suitcase in hand, "you've pretty much accepted me on faith, Chellis. That means a lot to me, a lot, I'm not kidding."

All he'd said to her in response was, "Welcome to Toad Hall!" And he hadn't been kidding about that, either.

Clearly, Elaine had been too jealous to accept it. Imagine that, her, jealous. The newspaper clipping (that *sacred* document), he'd discovered before Bethany had moved in, but Laney hadn't been thinking straight, an unprecedented occurrence. In her annoyance, she'd spliced together the timeline of the two events. But she had no right to be steamed even if Bethany wasn't his sister. It all boiled down to the fact that she didn't want anyone trespassing in her control zone, where she regulated the activities of her perfect husband, her perfect life, and her imperfect, factotum friend. The *harpy!*

The phone rang. So yes, he stood up. Stood up, marched over to it, and whipped it out of its cradle. He'd tell her a thing or two, tell her what's what, tell her to take a long walk off a short –

"Chellis?"

"Huh? Who's this?"

"It's Moe. Are you all right?"

"Moe? Moe! Yeah, yeah – I'm fine."

"Golly, that's a relief. We were getting really worried, Chel. Like, *seriously*. I told Hunt that you'd been in to visit with him for hours and hours before he regained consciousness."

"He *has*? That's fantastic, Moe. When? When did it happen?"

"Six days ago."

"*Six* days?"

"That's right, he's out of intensive care and everything and he keeps asking about you. I think he's getting kind of frantic, which really isn't good for him. He says this is so not like you that something has to be wrong, that you'd at least call."

"Moe, I'm so sorry. It's not that something's wrong, but mind-blowingly right. I've been, cripes, I'll explain when I get there. I'll leave for the hospital in five, no, give me ten. And Moe, tell Hunt I can't wait to see him. I'm going to bring someone with me, too, someone I want you both to meet. Someone *very* special."

18

Smoke Point

"SO WHERE'S THE NEW GAL?" Hunt wanted to know.

"Yeah, Chelly," said Moe. "I'm so excited for you. It's about time, too. You've been on your own for so long."

"Hold on, you two." Chellis raised his hands to block the mistake, nevertheless amused by the matchmakers' supposition. Couples!

"It's even better than that," he said, proceeding to explain about Bethany, his sudden sister. Unable to conceal his excitement, he began waving his arms around like the conductor of a bone-rattling, blood-pumping symphony, as he told them about her arrival, her taking up residence with him, her help in fixing up his place, her bowling score, her whole delightful self.

"Far *out*," said Moe, giving him an energetic, congratulatory hug (he loved all these hugs he was getting lately – more, more). "That is *so* amazing."

Hunt was an iota or ten less amazed. Which Chellis noted, but put it down to the dampening effect of the meds he was taking, or the resultant trauma of his illness. Amazement might not dawn on him for some time, very likely when Moe announced her maternity scheme. Hunt repeated, "So where is she?"

"It's the hospital, she had to beg off." Chellis shrugged. "She can't face it. Had a rough time when her mother, *our* mother that is, was passing. I'm supposed to tell you, though, how much she's looking forward to meeting you both."

"I can't wait to meet her." Moe was beaming. "Does she look like you? Do you have a photo, Chel?"

"As a matter of fact I do. Not a great one, she's kind of shy, hates to get her picture taken, well who doesn't? But I picked up one of those disposable cameras at the drugstore and snuck a quickie." He withdrew a snap from his shirt pocket and handed it to Moe. His friends would assume that he brought it along on purpose to show them, but the truth was that he carried it everywhere with him. When he wasn't with her anyway, because he wanted her always to be so. Otherwise he had to hide it, since the other ones he'd taken of her had disappeared. He couldn't understand it, they weren't that bad; it was impossible for her to take a lousy picture. In this one he'd caught her in the kitchen. Bethany had been in the process of decapitating a trout, and she'd turned to face the flash with a prettily annoyed look of surprise.

"She's gorgeous," enthused Moe. "And I do think you *are* a teeny bit alike."

"Nah, she got all the looks."

"Let me see," said Hunt.

Moe gave him the photo, after which she trailed her fingers lightly over his forehead, his emergent dome her fond talisman. Either that or she was attempting to smooth out the frown that appeared as soon as he saw the image. Frown notwithstanding, Hunt stared at it for several beats of Chellis's heart with a completely neutral expression. Chellis was disappointed, but understood his pal's lack of enthusiasm. It wouldn't do for Hunt to start salivating in front of his partner.

Hunt grunted and handed it back to him.

"Well, what do you think?"

"I don't know," said Hunt.

"Honey, you're tired," said Moe.

"Yeah, you must be wiped," agreed Chellis. Which shouldn't have stopped Hunt from faking some happiness for him, for expressing *some* wonder at this totally unexpected family reunion. Or was he jealous, too? What was it with his friends? "Hunt old buddy, I'm going to let you get some rest. You've been to hell and back, long trip. Sure am glad you didn't buy any real estate down there."

Hunt smiled and they clasped hands.

"When are they letting you out of here?"

"Couple days, I think."

"The sooner the *better*," said Moe.

Chellis checked to see if there was a lascivious gleam in her eye, but she appeared to be unambiguously expectant.

"Great, that's really great. *He's* our miracle baby, eh Moe? I'll be back tomorrow, so let me know if there's anything you want. See you guys *mañana* then, and in the meantime, uh, don't do anything I wouldn't do."

"That gives me lots of wiggle room," Moe grinned.

Wiggle room, he thought on his way out, *yikes*.

As soon as he was gone, Hunt shot Moe a troubled look, and said, "Bebe."

"What's that, sweetheart? Did you say . . . ? Gosh, *how* did you guess?"

*

When Chellis arrived home, Bethany greeted him at the door with a grin and a frosty pitcher of martinis, much as suburban wives in the fifties were instructed to do. Regrettably she'd skipped the Saran Wrap. "Arsenic hour!" she announced.

"Already?"

"Too early?"

"You jest."

"Sit on the porch?"

"Too hot, don't you think? Cooler inside, I'll put on some music."

"Okay, then you can see the weird, cube-thing your dyke friend brought over."

"I have a dyke friend?"

"That Elaine person."

"Elaine? She's not a lezzie."

"Could have fooled me."

More jealousy! The greenest of emotions, sick green, khaki. Chellis would never in a mil have imagined that his person, his pathetic stretch of flesh, would become such a contested battleground. Suddenly everyone wanted him? Or wanted their edition of him.

"She brought something?"

"Come see."

On the coffee table's glass top sat a plain chrome cube, about the size of a medium Rubik's, but more puzzling than one of those maddening toys, for it gave no clue as to what its function might be.

"What is it?" he asked.

"Dunno. She said it was a housewarming present. That's all. She walked in, plonked it on the table, and left."

"God, don't touch it. I should probably call the bomb squad."

"What's her problem anyway?"

"You. She'll get over it. She's never met a problem she couldn't solve."

"I'd be glad to be friends with her."

"That's my sis, magnanimous through and through." He reached for the pitcher.

"I don't know about that. But I do know that you could use some lessons in female wrangling."

"Precisely what I've always thought. Send in a herd of the unruly creatures and I'll do my best. Sit!" He pointed to the couch. "Is that how it's done? Drink!" He filled the arty and grossly expensive-plus-tax martini glasses and handed one to her. "Her gift is either purely symbolic and she's telling me I've turned into a bourgeois square, or it's some sort of regulatory device. Just wait, if I have more than one of these fine libations you've concocted, which I absolutely intend to do, I bet you anything an alarm will sound." He studied the cube. "I better give the old Puritan a call, get the instructions. Or destructions, more like."

"Don't." Bethany sipped and smiled. "That's what I mean about the wrangling. It's exactly what she wants. She snaps her fingers and you jump. Same with that employer of yours, that Mrs. Havlock you were telling me about."

Yes, he nodded, he had told her about Mrs. Havlock. Told her everything. Almost. When Bethany had asked him what he'd found out in Kinchie, he'd replied, "Nothing. Red herring." Which had then allowed him to provide his own red herring by telling her about the provenance of that phrase. He didn't feel as if he was being disloyal to his sister by holding back a snippet of information that only concerned Mrs. Hav. He was keeping it in reserve for her return.

"I think she's set you up."

163

"In this, you and Elaine are in agreement. But why? We have a symbiotic working relationship, we get along just fine."

"Chellis, men don't have a clue about what women are really up to."

True enough, he supposed. Only another female might best understand the machinations of a member of her own sex. "Agreed, so why?"

"For inspiration? Or kicks? Simply to see how it plays out? She's a writer, good chance she's unstable, most of them are basket cases. Ever meet one in person, other than her?" Bethany pointed her index finger at her temple and made a small circling motion, a gesture he hadn't seen in years. He found this extremely cute.

"She seems pretty sane to me."

"*Seems*, Chellis. Nothing is as it seems, right?"

"Hey, I learned that in Eng Lit, too. Do you realize that both of our half degrees add up? Like us? Together we're a learned unit."

"We are! So let's use our smarts here. You have to see that she's getting her jollies by playing with you, seeing what she can get away with, weaving some sort of web in which you're getting more and more entangled. She's creating a fiction with a real live person in it."

"Nah."

"*Mais oui, mon frère*. First she tries to unnerve you with the gory forensic research and that horrible title of her new book, then she sends you off on a fool's errand and makes you think your life is in danger by hiring some lowlife to clunk you on the head. In the meantime she stages a disappearance. That *you're* being fingered for. Just wait, they'll pin that murder on you, too. That publishing guy? Also part of her plot."

"*You* should be the writer."

"No thanks. I'm not that desperate."

"If I pour you another drinkie, will you at least promise to provide me with an alibi when required?"

"Darn right I will. No one's going to intimidate you with me around."

"Most excellent sib!"

"And that guy you mentioned, what's his name? Rick?"

"Dick. Dick Major."

"He's involved."

"That I can believe. How, though?"

"Dogsbody."

"Well I can assure you that Bunion and Hormone won't like sharing their biscuits with Dick. They'll tear him to pieces."

"Good," she said, with a surprising amount of conviction.

"Speaking of nourishment, what should we make for dinner?"

A homey, everyday question that any old domestic boot might ask. But he felt a genuine thrill when he asked it, a thrill of pride that he had someone so close to ask it of, his fellow nestling. Food was an intimate subject after all. Think of where you put the stuff!

"Aren't we having it?" Bethany held up her empty glass. While he'd been musing, she'd beaten him to the bottom.

"Hey, you're a bigger soak than I am. The sipping sibs. My dear, do have another serving."

*

An hour later they were still gabbing and Chellis couldn't help but think that he was the guilty party, the one who had prolonged it. But this ritual, their pre-dinner yakfest – sitting around shooting the breeze – it was his favourite part of the day. There seemed to be no end of things to talk about. They'd had spirited discussions about magnetic therapy, the latest Woody Allen film (there always was one), the war in the Middle East (ditto), and speculated about when the ebb to the right (and the accompanying undertow that dragged almost everyone with it) was going to flow back to the left. He for the *when*, she for the *if*. They veered easily into more personal topics, often comparing their childhoods, which made Chellis even more grateful for his permissive one. Bethany told him more about their mother, which admittedly didn't give him a great hankering to wish her back from the grave. He did feel truly sorry that she'd had such a crummy life, and for his part it was comforting to know about her and oddly fulfilling. Bethany was helping him develop a posthumous relationship, a connection that was something to hold onto, a guide that helped him find his way. Not that she solved all the mysteries of his truncated bio.

"I wonder why she called me Baby Beith?"

"Your father's last name? She never said, never called you that. Didn't make it any easier to find you, that's for sure."

"But you did."

"I did."

"Bet you're sorry."

"Only if I don't get dinner."

"God, it's getting late. Night already. I've almost gone beyond it, I'm practically glued to the chair."

"Me too."

"It's so quiet. No calls. Nary a supper time solicitation, that's got to be a first."

"No free trips to Hawaii."

"No charities with their begging bowls, no credit card offers from the impoverished big banks who call every day because my sucker status is so well established. How's the job search going by the way? How callous of me, I forgot to ask."

Bethany had been spending hours daily on his computer. Grit and application, qualities only available apparently in his family's recessive gene package.

"Revised the résumé *again* today. Definitely left out the summer I spent stripping."

"Paint?"

"No, silly."

"*That* kind of stripping? You didn't, did you?"

"Afraid so. If I hadn't had so much to drink, I wouldn't be telling you."

He glanced quickly behind her, where he could almost see Elaine standing, hands on her hips, mouthing, *What did I tell you?*

"You can tell me anything," he said. "You realize that, I hope. Who am I to judge, it's good money, lots of students do it. Wasn't it awful, though, all those slimeballs leering at you and . . . all that?" He could feel his cheeks rouge-up like a schoolboy. The one area they hadn't covered in their chats was their respective love lives. He didn't want to know. She was his little sister, untouched by groping male paws.

"One's thoughts are directed elsewhere."

166

"Brave girl."

"Men *are* creeps," she said quietly. She dropped her gaze to her hands that were resting open on her lap, palms up, her body language a declaration of her vulnerability. Then she raised her eyes to meet his. "But there are some exceptions."

"Me? I'm as creepy as the rest."

"What you are," she said, with the slightest slur, "is mucho hunky."

"Ha, ha. Good one."

"No, I mean it." She rose from the couch and moved over to him. She bent toward him, placing her hands on his shoulders. "I shouldn't say this . . . but sometimes I wish we weren't related."

"Yeah? You're kidding? Okay, all right, I have to admit you're pretty hunky yourself." He ran his hands up her bare arms. "Beauty biceps, you work out, it shows." She bent closer, while his hands continued their trip up her arms, her shoulders, her neck. He stopped, yanked his hands away. Hot, hot! What was he doing?

"Want to wrestle?" She took hold of his recoiling hands and pulled him to his feet.

He couldn't stop himself, talk about magnetic therapy. He caressed her face, combed his fingers through her thick, faintly scented hair. What was that fragrance?

"I wouldn't mind," he croaked. Her earlobes, they'd be delicately chewy, *al dente*. His hands detoured south. "Your, uh, chest, it's so white. Like, I don't know . . . a graveyard at night."

"This is a compliment?"

"You bet." He ran his hands over her breasts. Marvellous. *Help.* He placed a finger on a button of her sleeveless blouse, third one down from the top that was straining to hold the fabric in place. A black, skimpy bra peeked through. If he undid the button, he knew he would be undoing much more than a blouse. He ran his finger around its rim, around and around . . . *oh deep, profoundly deep, shit.*

19

Uh-Oh

CHELLIS WAS STANDING in a phone booth ramming change into the coin slots and dropping most of it on the floor. Copper and nickel alloy rained down, a demotic version of Zeus's spendthrift visit to Danaë. He did not much feel like Zeus. He felt more like one of those mythological guys who were ripped to shreds for their sexual presumption. He also felt all prickly and cold, as though he were standing exposed in this glass case wearing nothing but a panic crinoline, a scratchy, fright-tutu raying out around him.

He had fled from the scene of the aborted seduction with absolutely no dignity and an excess of awkwardness, while mumbling something about having to make an emergency run to the drugstore. Farclas wasn't exactly the Ozarks, but the general idea was that he was reluctant to father any relations that were quite *that* near. Bethany had always – in the week he'd known her – been incredibly understanding of his foibles and klutziness, but he had to think his precipitous departure had completely blown that. She'd be relieved to be shot of him, fed up and likely furious for being so rudely rejected. Good, maybe she'd leave . . . for it hadn't been any high-minded scruple about diddling his own sister that had sent him bounding away like a terrified rabbit. No, he'd been more than eager to sample that forbidden fruit. (Forbidden vegetable? Somehow that didn't sound quite so sexy.)

After flying through his front door, he'd rushed over to his estranged neighbours' house in the hopes that they'd take some pity on a desperate man and let him use their phone. He *was* having a heart attack, albeit a metaphysical one. On nearing their front door, however, he'd heard a couple of deadbolts slam into place inside. Only then had he noticed that they, or someone, had marked up their door

with graffiti, a ragged script in black Magic Marker had defaced the delicate cream paint with the message: REAL OR NOT. Such an interesting statement, especially as it pertained to the residents within, but he simply didn't have the time to entertain it. Evidently they were in more need of help than he, but he was not presently standing in the phone booth for the purpose of finding them immediate psychiatric care.

Finally, he'd fed the machine enough cash to make his call.

"Elaine?"

"Chellis! There you are. I've been trying to call you for hours."

"You have?"

"Did that rotary of yours need a nap, poor old thing?"

"I . . . don't know."

"What do mean you don't know?"

"I'm calling from a pay phone."

"Why?"

"The *button*."

"Excuse me."

"The buttons on Bethany's blouse are the *same*. I found one at Mrs. Havlock's, outside in the garden, when we were there poking around. I put it in my pocket and forgot about it, forgot to mention it even."

This declaration was met by a contemplative silence at the other end of the line. Elaine then said, "What were you doing staring at her buttons?"

"Nothing! They're . . . noticeable."

"They're big buttons?"

"Small, she has *small* buttons. On this blouse she's wearing."

"You must have been standing very close to notice. Is she still wearing the blouse? Or did you have to remove it to get a better look at the buttons?"

"Stop it, Laney. The point is – "

"You don't have to tell me what the point is. She's trouble. That's why I was trying to call you. I saw some guy go into your place today while you were at the hospital."

"You were hanging around spying on my house?"

"Made a delivery, remember? But this was later. Just happened to drive by."

"Uh-huh. Love the cube, by the way. So what guy?"

He felt a sudden rush of the green emotion himself. Despite everything. And when he considered – less panicky now that he was talking to Elaine – this 'everything' did not rest on a very substantial base of incriminating evidence. A button! What did that prove? Hundreds, thousands of women wore similar denim tops. What were the odds? The buttons on her blouse were identical to the one he'd found, but so what? Probably nothing but a coincidence. The button that had flipped him like a tiddlywink out the front door could be as blameless as any of its zillion docile mates that populated the world, their working lives spent doing and undoing, doing and undoing, then retirement in some granny's cookie tin. Before fleeing, he should have at least done a quick survey of the whole button terrain to see if any were missing.

"Tough-looking dude. She have a boyfriend, your 'sister?'"

"Not that I know of. But why shouldn't she?" This he asked with a faux-rational calm, although there was a giveaway surge of static on the line caused by his hyper-agitated brain waves.

"Chellis, you're being willfully obtuse. Surely she would have told you, since you two spend so much time together, supposedly talking. Come on, it's *all* dodgy. Including that clipping. I checked in the Library Archives, the old newspapers, and there's a page missing from the *Gazette* that corresponds with the time that ad would have appeared."

"My, but you've been working hard on this case."

"Someone has to. You've been too busy mooning around like a sick puppy."

"Calf."

"What?"

"Sick calf. If you're going to resort to clichés, you should get them right."

"Fine. Calf. Better a sick one than a dead one, but it's time to wake up."

"And smell the coffee?"

"*Yes.* Come stay at my place for the night. You're not safe as long as she's at yours."

A sleepover at Elaine's! What he would have given for this invitation a mere week ago.

Speed of light he would have appeared on her doorstep, tooth-brush in one hand, the other a free agent.

He sighed. "Elaine, I found the clipping *before* she moved in."

She sighed competitively and forcefully, apparently trying to blow the dust out of his head. "You don't suppose she could have slipped into your place before arriving at your doorstep, do you? When you were in Kinchie, say?"

"Impossible. Place was sealed up tighter than a drum."

"I thought you didn't resort to clichés?"

"Tighter than Vaughan's – "

"Don't go there!"

"God, I wouldn't dream of it."

"Face it, your rickety old house is *not* secure. An ant could break into it without much effort."

"Sounds far-fetched to me. But while we're on the topic of criminal behaviour, you didn't destroy Dick's wallet, did you? It might come in handy."

"What do you mean, I don't have his wallet. I wouldn't touch his filthy wallet if you paid me. If you paid me, Christ, another one."

"Don't fret, speech is mostly hackneyed prefab anyway. So you don't have it?"

"I don't. But I bet you I know who does."

"C'mon Laney, you want to blame her for everything. Just because you don't like her. Next you'll be saying she bumped off Mrs. H."

"She probably has, which is why you should come stay over. You could be next."

"Who's the neurotic one now? But thanks anyway, maybe I will. I dunno, don't wait up. I need to get some air."

"Chel, watch your step. I do care about you, honestly, I hope you know that."

Right, the very emotional boost he needed: a tepid, watered-down version of the L-word. Spoken like a real sister.

*

Walking and thinking. Again. He and Aristotle, he and Thoreau, he and Werner Herzog. He all alone without the consolations of phi-

172

losophy, nature, or a film in the making – or any of those smart, ambulatory guys to keep him company. He wandered around, up one street and down another, a smudge in the night, a stain on its purity. He passed house after house with windows aglow, lit with inner warmth and joy, inviting him to peer in, to be an honourable Peeping Tom who thrilled to the secret good revealed, rather than the naughty. Forget it. He was a terminal outsider to whom no secrets of familial solidarity would ever be revealed. Not only a misfit, but a maimed one. He didn't stumble or drag one foot behind or bleed in an unseemly manner on the sidewalk, but was one of the walking wounded nonetheless. His faith in his half-sister had taken some serious hits. *Feck*. If what Elaine said was true, if Bethany was up to some monkey business, then he could have bedded her without the least compunction. *Une liaison dangereuse*, indeed. Maybe he was making a film after all, a snuff, in which he was slated to be the unwitting star.

Chellis took a deep breath and practically choked. He felt as though he'd internalized that damn button, swallowed it like a bitter pill and now it was stuck in his craw, undissolved. And yet, with apologies to Sherlock, one measly button proved dick-all. What about those other dicey details? His phone could have been left off the hook, easily, accidentally. He hadn't searched very hard for the wallet. Rennie herself could have stolen the newspaper clipping from the Archives years ago (the sort of thing she *would* do). The gentleman caller Elaine spotted may only have been a vermin exterminator, seeing as Bethany had talked about getting someone in after she woke up one night to find a mouse gnawing on her hair – whereupon she broke *his* record for the bathroom dash – a physical accessory of hers he wouldn't have minded gnawing on himself. He walked on. *Wee sleekit, cowrin', tim'rous beastie*. It didn't do to identify with a mouse, he supposed, especially if her preference was for rats.

He neared his own house, unable to resist the homeward tug on the old heartstrings, those strings playing a few throbbing riffs as he headed down the front walk. No light was spilling out of his windows to give him a cheery welcome. The place was completely dark. His car was still in the driveway, which only meant it hadn't been worth ripping off. If that had been her plan, to take off, to vanish into the mysterious unknown from whence she had come, then she had done it without any earthly mechanical assistance. Unless someone had swept by to aid her flight. Unless the resident mice had been turned into footmen.

Soundlessly he approached the porch, easy enough as the encroaching crabgrass provided a cushiony outdoor carpet. He'd known all along that the stuff would eventually serve some worthwhile purpose. Instead of creeping up the steps, he walked around to the side of the house to see if there was any action in the living room. A faint light did show through that window, a pale bluish glow. The TV? Bethany rarely watched the tube, said it was a drug for cakeheads, a sentiment with which he had agreed heartily, and on account of it, to his sorrow, had missed two new episodes of *The Simpsons*.

He peeked in. The light wasn't coming from the TV, but from Elaine's cube. It sat dead centre on the coffee table, softly glowing (it was a lamp?), and lending an eerie, science fiction ambience to a room that Chellis realized he didn't like very much anymore. He wanted his old organically evolved one back. He hated glass coffee table, and swag drapes, and leather club chairs . . . not that he had one, but he *might* have, the setting was perfect. Laney had been right about the couch, it was crap with nubs. But, he had to admit, he still liked the woman who was occupying it, liked her all the more because she looked as bereft as he felt.

Bethany was sitting accordion-style, hugging her knees, chin resting on her kneecaps, staring at the cube. Her expression was one of sheer misery, and he wondered if the cube was responsible, wondered if it radiated some sort of hypnotic, downer vibes. But no, he also had to admit, *he* was the reason she was miserable. This was the effect that being a shithead had on people, people who loved you, who cared what you said and did. And didn't do.

He thought, *what if, what if, what if* . . . Laney was as right about the fabric of his sister as she had been about that of the couch? Bethany's moral upholstery. He stepped back into the darkness, letting the night enfold him like a voluminous Zorro cape. He didn't want to do anything hasty, he needed to think this thing through.

Immediately he stepped forward again and tapped on the window.

174

She looked up, startled.

He tapped again, and her head jerked aside, a flicker of fear in her eyes as she peered at him, momentarily not recognizing who it was.

He waved, grinned, shrugged. She smiled tentatively with a childlike uncertainty, and he was undone.

Once in, she hugged herself rather than him, and said, abashed, "Chellis, will you ever forgive me? That was all my fault, what was I *thinking*, I'm so sorry."

"Hey, hey, no. My fault entirely. Forgot myself, total lout, too many martinis."

"That's for sure. The drinks, I mean."

"And because you're . . . so dishy."

"I am not."

"You are, believe me."

"I'll leave. I'll leave in the morning. I've ruined everything."

"Nothing's ruined. Let's hit the delete button on this one, forget it happened."

"Is that possible?"

"Anything's possible."

Little did he know that this hoary bit of optimism, this gung-ho despoiler of many lives, was soon to pan out.

"I felt so bad when you left, so stupid."

"Me too. Talk about overreacting."

"I didn't think you could run that fast."

"Yep. I hold the world record for the fastest chicken run."

She gazed at him, tears imminent he feared.

"Look, Bethany. Let's not keep beating ourselves up over this. Nothing happened, except for me getting some exercise. Not a bad thing, all in all, and now I'm starving. How about that dinner? Have you eaten?"

She shook her head. "Couldn't."

"How does an omelette sound? Wait, they don't make a whole lot of noise, do they?"

She laughed. *Yes!*

*

After dinner they resumed their former places in the living room, and resumed drinking, but only a comforting and chaste tipple of single malt before hitting the sack – separately. Did he regret this? Yes and no, but of the two ways for them to continue to be together, he preferred sib over sex. How often is someone gifted a sister? As for all those unfounded suspicions, that's exactly what they were.

"You didn't try to call when you were out, did you?" she said. "I unplugged the phone earlier today, then wouldn't you know, forgot all about it. This furnace cleaning company kept calling and calling, they wouldn't give up, had this loopy sales guy."

"Annoying, *geez*. I suppose I should get an answering machine."

"You're the only person in the Western Hemisphere who doesn't have one. But I like that."

"I'm a rebel."

"You *are*." She raised her glass. "Here's to you Braveheart."

"Speaking of rodents, did you happen to have an exterminator drop by this aft?"

"Exterminator? No." She frowned. "Jerry came round, though. That guy from the Caledonia, remember?"

"Ah, our supplier." Make that, Aha! "Buy anything?"

"Too expensive. His prices have gone up."

"We'll survive."

"We will."

Chellis wasn't able to check out the button situation by doing a count on the sly. Since fingering the button that had set off the alarm, if only in his own head, she had donned a sweatshirt. Not that he was worried about it. They had reconciled and restored their relationship to its former integrity, aided some by the whisky. Dreamily, he swirled the golden liquid in his glass, a substance so pure and powerful it might have been siphoned from a halo.

The front door opened abruptly and banged against the wall of the entranceway.

They glanced quickly at one another, startled.

"What was – ?"

"The wind?"

"There is no – "

Someone was moving rapidly down the hall, footsteps hitting the floorboards hard enough to crack the wood.

If Chellis had time to think, he would have thought it was Elaine, come to drag him off to her place by force. But he didn't, and it wasn't.

A woman stood in the entranceway to the living room. She was sixtyish and a fright, with scream red hair, a sideshow sartorial style, much of it in lime green and hot pink, and skin that had obviously spent too many hours frying on a tanning bed. To top it off, she was giving *him* the once over.

She said, "So there you are. Long time no see, mister. Mind if I smoke." It wasn't a question. "Move over, eh." She clacked toward them in her silver high heels. (If she was supposed to be his fairy god-mother, he was appalled.)

This order was addressed to Bethany, who was staring at the woman with an ill-disguised mix of incredulity and offense. She scooted over to a distant end of the couch and directed a questioning gaze at Chellis, who was equally dismayed.

"Excuse me but, um, this is a private home," he began. "You can't just waltz in here and – "

The woman shot him a stern look, "Don't give me any lip." She unsnapped her orange, pumpkin-sized vinyl purse, dug out a package of smokes, and lit up. "Who's the broad?" she nodded at Bethany, smoke spiralling out of her nostrils.

Chellis had never believed that people actually dropped their jaws in response to a gobsmacking experience, but he felt his fall and swing loosely in the vicinity of his Adam's apple. He hauled it back in place to speak, to set this multi-coloured crone straight.

"*Listen* lady, I'm sorry, but you'll have to leave. You've made some sort of mistake, I've never met you before in my life. Unless . . . are you a friend of my mother's, of Rennie's?" That had to be it, some old acquaintance of hers. "Okay, I get it, you must be from out of town. I hate to have to tell you this but she's no longer – "

"I am your mother."

"What did you say?"

The woman reached out and pulled Elaine's cube toward her. She flicked some ash on top of it. "You deaf or something? Like your old man, heard what he wanted to hear, didn't he."

"Who *are* you?"

"Name's Fiona Gordon, guess you don't know that, eh. You coulda done a little looking yourself for your poor old ma."

"I *do not* believe this. Why do these things happen to me? You *are not* Fiona Gordon. You *can't* be. It's impossible." He was staring at her intently with an almost violent dismissiveness, trying to will her away, trying desperately to erase her. He closed his eyes, counted slowly *one . . . two . . . three*, opened them. Didn't work.

"No? Last time I looked I was. What, I gotta prove who I am to my own kid?" She stubbed out her cigarette on the cube, which made a weirdly human groaning noise, and started rooting around in her purse. "Got my birth certificate right here. Got yours as a matter a fact." She produced a folded sheet of paper and waved it around. "Goodie gum drops, she turned tail." She let out a smoker's phlegmy cackle. "Not your type, son. Besides, I don't want no hanky-panky in my house. That's what got me into trouble, eh."

"What? *Jesus*, look what you've done!"

Bethany was gone. *Gone.*

20

Siblicide

ELAINE MET HIM at the door with a knife in hand, a long-bladed, evil-looking implement, the sort used for lopping off arms and heads in less politically sanguine countries.

"Oh, it's you," she said.

"You were expecting your in-laws? Or possibly Jack the Ripper?"

"I was about to commit an act of baking. Come in."

"You're not going to stab me for arriving so late?" He already felt sufficiently lacerated by the evening's events.

"Not as long as you tell me what you've been doing."

He followed her into the kitchen and watched as she savaged a loaf of sourdough bread and stuffed the mangled slices into the toaster.

"I don't think this qualifies as baking, Laney."

"It does in this house. So what's up?"

"S'up? As we cooler cats say." He told her about his unexpected visitor.

"My God, Chellis, this could *only* happen to you. What did you do when she pulled the birth certificate stunt?"

"I said, 'G'night Mummy, I'm off to play in the traffic. Help yourself to the Drāno."

"You didn't really?"

"I didn't really. I did what I always do."

"You fled."

"I did. I turned tail, as that witch so lasciviously put it."

"You looked at the certificate first, though? You did that, right?"

"No. She's *not* my mother. She could only produce reptiles. Besides, how hard it is to make a fake one? I've done the research on this identity theft business."

"Funny, you doubt this woman, who could in fact be your birth mother. Think, what's in it for her?"

"Who'd want me for a son?"

"Exactly. And yet without question you believed everything Bethany told you. Hmm, I wonder why."

"Don't nag. Take pity, eh. Can't you pretend I'm a broken robot?"

No pretense needed, he *was* a broken robot; he could feel his inner assembly shuddering and snapping as he shifted on the kitchen stool. The button-sized nugget of doubt about Bethany that had lodged in his chest earlier had expanded and had filled him, not with more doubt, but with despair.

"Poor Chel," she said, taking in his forlorn expression. "One order of pity coming right up." She fixed them both plates of buttery toast with crispy burnt extremities and cups of hot chocolate, mini-marshmallows melting on top. They sat in silence for awhile, attending to the snack, Chellis drawing maximum comfort from every last fat molecule and sugar crystal.

"I suppose this is a secret recipe."

"Been in the family for years. I'll never divulge it."

"Tell me this then. Why did Bethany run away?"

"You need to hear the obvious, don't you? I can understand that, believe it or not. After all the emotion you've invested in her, it's got to be rough finding out she's a fake. You think you can't let go, Chel, but you've got to. This Fiona Gordon's arrival blew her whole story. Her whole *improbable* story."

"Maybe." He picked up a stray toast crumb with his finger.

"Not maybe. Admit it."

"Mmm."

"She's not your sister."

"Innocent until proven guilty."

"Open your eyes, Chelly."

"Will that help? I'd rather close them for a long, long time. Do you have any knockout pills?"

"I'd gladly knock you out myself, if I thought it would help."

"I'm worried about her."

Elaine dished out one of her higher-end, exasperated glares. "I'd worry more about what she was doing in your house."

He evaded the glare, suddenly finding everything in the room, minus Elaine, diverting. He surveyed the kitchen, Vaughan's kingdom, which was much messier than usual, dishes piled in the sink, newspapers scattered on the floor, Elaine's toolbox open on the counter. "Where's the master of this one, by the way?"

"Out. Working on a case."

"Vaughan working? At this hour? I'd spend a little more time worrying about that if I were you."

"You're not. Damn, I just remembered."

"I *am* you?"

"No, dummy. Hunt called, he's been trying to get in touch with you. Is your phone still out?"

"Uh, it shouldn't be . . . that is, I don't know." Bethany hadn't plugged it back in? "I told him to let me know if he needed anything."

"He said it was urgent."

"Urgent? Must have something to do with that book pile at his bedside. He needs some masculine reader relief, something involving swimsuits. Either that, or he's cottoned onto Moe's grand plan."

"What might that be? I almost hate to ask."

"She's pre-pregnant. It's a girl. A case of wishful insemination."

"Someone should lock that woman up."

"She's too happy."

"By far."

"I'd hate to wake him, can't be that urgent." He was too weary to work up the required degree of concern. Guilt for not calling would have to suffice. "I'll go to the hospital first thing in the morning."

"You want to borrow a pair of Vaughan's pyjamas? I'm afraid he doesn't have any Wallace and Grommet ones."

"I'm prepared to suffer in silk."

*

He did, too. The night and its medley of torments came to visit. Initially, sleep snubbed him, or simply failed to recognize him in Vaughan's XL, posh, sapphire PJs, which also made him sweat copiously, behaviour more appropriate to a peasant – or a sprinkler – than a valued overnight guest. The creepily soft material clung to him like a layer of sodden blue skin, and with his restless tossing and turning he got all tangled up (in blue!), hog-tied in silk. Only his head was free, which was a laugh if there ever was one.

Eventually, thinking he'd get up to make himself some warm milk, or use Elaine's Samurai sword to commit *seppuku*, sleep yanked him abruptly into nightmare. He refused to cooperate. His dream was so unsubtle, symbolism flashing in neon, that even though he was unconscious he was offended. Without fail, he skipped similar, tediously relevant dream passages when he came to them in his wakeful reading-life, so did likewise with his own midnight composition, which involved carrying some dead woman over the threshold of his house. He willed himself awake out of sheer annoyance, but then was carried rapidly back to dreamland by following the image of a school bus that was packed with swarthy, bearded men all wearing wedding dresses and yukking it up amongst themselves. He woke again shortly after, mouth flung open and snoring whacking great holes in the walls of the guest room.

He choked and stuttered to a stop. It felt as if he'd inhaled his tonsils. Or swallowed his chin. Had Laney heard him? He was deeply, squirmingly embarrassed. How could he steal her from the Big V if he snored like an old fart? Was he *already* an old fart? Didn't women have to fall in love with you before your gut started to hang pendulously over your belt and you left all your hair in the sink and your teeth in a glass by the bed? If your honey signed on when you were still boy-fresh and svelte, then she wouldn't have the energy or the attitude to leave later. She'd be stuck to you with nostalgic glue, that fond, sentimental adhesive.

It then occurred to him that he hadn't once thought about stealing Laney away in the last week. He'd been disloyal to her. He'd committed a rare form of adultery, premarital and wannabe. He was as bad as Moe. If only he could be as good as Moe. What were Vaughan and Elaine doing right now? He listened and all was silent . . . not a mouse was stirring, not in *this* secured domicile, and not with Noir on the job (Pinky was terrified of mice, such a wuss puss). The only thing making a racket was his own brain. *Don't think*, he chided himself, then began to wonder if the mother imposter, that coven-of-one, had set up camp at his place. He wondered where Bethany was, what was going on, what was, what . . . .

Chellis parachuted into wakefulness again, the pyjamas adhering to him like a gaudy bruise suit. He heard a thin, needling noise near his head. A mosquito? *Christ*, not that. The only sort of female who would find him desirable had found him. She sounded close, homing in, so he hunkered down under the covers. She whined on and on, clearly smitten, out for his blood. He threw the covers back, sat up and switched on the bedside light. "You go girl," he said. "Find Vaughan. West Nile delivery? He's your man." He checked the room, peering up at the ceiling and in the corners, but couldn't find her. He then realized that the noise was issuing from a small digital alarm clock that sat beside the lamp. It was flashing 5:00! 5:00! 5:00! and emitting the ulta-irritating mosquito aria. An array of buttons were clustered on top of the alarm, so Chellis reached over to press one. The alarm didn't stop, but immediately switched from insect sound to human, a woman screaming in terror. He hastily hit another button and got an air raid siren, loud enough to wake the dead and send them scurrying down to a deeper level of oblivion. The next was the sound of a car hitting the brakes, skidding, screeching . . . he cut that one off before the crash, but the next was worse: the gut-wrenching agony of an animal caught in a trap.

"Did you like my Alarm Alarm?" Elaine asked cheerily. Early morning and she was getting the coffee started.

"No," said Chellis. He stormed through the kitchen and kept on going.

*

"Disembogue, man."

Chellis considered this to be a winning opener. Spit it out, tell all, unleash the news, lighten your burden, let'er rip.

Hunt responded with a crotchety, almost wifely complaint, "Where were you last night?"

Unless the surgeons had also removed his affable organ, Chellis reckoned that Hunt's grumpiness had more to do with the meagre post-heart-op breakfast he'd been served than his own neglect. The set of playhouse dishes that sat on his bed-table had contained nothing but the white, the thin, the bland. Now they contained nothing at all, having been scraped, and possibly licked, clean. Hunt had been rendered shrewish in suffering a shrew's constant hunger. Chellis realized too late that he should have smuggled in some contraband for his buddy. A pat of butter, golden key to the kingdom of satisfaction, would have been most welcome. Even the word 'pat,' especially in the plural, is consoling.

Seeing as Chellis was musing over the breakfast tray, Hunt said, petulantly, *"Skin* milk. That's what our daughter calls it."

"Your – ?" Chellis understood that they grew up too fast, the kids, but *carumba*. He hadn't pulled a Rip-Van-Winkle last night, had he? Having spent the night in Laney's theatre-of-cruelty guest room, he'd barely slept.

"According to Moe. She's thinking ahead."

"Usually a commendable policy, but don't the little ones get to come up with their own adorable mis-sayings?"

"That's Moe for you. She's pretty thorough once she has something on the go."

"She is." Chellis didn't want to think what kind of mother she'd make. One of those helicopter parents who hover and hover, until some other project snags her attention? No, not this time.

"So where were you? Why didn't you call?"

"Elaine's. Long story."

185

"I'm listening."

Chellis was therefore the one to disembogue. He didn't gush, though. What he related was a modest, if peculiar, stream of events, a stream upon which his sister had been carried away. A stream that also seemed to have an unfathomable undercurrent.

"You're lucky," Hunt said after he heard the tale.

"Lucky? I'm *lucky?*"

"Last night, talk about worry, I thought you might've been . . . well, let's just say I know her."

"Bethany? No you don't, how could you?"

"Sort of."

"Wait a minute, Hunt. Was this . . . did you see her at some strip club? She told me about that gig, confessed all. Why you sly dog, getting trashy kicks in some scummy dive. Didn't know you went in for that sort of thing."

"We both go in for that, Chel, remember? But no, that's not it. I met her a couple of weeks ago. Saw her, anyway."

"So? She was in town hunting for me."

"Wrong again. She was in Claymore, house-hunting. With Dick Major."

"What! You're crazy."

"I saw her. I dropped in on Adam Smith's open house to talk over a deal for a client of mine, and came in behind them. They didn't see me, I don't think. Did I want to talk to Dick, rehash old times? No thanks. So I ducked into the mud room, kept out of their way while they looked around."

"Adam Smith is dead."

"Not this one. He got a serious boner eyeing her up. Tried to hide it behind the realty spec sheets."

"That was someone else! Some babe of Dick's. Get serious, Hunt, you've never met my sister. All you've seen is a photo, and not a great one, either. Doesn't even look like her."

"I overheard Dick calling her Bebe. She ever use that name?"

*

Chellis drove home at a speed appropriate for a funeral procession, a solemn, respectful, and sorrowing velocity. More deceleration was involved than acceleration, more old codger at the wheel than hot dog. He caused some disturbance on account of it, as all the other hurried and harried drivers overtook him with horns blatting and hands expressing their dismay. Their rude dismay. He didn't notice. He didn't care. Bethany was dead, gone, kaput. He'd pushed her down the hospital stairs himself. (He broke her neck trying to reach her heart.) What he'd actually done was given her a fatal overdose of his home-brewed acrimony. He'd washed his hands of her, but not quite his mind, where she hung around still, looking so lovely, so convincing, so his.

Did he believe Hunt? Yes, yes, fuck.

Fool.

After what seemed like days, he pulled into his driveway and sat for a spell with his forehead pressed against the steering wheel, trying to draw some succour out of the vinyl. If his "mother" (had scare quotes ever been more apt?) was still in his house he thought he might as well kill her, too. Sister, mother, his ever-constricting family circle of female fictions. Finishing them off would be easy: simply close the cursed book. The end.

He trudged leaden-footed into the house, like Herman Munster only a lot less jolly.

She was there – of course she was – clacking toward him in her silver heels with a ciggie in one hand and a can of coke in the other. A grotesque replacement for the other greeters – Bethany, Elaine – he had encountered recently.

"Lord, you're a disappointment," she said.

"No argument there." He breezed past her, resisting the impulse to elbow her into the wall. What was it about the post-menopausal wearing leopard-skin leggings and bug spray perfume that brought out one's more goonish tendencies? He strode into the living room and stopped short. It was a mess, stuff tossed all over the place, books on the floor, CD's scattered, couch cushions upended as though she'd been trying to build a fort.

"*Gee-zus*, what happened here? You have the hag's book club over last night or something?"

"Watch your mouth. What d'you expect? Cops all over the place."

"Cops?"

"Yeah, cops. And if *I* was gonna bump somebody off, *I'd* be a little more careful about it, eh."

"What's in that coke?"

"Don't get smart with me. I saved your ass."

"You did, eh? How can I ever thank you?"

"You can start by showing some respect for your old Ma. I'm not the joke you think I am. You could start by cleaning up your room once a year, huh."

"You were in my room? Snooping in *my* room?"

"Damn good thing too, or they woulda found this." She set her stimulants on the coffee table, snatched up her orange purse and unclasped it. From its depths she then pulled out a man's white polo shirt. Although not pure white, for when she held it up he saw that it was splattered with dried blood, as if the tiny alligator logo had suffered a massive hemorrhage. "Found this in a garbage bag in the back of your closet. *Great* place to hide it, eh. You musta got your brain cells from your old man's side."

"That's not my shirt. Corporate logo? Leisure wear? Who do you think I am, some sort of accountant? Forget it, I wouldn't be caught dead in one of those."

"Good *Christ*, son. Oh, *duh*."

21

More Cutlery

"CHEL, OPEN UP."

"Why? Do you have to go?"

"No, but you've been in there for over an hour."

"Can't."

"You should eat more fruit?"

"Very funny. Listen, will Vaughan bail me out?"

"Of the bathroom?"

"The slammer, Laney. The clink. I'll need a lawyer."

"Vaughan does patents, not criminal law."

"I'm *not* a criminal."

"Agreed. So come out." Elaine rattled the doorknob. "It's only me out here, not the police. We have work to do, you're wasting time."

"They'll see me, they'll reach across town with the long arm of the law and nab me and the next thing you know I'll be reclining in an electric chair. In Texas. What work? I refuse to be an experimental subject unless it involves me getting a face transplant."

"Done."

"On second thought . . ." Chellis unlocked the bathroom door and peeked out. "Za za zen! That's a sexy getup."

"I'm undercover."

"Hardly."

"So what do you think?"

"You look absolutely – "

"Beautiful?"

"Nope, that is – "

"Fat?"

"I don't think anyone can be *absolutely* fat, although I could be wrong. But what's the story here? Wait, let me guess, you've invented a new method of contraception and you're getting me all het up so we can test it out."

He *had* seen her fiddling with a condom-sized device when he'd passed rapidly through her kitchen once again, this time with nary a word, to take refuge in the Champion's loo. It was the safest hideout he could think of, seeing as no one else in their right mind would dare set foot in it. Once in, he'd resisted the temptation to weigh himself, touch the towel bar, or wash his hands. He'd opted for standing frozen at the mirror and, using his Romper Room inside-voice, asking it repeatedly how he'd gotten into this fix. No answers had been forthcoming, other than those that Fiona had proffered, if she was to be believed. But then, why else would some guy's bloody shirt turn up in his closet, if not to incriminate him?

"Could tell that little gal friend of yours was up to no good the minute I set eyes on her," Fiona had said. "Sure as shit."

She had also said that the cops had taken some things of his and that he'd better get lost because they'd be back. "Listen to your mother for once, eh." She may have said this because she was planning on cleaning him out herself, but he'd taken off as ordered by the ersatz maternal unit.

"Is that a catsuit? You're not competing with Noir for Vaughan's attention, are you?"

"Don't be silly." Elaine tugged down a snugly fitting, spandex sleeve, a tweaking that somehow made the whole ensemble fit even more snugly.

"And you've grown your hair! How did you do that?"

"Wig."

"That's cheating. So okay, I give up, what's this in aid of? You're embarrassed to be seen with me? Manqueller of the day."

"What's a . . . what did you say?"

"Translates as murderer."

"They can't pin anything on you, Chel. You didn't *do* anything."

"I'm pinned already, tail on the donkey. Ass, more like." He gazed at his funny friend – she looked wonderfully ridiculous, which helped him feel less conspicuously ridiculous himself. They were true partners, after all. "That was your specialty in the good old days, wasn't it? Remember those wild birthday parties at my place?"

She nodded, smiled. "I hated them. And loved them. Do you want a disguise?"

"I'll go as myself. No one will recognize me in . . . Morocco? Uh, Norway? Where are we off to?"

"Claymore."

"Claymore? Not *there*. You've knocked my heart into my loafers. Why, for God's . . . no, don't tell me, I know how your mind works. Its outlying regions anyway, if not its throbbing urban centre. Hunt told you about the house, right, the love nest, and you want to catch Dick and Bethany there so you can report back to Di, the wronged wife? Who will then skin Dick alive."

"How astute."

"I'm not going. You think I want to see Bethany again? *Ever?*"

"The double-crossing bitch."

"You said it."

She *did* say it, and greatly enjoyed doing so.

"We don't even know if they took the place."

"They did, or she did anyway. I checked it out at the realtor's."

Chellis slipped his hands into his pockets, stared at the floor, thinking about those days Bethany had rushed out of the house for "job interviews." He also thought about some troubling details vis-à-vis the events of the past few weeks. Details that didn't add up, or might have if he hadn't been so besotted and determined to ignore them. As well, there was the not insignificant detail of the bloody shirt, although Fiona herself may have pulled that out of her bag of tricks to serve her own mysterious motives. Taking into account what he did know, he did some elementary math on the spot, some figuring of the one plus one equals three variety, and said, "What a nitwitted fellow am I." *Sure as shit.* "Laney, you're right, we do have to go to Claymore, and *pronto*. Your car or mine? Wait, hang on." He touched her arm lightly. "Do you smell something burning?"

By the time they'd hustled outside, they discovered that his first question was no longer relevant, while his second was all too. Yes, something was burning, and doing so consummately, as if it were made of paper rather than metal and glass. (Make that plastic and fibreglass.) Chellis had parked his much maligned, but worthy vehicle by the curb in case he had to make a quick getaway, and now it was getting away all on its own as it disappeared into another element. A great little ball of fire.

He grabbed Elaine's hand and began running, pulling her toward her car, parked in the driveway.

Contrary as usual, she dug in her heels and insisted on calling the fire department.

"Don't worry, they'll find it." He gave her arm a sharp tug. "What you need to worry about at the moment are projectile auto parts."

"Ow! Watch it. Let go!"

"I hate to tell you this, but gas cylinders are going to start blasting off my car like rockets. The bumper, too. No kidding, you can get impaled. Tires exploding, poisonous gases. No end of fun. So are you coming?"

"How do you know all that?" Elaine asked shortly after, gunning it, her ritzy, soft-focus neighbourhood blurring as they zoomed by. She was in such a rush that she even made her SmartCar zoom. Chellis himself had the unsettling sensation of being trapped in a blender.

"Lazar got his Lamborghini torched once. I'm the one responsible for the fantastic authenticity of the crime. I sometimes wonder what the fictional bad guys would do without me. You didn't read that one?"

"Guess not. But Chel, what about the real ones, the bad guys who don't need your research skills? *What* is going on? I mean, your *car*?"

"They are becoming a bit of a problem, aren't they? We'll simply have to put our pretty heads together and see what we can do." Bravely spoken, he thought, if nothing else.

*

When they passed the Claymore town sign with its smattering of rusted bullet holes and visitor-discouraging, *piss-off* subtext, they did shift closer to one another for protection.

"What a place," Elaine shuddered.

"Home of the depraved."

"Do you remember the Claymore hockey team that used to come to play our high school?"

192

"Do I remember Charles Manson and his team players? What were those Claymore guys called? Satan's Iceholes, something like that? They used their skate blades for cutlery in the cafeteria."

Elaine white-knuckled the steering wheel. "I checked out the street on MapQuest, 17 Boswell, shouldn't be too hard to find."

"You found Claymore on MapQuest? The vile thorp wasn't censored, lurking somewhere on the undernet? Well we'd better find this house before *your* car gets incinerated. Or melted down for tools. A SmartCar's pretty advanced for people still living in the Iron Age."

They crept along through enemy territory searching for the street. The houses they passed weren't much different from the general Farclas variety, modest post-war bungalows and sixties' ranch-styles, but they only had eyes for the most discordant and delinquent of details: a barbeque with a missing wheel parked on a front lawn, icicle lights left up since Christmas, a fly swatter dangling from a doorknob, a twin set of scraggly meatball shrubs flanking a cement stoop, a lidless can of whipping cream sitting on a window ledge beside a pink plastic back-scratcher with all but one finger missing – and guess which one.

"The true classless society," observed Chellis.

They drove around for awhile, closely scrutinizing the street signs, amazed that there were street signs, until Elaine announced, "This is it." She turned sharply onto a secluded and lushly treed side street. "Boswell Drive."

"Drive? Claymoronians don't *have* Drives. Or Crescents, or Ways. The whole place is on the other side of the tracks."

"True, but pretension is ubiquitous, as you might say, and as I recall *did* say when you first saw my new house. But feast your eyes on that, over on the left, number 17. The stone one with the wisteria trailing off that wrought-iron pergola."

"That's not wrought iron, it's an inferior polymer. So is the wisteria and the stone. All synthetics."

Elaine parked on the curb opposite the house.

"Curbs, already," said Chellis. "I wonder if they have running water."

"Focus, Chel."

"I am."

"On the job at hand. What do you think?"

"I think we're sitting here in full view of whoever is in the house."

"Hence my disguise."

"This is logic?"

"Someone's coming out." Her voice dropped to a whisper.

Out of shirker's habit, Chellis instantly slid down in his seat and compacted himself into a wad of self. Elaine meanwhile snatched a container of dental floss out of her bag, snapped off a line, and began vigorously flossing her teeth.

"What are you doing?" Chellis wrenched his head sideways. "Apparently I did take too long in the can."

"I'm being inconspicuous. Nothing but a girl going about her daily hygiene."

"Hardly noticeable at all."

"Yeah."

"So who is it?"

"That guy who was at your place when you were out visiting Hunt. Some biker dude by the looks of him."

"Jerry."

"You know him?"

"He's a businessman. Funny cigarette business."

"Ew, there's something wrong with his face."

Chellis peeked over the dash. "*Acne vulgaris*. Also he has eyes on the side of his head, like a turbot . . .and *Jesus H. Christ*, do you see *that?*"

"What?"

"He's got Uncle Bob! On his back, he's wearing Uncle Bob!" So, another wound compliments of the treacherous and twisted sister.

"*Stay* down, he's looking this way." Elaine dropped the floss and flipped down the sun visor. She made a show of gazing into its mirror (a card with the periodic table on it was in fact taped over the mirror) and fussing with her hair. "Doesn't suspect a thing, thinks I'm just some dumb broad. Brilliant, he's getting into that muscle car parked in the driveway."

Chellis chanced another look and saw Jerry back out onto the street in a car that was all sleek sinew *and* muscle, a brand new, black Saab. He cruised away in lordly disregard of Elaine's jam jar on wheels. The sight gave Chellis cause to ask himself why every male he encountered these days drove luxury cars, even guys like Jerry who as he recalled didn't indulge in other luxuries, like deodorant. What would his insurance buy as a replacement for his torched baby, he wondered? A skateboard?

"Let's go," said Elaine.

"Go?"

She was already climbing out of her bubble of a car, handbag slung over her shoulder. "Let's check this place out."

"Laney! There are sneakier ways of going about this. We have to be careful. What if they're in there?" Those two snakes, entwined around one another. Although he hated to badmouth snakes; calling someone a *human* was usually the more apt condemnation.

Protest, even common sense, were of no avail when Elaine had a head of steam up. She was walking briskly toward the house next door to number 17. A few strides along and she vanished into their shrubbery. Chellis clambered out and ran after her, trying with all his might to shapeshift into a candy wrapper blowing across the street. Mind over matter. Mind would be flattened into matter if they got caught. He should have told her what was really going on here. What he *more* than suspected. What he knew.

Something else he knew, common knowledge in Farclas, was that the entire citizenry of Claymore were on welfare, and prospering by it, too, considering the upscale digs on this street, including the twee Cape Cod next door to the house of sin. The Cape Cod appeared to be uninhabited, but he didn't think so. The suds-guzzling residents within were simply immobile, stuck to the floor in their own vomit. That or too lazy and boob-intubated to get up and take note of a stranger rustling around in their forest of rhododendrons, as Chellis himself was doing in hot pursuit of a handbag-toting girl detective. (Did women have to take their purses with them *everywhere?*)

Chellis assumed that Elaine's paparazzi-plan was to snap a few photos of 17 Boswell from the vantage of this green cover. With luck, she might catch the two lovers leaving or arriving, or, with surreal luck, she might catch them sunbathing in the nude by the backyard pool (pool!), Dick sucking on Bebe's toes. As usual, he assumed wrong. When he did spot Elaine, he was aghast to see that she was

taking a much more direct approach. She was dragging a stepladder, pillaged from the Cape Cod's twee, matching gardening hut, and heading straight for the den of iniquity.

Elaine motioned to him to come and help. She was dragging the ladder toward the back of the house.

"No way," he hissed. Then he dashed over to help anyway, before she made a death-summoning racket setting it up. "Laney, this is insane. There's more going on here than you think."

"Such as?" She dug her cell out of her handbag and flipped it open, exposing its camera feature, a technology that made Chellis feel ill, given the speed with which it had spread throughout the world and considering the zillion private worlds it was capturing, exposure by exposure, the majority stupefyingly banal. "Hold this, will you." She shoved her purse at him, and having placed the ladder beneath what she must have guessed was a back bedroom window, climbed nimbly up. She didn't climb as far as the window, but reaching up held the camera close to the glass. She snapped a photo of the interior then climbed back down. Nothing to it.

Except that there was. Together, they gazed at the viewfinder and the image she had captured.

"Such as *that*," Chellis now could answer.

"My God, what's Mrs. Havlock doing here?"

"Writing," said Chellis. "With a knife to her head."

"Hey Chellis," a voice came from behind, but not far enough behind, not far enough for a cornered creature to make a run for it. "Man, I *love* your bag."

Chellis turned. "Gee, Jer . . . thanks."

22

Scheherazade

"YOU'RE BLOODY LUCKY she didn't stick a knife in *your* head, too."

"Good point."

"How does he fit into all this? Victim number one?"

"Let's ask."

Glib was presently going to have to temp for any earnest expressions of raw fear. It might even keep him from filling his boxers. Refusing to take anything seriously did have its uses, even when one was on the verge of being planted in the backyard or made to walk the pool's plank in cement swim shoes.

Jerry had expressed a very convincing invitation to enter the house, followed by an emphatic suggestion that they spend some quality time – a quantity of time no long appeared to be an option – in the basement and in a room that was unfurnished, unfenestrated, and locked.

Both he and Elaine were pacing, passing one another as they circled the room or crossed it kitty-corner, do-se-do, practising their square dance of death. Their mental activities, however, weren't that well partnered, in that Chellis was worrying hard, trying to burrow into an invisible and inaccessible safe room, while Elaine was thinking hard, trying to find a way out.

Besides being aggrieved about Mrs. Havlock, who was not gadding about the country after all, the only other strengthening emotion Chellis was able to summon at the moment was indignation about Uncle Bob, also in captivity and equally passive. If only his leathery old pal were more like that man-eating shirt Hercules's wife gave to him, the homicidal garment that ripped his hunky flesh right off his bones.

While still outside, Jerry had divested Chellis of Elaine's handbag, so that shamanistic resource was lost to them, too. Unless, like the Almighty Himself, she could conjure up a destructive invention out of the dust balls that roamed the edges of the room. Evidently thugs weren't given much to housework, only ridding houses of the harmless human element.

They stopped pacing and stared at one another.

"Damn," said Elaine. "He's got my new window opener."

"Is that like a can opener?"

"It's a remote. I was working on it when you ran through the kitchen. Press a button and *zim* your window flies open. Handy for old ladies."

"I feel like an old lady, but perhaps you've been too deep in thought to notice that our prison has no windows? A can opener would be more useful. We could knock ourselves out with it."

"Tell me what's going on with Mrs. Havlock, will you? I don't get it."

"That makes two of us." Which would have been ideal under normal circumstances. "They're forcing her to write something, as we observed. Imagine trying to concentrate with a knife flashing around your head about to slice it up like a melon." Chellis was still staggered by the image that had been displayed on the camera phone, which, naturally, had also been taken away from them: Mrs. Havlock seated at a small metal table, fingers working the keys of a laptop, while Bethany, weapon of choice in hand, had either been dictating something to her, or simply threatening her. The knife, a stylish stiletto and not some crude utensil rustled up from a kitchen drawer, had been positioned a breath away from Mrs. H's temple. Gun to the head was the usual formulation, but the firearms conjured tended to be figurative and drawn from a self-manufactured arsenal. Like most writers, Mrs. H might even be accustomed to the feeling, which could explain her remarkable air of calm. "Writing what, though? A new will? Some crackerjack manifesto that will get great reviews, but is published posthumously?"

"God. Where's Dick, do you think? I thought he'd be here."

"Out getting us pizza, is my guess."

"This whole thing is fucking nuts." She scratched her head.

"Now look what you've done, your wig is crooked." He reached up and straightened it for her. Gave her a soulful look. "You *are* beautiful. Even under a bushel of someone else's hair."

"Chelly." She slipped her arms around him, pulled him close. "Are you scared?"

"Shitless."

"Don't worry, *don't*. I'll think of something."

"I know you will." He broke away, gazed at her for an ardent moment. "I'm entrusting my life to you. Keep it safe, will you, while I go to the john."

"You can't hide in the bathroom again!"

"Nature calls. Where is that minder of ours? Oi, Jerry!" Chellis walked over to the door and began to pound on it. "Emergency here!"

Jerry unbolted the door and thrust it open, a SWAT team of one, but not a member of the redemptive side. He was holding a handgun – no theatrical knives for him – which he pointed at Chellis's chest. "What seems to be the problem?"

"Not my heart, or I'd ask you to fix it. Is that shiny piece of hardware registered by the way?"

"Sure, I'm a model citizen."

"Excellent. I find that under these stressful circumstances my bowels have loosened, and therefore I require directions to the men's room."

"Jesus. Ed said you were chickenshit."

"Ed? I know an Ed? An Ed who has opinions about my person?"

"Edna."

Chellis delivered a blank look that was soon enough filled with Jerry's own ravaged features. It seemed that the man had been scrubbing his face lately with steel wool, which was no way to treat a suppurating case of acne, however entrenched. "Are you telling me . . . are you saying that Bethany's real name is *Edna?*"

"You got it." Jerry squinted at him. "What's so funny?"

"Nothing, nothing." Chellis sucked in his lips. Edna!

Somehow this demystifying piece of information emboldened him, and he felt even bolder once inside the junior league, basement bathroom. Bolder but desperate. Anxiously, he searched the room for something, *anything* that might be useful. Toilet paper? He could compact it into a ball and stuff it in Jerry's mouth and then . . . die. A grungy, yellowed toilet bowl brush was leaning against the wall, but this didn't strike him as a particularly great weapon, either, even though there was something cheering about the levelling and democratic demands of bacteria. Jerry could pump the bowl full of bullets and still not kill a thing.

"Hurry up in there." Jerry rapped on the door with the butt of his gun. "And don't stink the place up."

"Coming!" Chellis reached over to the handle of the toilet and flushed, then turned on the tap and began to run the water full blast. A bar of Dove, the milquetoast of soaps, sat in a puddle of muck on the counter beside the sink. A thin, pinkish hand towel lay crumpled and stiff beside it. He crouched down and opened the door of the cabinet below. It was completely empty except for a weapon of mass destruction that had been tossed carelessly into a corner. He snatched it up and slid it into his pants pocket.

Once back in the room, Chellis and Elaine barely had time to consult before Jerry returned. "Ed wants to see you. Move it."

Bethany – it was hard to get used her new nominal guise – was waiting for them upstairs in the living room, seated in a midnight blue, wingback chair. Velvet. It was the classiest chair amongst an oddly-matched family of furniture, although this didn't seem to matter much, as he and Elaine were not invited to take the weight off their feet. She was dressed more conservatively than usual, in a businesswoman's black pantsuit, although she had retained the pointy green shoes of her former role. Her killing accoutrement was nowhere in view, which could only mean that she found them totally harmless.

"Edna," he said.

"Chellis," she smiled. Not unfondly, he didn't think.

She turned her attention to Elaine. "And who are you supposed to be? Madonna? The *aging* Madonna."

Elaine said not a word, but increased the voltage of evil eye she had fixed on Evil Edna.

"So Bethany, I mean Bebe, no, *it's Ed*, how does one keep track? You've been up to no good."

"Shut your face, asswipe." This classic, guard dog comment (and mixed metaphor) came from Jerry, stationed directly behind them, *his* weapon at the ready.

"It's okay, Gerald," she said. "He never knows when to shut up."

"He's a prick." Jerry again.

"He's more sap than prick. A wimp, a stooge, a buffoon. One could go on and on."

"But one can't find one's thesaurus?" offered Chellis.

"To get back to your original question, I'm actually up to great good. For myself."

"How is that, Eddie? I'm dying to hear."

"Don't call me Eddie, I don't go in for childish diminutives, *Chelly*. You're right about the dying, though. Sorry about that, I've gotten kind of used to having you around. Like a pet. You don't make a half-bad curry, either. But you fit into my plans so well."

"Enlighten me and I'll make you another curry. I might even bark."

"Someone has to take responsibility."

"For Jude Thomas? An old flame of yours you stomped out?"

"He was useful. I learned a lot about the publishing world from him, and learned a lot about Mrs. Havlock. He was obsessed with her, it was a little weird. He also got in my way, tried to stop me doing what I wanted to do, typical male. I bet you don't know that I've written a novel. It's *amazing*."

"You don't say? Then don't also forget brilliant, rivetting, shocking, astonishing . . . you'll have to find that thesaurus so you can write your own blurb."

"Why would I need to do that?"

"Because your book is bound to be a pile of doggy-do and no publisher will touch it."

"Funny, that's more or less what Mrs. Havlock said when I first sent my manuscript to her. She scrawled some derisive comments across the front page and sent it back to me. But you know what, she didn't even read it. I could tell. So I wanted to make sure that she *did* read it, you see. I wanted her to read it and read it and read it until she had it memorized, and then I wanted her to rewrite it until it was up to speed, according *to her*, since she's such an expert, such a successful award-winning author herself."

Out of all the unsolicited manuscripts that poured like a Niagara onto her plate, beginners desperate for help and endorsement and a leg-up, trust Mrs. Havlock to somehow single out for her ire the one sent by a psychopath. "She's your ghost."

"She *is*. Having reached the end and having crossed the deadline, she's that indeed. There you go Chellis, you're not the only one who can make execrable puns and get away with it. I'm also her long-lost daughter, by the way. I'm the product of a quickie affair, given up for adoption years ago, and terribly crushed to have lost her so soon after our tearful reunion."

Chellis's gaze dropped to his boots. He felt sick and she was *sick*, their only likeness and connection. "Right, of course," he said quietly. "You scooped up documents at her place."

"Including that nifty little clipping about you. Don't ask me why she had that. Strange woman. Speaking of weird ladies, how's your mother? What a gem. On the bright side, there'll be someone to inherit your new furniture. The thing is, Chellis, you're destined to be Mrs. Havlock's fatal date. Work relationship gone bad, that sort of thing."

He shrugged. "In for a penny . . . ."

"Murder-suicide is the best scenario, I think. Can't keep you around, I'm afraid, you do like to blab."

"You're scripting this as you go?"

"Makes it more interesting. The research I did while I was living with you was extremely helpful. And guess what? You're in my book! You'll live on, so don't be upset. I've immortalized you."

"Can't tell you how thrilled I am to hear that. I'm curious, though. Fiction aside, that mother we wept tears over, was she yours?"

"Mm-hmn. Mine and Gerald's. She wasn't as hard done by as I made her out to be. Merely stupid."

"Fat old whore," muttered Jerry.

"Jerry's your brother?" said Chellis. "Jeez, you sure know how to pick 'em."

"When I was a girl he protected me from a lot of very bad men. When he could, he wasn't always around when mother was entertaining. I don't like men much, Chellis, except maybe for you, and you don't really count as a male. You can't even take advantage of something hot when it's offered."

"Unlike Dick Major?"

"Richard Major was the one who was up to no good." Her voice remained calm, but the subject obviously nettled her, everyone's eventual response to Dick. "He almost wrecked everything. After Gerald borrowed his car to abduct Mrs. Havlock, he had to make a few repairs to it. Richard hasn't been saying too much since, consciousness being a requirement for that. Thanks, by the way, for the wallet. We didn't think we'd see it again after Jerry lost it, and it's come in handy, no-limit credit cards, you've gotta love it."

Chellis glanced at Elaine to see if she was loving this news of Dick's demise, but she looked instead quietly horrified. As well she might be. The plot had thickened to such an extent that he could scarcely breathe.

"Did Jerry have to fix *my* car, too?"

"I didn't," said Jerry. "Touch *that* thing?"

"Something happened to your car? Chellis, you do attract the worst kind of luck." She grinned at him, dropping her eyes to the front of his pants. "Aw, how sweet, I see I still have a stimulating effect on you."

"Not at all, Eddie. I'm clean of mind *and* body. This is only a bar of soap. See!"

Chellis yanked Elaine's soap out of his pocket, spat on it – thus adding a spritz of superhero body fluids to its tacky consistency – and whirling around, slapped it across Jerry's bulging eyes, where it stuck fast. This slick move was coordinated with that of kneeing the man lightly, but serviceably, in his G spots, which allowed Chellis to snatch the gun away from him. Jerry began to freak, injured in face and gonads, roaring as he tried to yank the soap off his face without extracting his eyeballs, and Chellis began to freak because he had a gun in his hand. Unlike his BB Gun, this was serious and *weighty*. But Lazar had held lots of guns in his day, and lots of urbanites had, not to mention all those gun-loving farmers and hunters who slept with racks of them above their beds, and gun-toting was a *right* in the US . . . so with the collegiality of his fellow gunslingers fully behind him, he grasped the handle firmly and tried to point it in the right direction without shaking too much or dropping it on his foot.

Elaine, meanwhile, had not been idle. She flipped her wig – as planned. When Chellis attacked Jerry, she whipped it off and hurled it into Edna's face, and then with a few economical, *Kill Bill* moves had the astonished woman in an arm-lock and on the floor, knee pressed into her back. If Elaine's butcher knife had been handy, Ed's head may have been rolling across the floor instead of squashed into it, and she herself unable to shriek so violently in muffled rage.

What next? Chellis was racking his brain – rope? 9-1-1? what? – when an unlikely *deus ex machina* put in an appearance.

After a brief fusillade of raps at the front door, a woman, roughly Fiona's age, stuck her head in and gave them a filthy look. Chellis didn't think she was a representative from the local Welcome Wagon come to shower them with gifts.

"Don't point that thing at *me*," she said.

"I'm not," Chellis countered. "Look, could you – "

"I know you're criminals, I've been keeping an eye on this place. What have you done to that poor man?"

"We're not. He's not. Look, we need – "

"You stole my ladder!"

"*Christ.*"

"Don't you swear at me. You should have you mouth washed with – "

"*Shut up*, will you. Call the police, can't you see we have a *situation* here?"

"I called them already. Serve you right. Hear that? Sirens. My son's in the force, I'll have you know. He'll fix your little wagon, mister."

"I doubt it."

"Here he is! Don't worry, he'll make sure you're put away for years. No parole, tougher laws these days, it's life for you, buddy. Scum. Despicable human being. Call yourself a man? Hello, sweetheart."

Two officers and a plainclothes cop had rushed into the room. The plainclothes one stepped quickly in front of her, providing a filial screen.

The old bat said, "There they are, Artie dear, the ones I told you about." Proudly, she patted her son's shoulder, until something caught her eye, something that marred the impregnability of the fabric. She reached up and plucked it off, then gave it a critical examination. A long blonde hair.

"Good work, Ma." He eyed Chellis. "Mr. Beith."

"Inspector Foote? Arthur, I *knew* we'd meet again."

"Are you seeing anyone, dear?" Mrs. Foote enquired, unhappily.

"Nah, that's Trevor's hair."

"You're from Claymore?" Chellis said.

"Born and bred. Sure beats being from Farclas, if you don't mind my saying."

"Not *at all*." Chellis waved the gun airily. "Um, I realize this looks a bit fishy, but I can explain."

"You didn't steal my mother's ladder?"

"Well . . . ."

"Kidding." Arthur gave a nod to the two officers, who began to round up Edna and Jerry.

"What the – ?" one of them said, trying to tug the bar of soap off Jerry's face, while Jerry howled and thrashed around. Edna, on the other hand, seemed more than relieved to get away from Elaine, arm unbroken, and was giving the younger, more handsome cop a shrewd assessment as she proffered her hands for the cuffs.

"We were already on our way here when Ma called," Arthur said. "I believe you know a fellow named Richard Major. You might want to send him a little thank-you card."

"You better," interjected Mrs. Foote.

"Dick?" said Chellis. "You're still kidding, right?"

"No sir. He saved your bacon. Although you two didn't do a bad job here yourselves, I see. But tell me, did anyone save Athena Havlock's?"

23

Assuredly a Goddess

MOE'S PRE-ANNUNCIATION SHOWER was in full swing, mostly in the kitchen and mostly involving a number of friends, male and female, who were pouring volumes of alcohol down their gullets. Except for Moe, who was keeping her gestatory vessel unsullied and in receptive readiness. Potential life was the celebratory subject of the shower, and the almost-embryo, the spark-of life-to-be, the much-desired-daughter was the guest of honour. The provisional parents had received a range of gifts: a his and hers frothy black negligee (one size fits all), a package of oysters, a Club Med coupon, a half-used pack of Viagra, a pregnancy testing kit, a bottle of nitroglycerine tablets, and a DVD of the John Waters movie *Pecker*.

"One of my favourite films, definitely in the top ten," Chellis said to Moe. They were leaning against the counter, enjoying the swelling surge of talk and laughter. "It's not what you might think, if you're thinking porn, as I know you always do."

"Chelly! You're teasing me."

"Actually, a better choice might have been Andy Warhol's *Empire*. That would have sent you two scurrying off to bed in a hurry."

"The only gift I want from you is *you*." She tapped him on the shoulder. "I'm so happy you're still here, still . . . ."

"Alive?"

"What you went through! That horrible woman."

"You mean Fiona Gordon?"

"*No*. Although she wasn't very nice either, was she?"

Hunt made his way over to them, beer in hand. "*Mea culpa*," he said meekly.

"I should say so, sweetie," admonished Moe. "You shouldn't be drinking that."

"Couldn't find the fish oil. But I'm rendering my apologies to Mr. Beith here."

"I should say so, sweetie," said Chellis. "Fiona seriously ripped me off."

"*All* your stuff?"

"Only the new furniture and kitchen gizmos. Glad to be rid of it, if you want to know the truth. Unpleasant associations. I'll be able to live like the celibate monk I am, stripped of material possessions *and* maternal attentions. I can spend my days doing penance for betraying Rennie, my best and truest mother." He gazed at his friend and shook his head, amused. It had been a clever hoax. Hunt had been certain that the new-found sister was pulling a fast one and to prove it had come up with a ruse of his own. He'd hired a mother stand-in, apprised her of the situation, and sent her to Chellis's place to test the imposter's reaction. It had worked, causing the then Bethany to beat a hasty retreat. More hood, than sister.

"Who is she in real life?" said Chellis.

"Fiona? Her name's Brandy. She's Bev's sister, Bev from The Age Spot."

"Good God. Bev might have been my aunt! It boggles the mind. For a while there I thought the mother-from-hell was the one who'd torched my car, but turns out it was some Mafioso dude I encountered in the hospital waiting room when you were in having your heart retooled."

"You sure know how to make friends and influence people," said Hunt.

"It's a gift."

"Chelly," said Moe. "I don't think you should feel bad about Rennie. Done is done. It's time to move on. She'd want that."

"Is that your motherly advice, Moe?"

"It is."

"I'm taking it then. I'm moving on . . . into the living room. See you two later, unless of course you sneak off for some private canoodling."

They beamed at him and shifted closer to one another, Hunt reaching for Moe's hand. All hands would have to be on deck when they won the baby lottery, whenever that might be. Chellis knew he was going to love being an honorary uncle, not that he could top the masterly performance of Uncle Bob, presently flat out on the table among the bottles and bags of chips. Bob had been the one to smuggle Elaine's soap into 17 Boswell, soap that Jerry had unadvisedly tried before tossing it in the cabinet of the downstairs bathroom.

"He saved *our* bacon," Chellis had remarked to Elaine, once they were allowed to leave the police station (Chellis with his wallet!) after repeatedly recounting their story.

"*I* saved our bacon. It was my soap."

"Elaine, you imperilled our bacon, remember? On your headlong rush to perdition? We're lucky our bacon isn't green and stinking in some bag in the morgue."

"I should sell that soap."

"Yeah, any number of ethnic cleansers would love to have it."

Leaving the kitchen gathering behind, Chellis wandered into his nearly-deserted and despoiled living room. One of his guests had strayed and he wanted to reassure himself that she was all right. She was standing motionless by the window, staring out, but not unaware that someone had arrived. Her shoulders clenched slightly.

"It's only me, Mrs. Havlock."

"Darling," she turned around. "Lovely party, but I needed a minute. I was appreciating the gorgeous night, the stars – "

"And breathing?"

"That too."

"You had us all fooled, Mrs. H. Or Edna did. I was terrified when the cops went to search for you."

"Edna did enjoy her tormenting little games of cat and mouse. She was keeping me fresh for you, I believe. My executioner."

"I would have died first."

"Truly?"

"Yep, I would have checked out, then checked out the afterlife amenities for you."

"My dear concierge. I hate to say it, Chellis, but that might have been the best book I've ever written. She had some workable ideas and it was her framework, more or less, but I put the meat on its bones. I certainly polished it enough. I knew better than to end it in an inspirational rush. She wasn't half bad herself, really. As a *writer*."

"A passable plotter, let's say? What are you going to do with the manuscript?"

"Destroy it. After the police are done with it. Good riddance to excellent rubbish."

"You told me a fib." He wagged a finger at her. "About Dick Major."

"I did, didn't I? One doesn't always own up to knowing people in his business, but he was very helpful. Jude Thomas had been stalking me for some time, which is why I moved to the country. Richard took care of it for me, terrified the man, I expect. That's when Richard must have gotten involved with Edna, the girlfriend. He likely thought it was a straightforward affair with an irresistible babe, but then Thomas was murdered. Not that he knew she'd done it, not right away. She may have been planning on setting him up, or she may have fallen for him, I don't know. She certainly would have pumped him for information, about you for one, an old high-school acquaintance *and* my employee. In any event, the brother let slip a few details about their abduction plans and Richard came by to warn me. Unfortunately, they acted faster than I did."

"I thought I saw you with him in his car once, but it was hard to tell. On a TV newscast, weirdly enough."

"That would have been Edna, keeping out of sight, I don't doubt. The only ride I had in the ill-fated Lexus was with Jerry. I would have made a break for it when he stopped at the liquor store – Jerry isn't the sharpest knife – but the one *with* the sharpest knife was in the back seat, worse luck."

"They must have tried to bump Dick off shortly after that. I can't believe his car ended up in the drink again, and *again* he survived to tell the tale. This time he was so furious he told it in full. Dammit, I suppose I do have to send him that thank-you note."

"I'd send him a get-well card, if I were you. All the publicity about the crime didn't hurt me, on the contrary, but his wife, Diane, naturally wasn't pleased. He's back in the hospital."

"Ouch."

"On top of that he seems to have picked up a nasty case of lice. That's what one gets for associating with riff-raff."

"Ha, that'll teach him. I have to say, though, Mrs. H, I'm beginning to get the impression that women are dangerous."

"They *are*, dear." She patted his hand, then gave it a finger-crunching squeeze. "I'd be careful if I were you. Where is your friend, by the way?"

"While we're on the subject of dangerous women? Don't know, she's late. Probably working on some invention that will make Moe instantly pregnant. With sextuplets."

"We'll have to get back to work, too, Chellis. Submerge ourselves, it's the only way to process our ordeal. Did you get everything on that last list?"

"Shit, no. Sorry, the envelope's still sealed. I guess you could say I got distracted."

Athena had not let go of his hand, so gave it another mini-disabling, but fond squeeze. "Doesn't matter. My corpse walked."

"Your corpse? That guy under the bush?"

"I thought he was dead, but he got up one day, brushed the twigs and fallen leaves off his clothing and wandered off, his back to me the whole time. I still don't know who he was."

"The prig. He wanted all the attention. I did find out about that grave in Kinchie, mission not-so impossible as it turned out.

"The missing woman, Bethea Strange? Do tell."

"She ran off with the town's Presbyterian minister. You won't believe this, it's too good to be true, too wild, but his name was Reverend McGuffin."

"I don't."

"I kid you not, it was a fabulous scandal at the time, kept tongues wagging for decades. The spirited Bethea must have thought better of snuggling up to her mouldering hubbie for an eternity. But, and this is the interesting bit, it turns out that she was *our* McGuffin. Beside that gravestone was a smaller and much newer one, scarcely visible in the photo, that marks the grave of an infant named Bea Havlock."

"Good Lord." She dropped his hand. "Could this be true? She's not *mine*, if that's what you're thinking. Never heard of her."

"You don't have a long-lost child?"

"Chellis, I may have made a few mistakes in my life, but getting knocked up wasn't one of them."

"I thought not, or why would you need to send me up there to snoop around. My guess is that Jude Thomas sent the photo to you for whatever unhinged reasons he may have had, and that Jerry or Edna – probably Jerry – tried to stop me from finding the grave, seeing as she was going to pose as your daughter. Not that you couldn't have two long-lost children, but Thomas must have convinced Edna that the dead baby was yours and she figured it would be a snap to turn up the birth certificate, a genuine birth certificate. Once the murder-suicide hit the papers, she'd put in an appearance, playing the teary prodigal."

"They did search for my will, wisely kept at my lawyer's. And true enough, she also had me write some nonsense about a lost daughter, but my hand poisoned the confession with duress, I'm sure. My lawyer, Mr. Maroon, would *not* have bought it."

"Mr. Maroon? I'll be darned. He'd be too busy buying booze. But say, Mrs. H, why did you have that clipping about me? And *my* runaway mother. The one they found in your office."

"It was meant as a little surprise, dear. I was going to do some research on my own to see if I could find out something about her, but I didn't get very far, I'm afraid. Brick wall. My theory, though, is that she came from a town called Beith, in Scotland, or her ancestors did. She gave you something significant, you see. Something to go on. You could follow it up."

"I could . . . maybe. So I have peaty genes in my blood, you think? Makes sense." He wet his lips at the thought. "We should raise a glass to her, Mrs. H."

"Yes, *let's*. But first, I do have something for you. Seeing as I'm the only one allowed to provide the real *deus ex machina* around here, being the author and all." She slid her hand into the pocket of her jade silk jacket and brought out two keys attached to a silver ring. These she dangled in front of him and said, "Let's step outside, shall we."

When they did, Chellis marvelled. "That's *some* machina."

Crouched in the driveway, among the hybrids, the cheapies, and the gas-guzzling baddies was the compact, but elegant silver sports car that Athena had driven to the shower. A grown-up boy's dream.

She handed him the keys. "Here you go, darling, it's yours. I'll get a cab home."

"No possible way! You *can't*, Mrs. H., I mean, honestly."

"I can, though, Chellis. Don't quibble."

"I can't believe this. It's . . . gorgeous. Thank you a *gazillion*. You're a . . . a . . . ."

"A mere woman, Chellis, but one of means. Besides, I'm enormously grateful. Lazar couldn't have done a better job."

"That's for sure."

She narrowed her eyes and peered into the dark, having caught sight of a flicker of movement, someone crossing the lawn. "Ah, here comes Elaine, and looking, hmm, somewhat pugnacious, wouldn't you say?"

Elaine expelled a hard syllable of greeting as she marched past them and into the house.

"Yikes. Bee in her bonnet. We may need that drink, Mrs. H. I have a quarter-bottle of something ferociously phenolic in the cupboard. I've been saving it for a special, and/or trying, occasion. What do you say we go kill it?"

"Murder at its most satisfying, Chellis."

*

A few drinks did help to fortify him for Elaine's surly mood. With his insides aglow, he himself wasn't as surly as he might have been when she shattered *both* of his kitchen windows in demonstrating her newly developed window opener. Everyone else cheered and hooted at the spectacular effect, glass exploding into the night, while Chellis restrained himself from the extremes of passion.

"Shoot. It's back to the drawing board, I guess." She stood frowning at her all too successful window-opening device.

"I beg to differ," he said crisply. "But I believe it's back to the hardware store."

"Don't worry, I'll fix your damn windows."

"You did already."

"*Why* are people using Mike as an ashtray, I'd like to know?"

"Name's Bob, how could you forget? That's unfeeling, Laney."

"Dry up, Chel. Mike is the name of my security cube."

The chrome cube, returned by the police, was resting mid-kitchen table, its flat top piled high with butts.

"Is that what it is? It's bugged? The cops never said anything. Likely couldn't figure it out."

"A baby could figure it out."

"Why don't you give it to the prospective parents then?" He'd earlier seen her handing Hunt an envelope and conferring earnestly with him about something. Besides hoping that his friend had kept his life insurance up to date, Chellis was consumed with curiosity. But he hated to ask. Instead, he said, "What's eating you, anyway?"

"Nothing!" She snatched a chip out of a bag on the table and stabbed it into a bowl of dip.

"Could have fooled me."

"Anyone could fool *you*."

"Hey, don't choke on that, eh."

"Get lost."

"Look, it's my party and you can cry if you want to. Me, I'm *trying* to have a good time."

Her face took on a strained tightness, control caving, her lips began to twitch, tears crested her bottom eyelids . . . and she was gone, out of the kitchen in a shot.

Chellis ran after her. "I'm sorry, I'm sorry, what did I say? What is it?" *Why* did they have these marital spats without getting to have marital cohabitation, or any of the warm-and-cuddly fringe benefits?

She locked herself in the bathroom and wouldn't speak. He didn't want to hassle her further, so gave up, and walked back to the kitchen for another drink, sorely needed, as he had predicted.

Not long after, the gathering began to break up, especially since no one could get into the bathroom. Hunt and Moe had already gone, as had Mrs. Havlock. A chilly wind flowing through the open-to-the-world kitchen windows did a handy job of dispersing the diehard hangers-on, like Joe Caruso from down the street, who left with a joint tucked like a chubby pencil behind each ear. Party favours.

When Elaine reappeared, Chellis was sitting on a pop crate in the living room, rubbing his forehead and considering whether or not to take up smoking, seeing as Mike the Ashtray had an abundant supply of remainder ciggies on offer. He jumped up when she came into the room and extended his hands to her. They were buddies, were they

214

not? She moved toward him, more abashed than angry, and said, "I'm the one who's sorry, Chel."

"That's okay. You and Vaughan have a fight or something?" Impossible as that might be.

"I could strangle him."

She sounded as though she meant it.

"We don't do that, remember. We're the good guys."

"He's not. Chelly, he's in love."

"I would be, too, if you were my wife."

"With someone else."

Chellis closed his eyes and kept them closed for a few seconds. The news did not compute. When he opened them again, he said softly, "Elaine, you're mistaken. You've had a hard time, we've both had a hard time, all the stress of the past few weeks, the brain-scrambling trauma. Come on now, infidelity? This wouldn't happen to our uxorious Vaughan."

"He moved out tonight. I've known about it for a few days."

"*Christ*, you're serious? He left *you*? *You*? Who is it? Who's the slut, did he 'fess up?"

"It's Ewan."

"Who?"

"Ewan. The receptionist at the veterinarian's. I think you've met him."

"The guy with the cute bum?"

"God, not you, too!"

"I'm observant, that's all. Had to pick up the doggies for Mrs. H the other day. Ewan was bending over to fix their collars, and, ahh . . . but this is *terrible*. It's incredible. Vaughan! I've always admired him so much. I respect him, you know."

"I know."

"I can't believe he'd do this to you. What a total jerk!"

"He's an asshole."

"A *perfect* asshole." He paused. "I bet Ewan thinks so."

She stared at him, giving him an instant case of gaze aversion. "Chellis, you're making a joke? A very *bad* joke."

"Um."

"Forget it, I'm going home."

"Don't. You're upset. Stay and have a drink, we'll talk about it. I promise not to make any further use of my well-endowed wit."

"No, I should go, I'm beat."

"Why don't we take a spin in my snazzy new car?"

"You have a snazzy new car?"

"Do you like me now that I have wheels? Wheels that aren't hanging off the rims, that is?"

"Chellis," she gave his hands a squeeze, but without applying the same amount of elbow grease to the effort that Athena had earlier. "I like you. Believe me, I do. Why else would I buy my folks' old place?"

"Come again."

"The house next door, I bought it. Hunt told me it was going on the market and I grabbed it. It was a steal, you absolutely terrified your neighbours. They couldn't leave fast enough. I'm selling the place on Hitchcock and moving in."

Chellis was stunned. This sudden avalanche of good fortune was making him nervous. He began to tremble. He held on tighter to her in case it was all a fantasy and she melted away.

"Don't know how I'm going to put up with your jokes, though." Elaine smiled. "I do want to be neighbourly."

"Be neighbourly." He pulled her a little closer.

"You do realize, Chel, that you use your sense of humour to fend off intimacy. It keeps you at a remove, keeps you uninvolved."

"It's a way of not getting hurt?"

"Exactly."

"But then if I shut up you'll take advantage of me. You'll slap me silly."

"Promise I won't."

"There's an easier way to stop me from cracking wise." He pulled her closer still.

"Really? What might that be?"

"Kiss me."

24

Kiss of Life

OH *YEAH*.

Acknowledgements

WHILE SIDESTEPPING the almost hysterical sense of gratitude one feels toward just about everyone on managing to arrive at this page in the composition of a novel, I would be remiss if I didn't offer my heartfelt thanks to the home team, David Burr and Alexander Griggs-Burr, and to the fine gentlemen in literary search-and-rescue, John Metcalf and Daniel Wells. I would also like to extend my gratitude to those necessary administrative angels – long may they live! – the Ontario Arts Council and the Canada Council for the Arts.

About the Author

Terry Griggs is the author of *Quickening*, which was shortlisted for the Governor General's Award, *The Lusty Man*, and *Rogues' Wedding*, shortlisted for the Rogers Writer's Trust Fiction Prize. Her children's books *Cat's Eye Corner*, *The Silver Door*, and *Invisible Ink* have been nominated for multiple children's writing awards. In 2003, Terry Griggs was awarded the Marian Engel Award in recognition of a distinguished body of work. She lives in Stratford, Ontario.

About the Illustrator

Nick Craine has illustrated two acclaimed screenplay adaptations for filmmaker Bruce McDonald: *Dance Me Outside: The Illustrated Screenplay* and *Portrait of a Thousand Punks: Hard Core Logo*. His illustrations have appeared in *The Washington Post*, *The New York Times*, *UTNE Reader* and elsewhere. He is currently at work on a collaborative book project with author and book designer, Angel Guerra. He lives in Guelph, Ontario with his lovely family.

SORRY, I DIDN'T MEAN TO KILL YOU

Once again we meet staggeringly studly detective and internet-trained lawyer,
Marcel Lazar, in an enthralling, disturbing, and shocking tale of mistaken
identity, mistaken embalming, and other stupid mistakes of an enthralling,
disturbing and shocking nature. How did Clovis Chesterfield, lingerie
magnate, end up on the barbeque basted with Elmer's Hot Sauce and strangled
with a fake-fur chinchilla thong? An accident? The wily
Lazar thinks otherwise, but distracted by Chesterfield's
wife, Esmeralda Hicky, an ex-Zamboni driver
from Owen Sound and reasonably attractive
bombshell with big lips, he finds himself
embroiled in an enthralling, disturbing, and
shocking situation. This tender, well-cooked,
carnally-enriched tale of broken
dreams, machinery, and fingers,
is classic Greedham. Read it
and weep!